They were total strangers, five people who stepped into an elevator, watched the doors close, felt the car descend, and listened in horror as the cable snapped.

In a split-second they are trapped, maneuvering in instinct, fear, and desire. For William Whistler it is a situation to dominate, as he has always dominated everyone and everything in his life; Faith Greaff finds it an occasion for her subtle man-baiting mockery; Josie Swift, too lush, too sexy, is confronted with a past she tries to forget; to Charlie Latham it is a time for wisecracks, impersonations, and secret self-torture; and for T. T. Blades, a great quarterback facing the end of his career and the breakup of his marriage, it is a final refutation of a way of life, of a game that has led him to a dead end.

And that's the way a new game started—
<u>Game of Survival</u>.

# Game of Survival

Marijane Meaker

**PROLOGUE BOOKS**

F + W Media, Inc.

Published in electronic format by
PROLOGUE BOOKS
an imprint of F+W Media, Inc.
10151 Carver Road
Blue Ash, Ohio 45242
*www.prologuebooks.com*

eISBN 10: 1-4405-3927-8
eISBN 13: 978-1-4405-3927-5
POD ISBN 10: 1-4405-5810-8
POD ISBN 13: 978-1-4405-5810-8

This is a work of fiction. Names, characters, corporations, institutions, organizations,
events, or locales in this novel are either the product of the author's imagination or,
if real, used fictitiously. The resemblance of any character to actual persons (living or
dead) is entirely coincidental.

This work has been previously published in print format as a Signet Book by The
New American Library, New York, NY.

For Richard Van Vechten

# 1

That Friday morning in February, the United States Weather Bureau announced that in twelve hours, five to six inches of snow would fall. In New York City a prediction of four inches is a Heavy Snow Warning. At noon, when the first flurries began, a majority of employees in the seventy thousand commercial buildings of the city were notified that their offices would close early, and at four o'clock millions were already bound for home.

On West 44th Street, the Algonquin had rented all one hundred and fifty of its rooms, many to executive commuters whose business appointments delayed their departures to suburbia. By six o'clock the lobby and bars were doing their usual brisk business, but the desk clerk had been advised that orchestra seats were suddenly available at hit shows in theaters down the street; outside, traffic was sparse on the icy streets, the crowds were thinning; nearby restaurants had dozens of dinner cancellations, and at the corner, the Hippodrome Garage was already filled to capacity, with 648 cars for overnight.

The Gart Building stood next to the Algonquin and opposite the Hippodrome. At six-oh-five that evening, five people were still waiting for the elevator on the building's twenty-second floor. They were among the last to leave. One of them, Mrs. Raymond Graeff, had left thirty minutes before and then returned.

Faith Graeff was a plump dowager in her fifties, with a regal bearing and a gracious countenance, wearing a fox-fur cloche and a wool tweed coat from Bendel's. She had forgotten a Schrafft's cake; she had come back to retrieve it from the law offices of Yates, Oliver, Tyson & MacPheerson.

It was totally unlike her to forget anything, equally unlike

7

her to retrace her steps for something as trivial as a dessert, but today there was good reason for both: the reading of her son's will had put her thoughts in disarray; the cake was a special-order one, marking her pearl wedding anniversary. Raymond Graeff was on his way into New York City from Sneden's Landing to help her celebrate. They had a suite at the Dorset. After a small supper party down the street at the Museum of Modern Art, they would return to their hotel. She would order coffee in their rooms and produce the cake as a surprise. . . . If she could ever find the cake. Upon her return to the Gart Building, she had seen a note Scotch-taped to Roger Tyson's door: FAITH, CAKE IS AT THE DESK NEXT DOOR IN THE ALGONQUIN, R. T. . . . Which was where she was now bound.

As was Josie Swift, age nineteen, red hair and freckles, her claim to fame, before she met Senator Robert Anderson, that she looked like the movie actress Shirley MacLaine. She was an employee of Yates, Oliver, Tyson & MacPheerson, a bull-pen secretary from the general offices on the twenty-third floor.

Her date was at six-fifteen in the Blue Bar at the Algonquin; her date was the Senator. If no one looking at her would have believed that, neither did she. When she had first told her sister, last June, about him, Irene had said, "But he's not a genuine senator, I'll bet."

When Irene pronounced "genuine" it rhymed with "wine."

"He says he is; he's in the same Senate Bobby Kennedy is in."

It was true.

She would have preferred to wait out the hour between five and six amidst the old-fashioned luxury of the Algonquin's lobby, in an upholstered chair, gently patting the brass bell on the table next to her, summoning the waiter to bring her a Tanqueray Tom Collins. But she still felt everyone was looking at her pityingly or with disapproval; she still played with her hair or wrung her hands in public places. Her Galanos coat, her Guccis, none of the accouterments she had acquired since Bob had helped her improve her image, made any difference. She was a Lahaska Swift, which in Lahaska, Pennsylvania, translated as loser.

So she had waited out that hour in the ladies' room on the twenty-third floor of the Gart Building, staring at her reflection in the mirror, combing and recombing her hair, washing her hands half a dozen times, retouching her makeup; then she had emerged, anxious, nervous, excited, and suddenly, looking up into a strange man's face, frightened. She saw the glint of his thick glasses, a smile tipping his long thin lips, and

8

as he stood there, blocking the door leading back to the twenty-third floor, he spoke to her.

Which was when she ran, flew down the stairs to twenty-two, aware that he was following her, jumped the last two steps, landed hard, and flung open the door, relieved to see three people waiting near the elevator. Now he stood behind her with the others, so close that she imagined she could feel his breath on her neck; wordlessly waiting that way, wondering what he wanted from her.

He was Charlie Latham, age thirty-one. Despite his Ph.D., despite the academic career behind him, he was a mere instructor in a commercial writers' school. On the twenty-third floor of the Gart Building, in a cubicle the size of a closet, he taught writing to unseen students who answered Professional Writers' School advertisements, wanting to know if they had "creative potential worth developing."

Among them, one Lorine Fillmore Spring, of Toadton, Washington, who had sent a color photograph of herself, posed barefoot in an old-fashioned white peasant blouse with her breasts pressing forward, and a short, tight yellow skirt the color of her long hair: long legs, full hips and rounded belly, her waist pulled in by a wide red scarf, standing there in a field of bright-green and very seductive, very soft-looking grass. . . . And often, Charlie Latham imagined her sitting across from him—the office was so small their knees would surely touch—and always, when it came to File #3409, he regretted that he was an instructor in a correspondence school.

At P.W.S. Charlie did not have a reputation as a drinker; he had been extremely careful . . . about almost everything; his colleagues would have been as astonished to know of his intoxication now at six P.M. as Charlie had been to receive a wire, three hours ago, which began SPRING ARRIVED TODAY IN NEW YORK CITY.

For while Latham had followed the school's procedure with merciless rote, he had made an exception of Lorine Spring, penning unprescribed postscripts beneath his signature after a typist had copied the form he had specified. None of his messages had been too provocative, little more than single sentences like "How does somebody from Toadton, Washington, know so much about l'amour?" or "Bend more with your ardent bent, Miss S."; "Describe more in detail romantic scenes." Yet apparently they had provoked #3409 into materializing, which was the catalyst to Charlie's devouring three-fourths of a fifth of vodka.

He had waited until the other instructors had left; then he

9

had sat there staring out at the storm, planning to telephone her hotel, planning not to, planning to write her a note saying he was leaving on a trip, not to, planning as he made his way to the men's room to douse his head with cold water and sober up, planning to walk down to the Teheran for another drink and their bountiful hors d'oeuvres, planning to —but on his way from the men's room, near the staircase, as often happened those times when he was this far into the alcoholic logic, his plans abruptly made way for one dominant strategy—focusing snap, like that—when he saw the redhead, saw his opportunity . . . pursued it. Was now still in pursuit, waiting behind her, for her and the elevator.

Okay, what was taking the elevator so goddam long! T. T. Blades, age thirty-three, one of the lead quarterbacks in the league, six-foot-one, sand-colored, nearly white hair, green eyes, a broken nose, was due aboard the *Franconia,* leaving for the West Indies from Pier 92, in one hour.

His wife was already aboard. At lunch they had quarreled again; he had made it clear this was one second honeymoon the husband was not going along on. She took off four hours ahead of schedule, in tears, bound for her father's office here in the Gart Building.

T. T. roamed around their apartment alone, smoked, drank coffee, paced; then at four sent his bags along to their stateroom, sent a dozen roses from Wadely and Smythe, and a note: "Look for me, Love T." Then he put on his white cashmere coat and stood in the foyer cleaning out the pockets. A pack of cigarettes, a gold-point Tiffany pen, and that clipping from a Broadway gossip column which had appeared a few weeks ago: PINK-CLOUDING AT TOOTS SHOR'S, PRO FOOTBALL STAR T. T. BLADES, ON THE MEND FROM SHOULDER SURGERY, WITH GERGUS WIFE, ENDING ALL RUMORS OF SPLITSVILLE, NEVER LOOKED SOOOOO LOVERLY-DOVERLY.

That one had revolted T. even more than those items usually did; the same afternoon it had appeared, T. had bought their tickets to the West Indies.

He kept the cigarettes and the pen; then he called down for the doorman to get him a cab.

He directed the driver to the Gart Building. If he missed his guess, and Shirley wasn't still in Gib's office, the card with the flowers would tell her that her husband was going along on the second honeymoon; if she was with Gib, she could hear with her own ears what she had been dying to hear for the past three years: "I'm quitting football, Gib. Is there still a job opening for me here?"

She was not there; the only one in the office of Hockaday

10

Sporting Equipment, Inc., was T.'s father-in-law. A former football player himself, a former football coach, Gib Fitzgerald was now the manager at Hockaday.

"If you ever doubt your decision, remember this, T. You can patch up that battle-worn body of yours. The torn ligaments and torn cartilages, bum shoulders, and bad ankles—they all heal in time. But you can't always patch up a marriage."

He helped T. on with his coat. "Let your hair grow, T. Mr. Hockaday doesn't like the boyish brush cut. The way he puts it, he likes his customers to know that Hockaday men have outgrown games. Pick up some business suits, too; you know?"

Now as T. T. stood waiting for the elevator, he wondered if anyone would recognize him; it was not unusual for someone to call out, "Hey, aren't you T. T. Blades?" And then he would give whoever it was that bashful grin the sportswriters claimed he had, shove his large hands deep into his coat pockets until his fingers found the gold pen he used for autographing.

He sucked on his cigarette, noticing his hands were shaking; well, he had let go of everything now, but Shirley; why shouldn't his hands shake? Then he wondered if he could hold the pen straight if anyone did ask him for his autograph.

No one did.

He felt a sudden impatience to get on his way; he reached out with his thumb and punched the down button three times hard, though the red arrow above the elevator was already lighted.

For eighteen years football had been to him like breathing.

Before the musclebound fellow broke his concentration by hammering at the down button, William Whistler, age forty-two, five-foot-eight, one hundred and sixty pounds, president of Whistle Foods, Inc., had been secretly practicing an isometric exercise for strengthening the chin muscles. He often did this during free moments, for he was a man who was uncomfortable when idle.

While others might be disturbed over the snowstorm, Whistler was delighted at the thought of the added burden of trudging through snowdrifts as he walked from 44th Street and Sixth across to Sutton Place. The exercise would be good for him. Whistler enjoyed the challenge of obstacles, so long as they were obstacles he understood.

11

An understandable obstacle was a buyer you could not sell, competition you could not beat, a necessary capital outlay you could not raise; it was gallstones, a rent increase, taxes, fire, or missing a short putt in a highly competitive golf tournament.

It was not an unhappy childhood (who the hell ever had a happy one?). It was not chronic depression. It was not anxiety. It was not regression, repression, aggression, or obsession. Those things were sandtraps; you avoided them or extricated yourself from them.

That was what he could not get across to Ben Hyde; it was the real reason he had stayed late at the office this evening. Tomorrow, when Ben arrived to do belated work on disentangling Whistle Foods from a congressional investigation of air pollution, he would find the letter Will had just composed, requesting his resignation.

Firing Ben was the last thing Whistler had wanted to do. Ben had been with Whistle Foods since the early days, when he and Will would be out at five in the morning (because a restaurant was busy by ten) showing a chef how to cook frozen chili. They used to work fifteen hours a day then, with a salary of six dollars apiece, out of which they paid for their car expenses, meals, and lodging. In those days Will would never have dreamed he could do without Ben; they were as close as brothers.

Ben's psychoanalysis had changed all that; the years of self-absorption had told on him, were still telling. It had been a session with the analyst which had kept him from going to Washington on this pollution business, a session that could cost Whistle thousands of dollars, if the hearings forced alterations in the New Jersey plant.

Ben's failure to come through on that had been the catalyst, but firing him had been in the wind a long, long time; it was somehow fitting that the elements unleashed their storm just at the point when Will could no longer contain his own fury.

Where was the old Ben Hyde, who could push through a line of frozen tamales during lobster season in New England or sell frozen diet dinners in the heartland of hog country?

The musclebound fellow standing beside Whistler waiting for the elevator reminded Will of the sort Ben was now; there he stood, obviously as healthy as an ox, clearly in some desperate hurry. Why in the hell didn't he just walk down the twenty-two floors?

Will Whistler would have, if getting someplace were that important; so would the old Ben Hyde.

12

# 2

The car moved from twenty-two to twenty-one. Faith Graeff was picturing the cake—chocolate fudge with white icing; on the top in candy-red script would be a little F. Graeff original:

> Let flags unfurl,
> For it's our pearl.

Smiling to herself, pleased that she had taken the trouble to make this a very special evening for Raymond and herself, she was suddenly jolted from her complacency by a violent motion of the car, which pitched her forward, causing her to fall to her knees.

"We're falling!" Josie Swift cried out.

At the same time, there was a great noise which reminded William Whistler of the rattle of an anchor, as it was being loosened from a large ship. Then both the car and the noise stopped.

T. T. Blades helped Mrs. Graeff to her feet. "Are you all right?"

"I've run my stockings," said she. "How annoying!"—for appearances were important to Mrs. Graeff.

Whistler turned to the redhead, who had grabbed his coat sleeve during the confusion. "Okay?"

"Yes."

"Good."

"What happened?"

"I'm not sure."

"We fell."

"No. We couldn't have."

"I could feel the car falling."

T. T. Blades said, "It sure felt that way." He punched *Alarm*, then *L*. The alarm rang but the elevator remained stationary.

"Who's going to *hear* the alarm?"

"There's a maintenance man on duty all night," Whistler answered. "He'll hear it." He sounded more confident than he felt. He seldom remembered his dreams, but there was a recurrent one which always awakened him, and though the scenes and circumstances changed from dream to dream, the result was the same: he was falling. A moment ago his insides had given, as they did in those dreams, and he could feel the falling too. But his practical side said the same thing he had told the redhead: they could not have fallen.

T. T. said, "My father-in-law is still up in twenty-two-oh-six. Can he hear the alarm?"

"That's pretty far down the other end of the corridor," said Whistler. "But it's possible."

Blades hit the alarm button again.

Whistler looked the others over; besides the redhead and the musclebound fellow, there was a solemn, bespectacled young man who seemed stunned into silence; and the gray-haired lady who had been knocked down. Whistler wanted to reassure her: he smiled. "These elevators have built-in safety devices," he said. "Don't be frightened."

"Thank you," she answered, "I don't think I am." She was never sure of an emotion like fear. An inveterate optimist, Faith Graeff was put off only by those things which were out of her control, and usually unconvinced anything ever was. Fear? Yes. Of floods, fire, earthquakes, hurricanes . . . and, she supposed, of *this*. A little. But she could not truly believe that in no time at all she wouldn't be trudging next door through the snow, inquiring after her cake. In fact, she was so sure she would be that she had already decided she'd have a vermouth cassis there in the Algonquin lobby before she started up to the Dorset.

She summoned a cheerful smile to answer the gentleman's, and added, "It's very thoughtful of you to be concerned."

"Not at all." But after writing that letter to Ben, guilty over it—never mind all the justifications—Whistler was most open to this show of cordiality, to the notion of his own thoughtfulness.

"If it's any reassurance to anyone," said he in a strong voice, "we can't get stuck here. We'll be moving soon." Now his eyes met the others', as he would in board meetings make a point of looking at each individual, conferring with the look his blessings, establishing his authority, while his tone of voice became more resonant: "I work here in the Gart Building. There's an automatic manual system on these eleva-

14

tors. If anything is wrong with the mechanism, we'll be lowered automatically to the next floor."

"How long does it take to go on manual?" T. T. Blades asked. He looked again at his watch. He had a vision of Shirley at the party in their stateroom, sneaking a look at her wristwatch. He could see that pinched look which came over her face when she was worried and near tears. He knew what would make it even worse would be the other Cougars and their wives, who would all be on hand for the sailing and entertaining the same question: where was T.?

"The manual device goes into effect as soon as it's established that the car isn't functioning normally," Whistler answered. "It shouldn't be long now." He remembered that once he had told Ben about the dreams of falling.

"A classic," Ben had said.

"What do you mean?"

"I mean, it's a classic. Like teeth falling out, flying, drowning; they're anxiety dreams. The falling one is sexual repression."

"What does that mean, it's sexual repression? Jesus, Ben!" And Will had laughed.

"You're afraid to make a misstep, afraid to slip. The symbolic meaning of falling is a circumlocution for giving way to erotic temptations."

"Oh, Ben. Ben. I'm in pain for you that you believe these things. Can't anything be simple, innocent, natural?"

"You don't mean, can't anything be that way; you mean, can't everything be that way."

Which was the way it went between them more and more; they didn't have conversations, they had debates. There was always an underlying hostility. Their quarrels were not the old sort, where they both let off steam and were hard-put to remember much about it days later; they were the niggling type, too personal, like the verbal fights of children, where anything went.

Now Blades was holding his finger on the alarm button nonstop. "I've got a boat to catch. I'm sailing for the West Indies in an hour."

Whistler said. "You'll probably just about make it." But the thing about the dreams which interested him most was their lingering mood; it was a sense of loss which stayed sometimes as long as late afternoon; he spent such days feeling melancholy, just on the outskirts of nostalgia for sometime, someplace, someone he could not identify....

That was all he had wanted to discuss with Ben; just calmly tell him that, as they used to talk things over for hours

15

evenings on the road . . . and not even that far back—four, five years ago, out fishing on the Sound.

There was another moment of silence while the alarm continued ringing. Charlie Latham was enjoying watching the girl. There were not many advantages to being as badly myopic as Charlie was, but there were two he could think of now: one, it was hard to see his bloodshot eyes through the swirls of glass; two, they were like sunglasses, in that it was hard for anyone to know who you were looking at.

She probably knew; she looked as though she knew, cowering over in the corner, fidgeting with her hands—in her coat pockets, out of her coat pockets, twisting her fingers through her hair, smoothing her coat, and every now and then, yes, a glance in his direction, then eyes down to the floor, happening so fast you had to be observing her very carefully, and the hands went to the mouth, covering her lips, perhaps stifling an outcry . . . for he had not done anything; he had only asked her how she liked the snow. Even if he had done something, now was no time to say anything, not stuck here like this, people beginning to worry, would they be safe?

Oh, he knew he was very bombed, knew that; a little drunkee, knew that, but he wasn't falling down or throwing up or bumping into anybody. He bet this: he bet his life he was not even swaying a little; the old facade was intact, and vodka leaves no trace on your breath.

Redheads. Liked them in particular because they were supposed to be so ebullient; think one of them would come up and, pow! lay one on you with a vengeance. Didn't, though. Never saw one to; weren't that many. What? One other redhead, bar up near Columbia, they were just sitting there putting money in the Piels brothers' till, and then . . . then, friends, she screamed, the way a blond would, the way a brunette would, the way an old woman with white hair would. Eeeeeek! like they used to put in balloons over the ladies' heads in comic strips when they saw a mouse.

Little girl, I dare you to look directly at me; *dare* you. Do it!

She wouldn't look at him. That was what he wanted; that was what those creeps always wanted. What'd they always find their way to her for? This wasn't news. They were always pulling up in cars or coming up behind her on the bus or moving in beside her at a counter, never mind if it was Lahaska, Pennsylvania, or smack dab in the middle of New York City: the creeps came out for her like cockroaches in the dark. What did they *want?* . . . And what if she had been alone with him now in this elevator? Fear of him loomed

16

larger than the initial fear that the elevator would fall the length of the shaft, they would be killed. The stocky man next to her had convinced her they were safe; when they reached the lobby she intended to stick with him.

The lady beside the creep spoke to the tall fellow with the pale-blond hair.

"What ship are you sailing on, may I ask?"

"I'm sailing on the *Franconia*."

There was a certain kind of person who could make Josie Swift feel as tacky as an antimacassar, just by opening her mouth, and this lady in the elevator was such a person. She did not need to say another word; Josie had already translated the slight British accent and the high-pitched tone into crystal chandeliers, governesses, family crests, coats-of-arms, butlers, gatemen, heirlooms—all the things Irene always said were "part and parcel of the genuinely rich."

Mr. Tyson, of Yates, Oliver, Tyson & MacPheerson, was the same sort of fish. Josie spent a good part of every work day wondering what she was doing wrong, or having what she was doing wrong pointed out to her.

Some nights when Bob called from Washington, she could not help sounding discouraged. "Oh, wow! How does anyone stand people like Mr. Tyson, Bob! You know what he said to me today? He says, 'Miss Swift, please don't wear a fragrance anymore.' I didn't even know what he was talking about. I says, 'A what? A fragrance?' 'A fragrance,' he says back, 'a perfume, Miss Swift. The surroundings are too close for it.'"

And always, as a result of that conversation, at day's end, Josie, in anger and defiance, reeked of Miss Blanc, a groovy gardenia fragrance, Mr. Tyson, that could blow your mind.

Mrs. Graeff said, "The *Franconia* is a Cunard ship, I believe. I felt so badly about Cunard's plans to retire *Lizzy* and *Mary*. Of course, I've always preferred the Cunard Line to any other, although my husband and I did take the Grace Line to the Indies one year. We sailed on the *Santa Paula*. It's nowhere near as large as *Lizzie* or *Mary*, but it's an amusing ship in its own right."

"I haven't been on water since I came back from Korea."

"Were you a soldier?"

"I was a Marine."

"So was I," said Whistler, "in World War Two."

Mrs. Graeff cooed and said, "I feel quite safe in this company; two Semper Fidelises for protection." She smiled back at Josie; Josie read it that she deigned to smile back at

17

Josie. And say, "You're not frightened, are you, dear? You look a trifle peaked."

"I'm just tired from filing."

"I see."

"You file standing up. I've been filing all day."

"Well, soon you'll be home safe and sound, all tucked into your trundle."

"No. I've got a date at the Algonquin Hotel."

The lady did not say anything to this; Josie said quickly, "At the bar. Like, not in a room or anything."

There was no monkey business between her and the Senator. When he came to New York he stayed at the Carlyle. She always met him downstairs in the lobby. He had found a room for her at the Studio Club when she came to live in New York; only young women stayed there, and no men got above the ground floor. The few times Josie had gone to Washington, he had always arranged for her to stay with married friends of his; he had not even taken her to see his apartment, which was across the street from the Senate building.

T. T. Blades socked his fist into the palm of his hand. "I've lived through a lot of tense moments in my career, but this one has me sweating. My wife's on that boat; this is our first vacation in six years, and if she has to sail without me, I think she'll go directly to Reno from the West Indies."

Things between them had been worse than bad for some time now; it had been six months since they had made love. A few nights ago, a while after the lights went out in their bedroom, he felt a surge of affection for her, the closest he had come in some time to any desire for Shirley. Just as he said, "Are you asleep?", so did she.

Then she said, "Needles, pins, roosters, hens."

"Huh?"

"Needles, pins, roosters, hens. If you say something the same time someone else says something, then you're supposed to say needles, pins, roosters, hens. *You* know that, T. We used to do that all the time."

"I forgot."

She sat up in bed and turned on the lights. She opened a fresh pack of Raleighs. It always irritated T. that she hoarded the coupons like a miser; she had as long as T. had known her. None of his salary increases, nor his bonuses, nothing had ever deterred her. She kept them in a drawer of the bed table, held in a fat package by a rubber band.

For a while she didn't speak. She just smoked silently. Then she said, "T.? Is it because of your shoulder?"

18

"Is what?" He pretended not to know what she was talking about.

She said, "Everything seems gone. . . . Even needles, pins, roosters, hens."

T. pretended to be falling asleep.

Now T. suddenly punched all the floor buttons, and the alarm; then his palm with his fist again. "Damn it to hell!"

Mrs. Graeff stiffened noticeably.

T. sighed. "Sorry," he said. "Sorry . . . I'm just so—"

"I know," she replied softly. Then she asked, "What *is* your career? You spoke of having so many tense moments during it, I was made very curious."

"I play football with the Cougars."

"I met Fran Tarkenton last summer," said Josie Swift. "His wife and him came into the place where I used to work at."

Then Whistler said, "I was once told a story about a football coach," and he chuckled to himself as he began recalling it. "It seems they were trying to make up their minds about this rookie. One of the players said, 'Coach, you can't take him. He's really stupid. I asked him how much four and four was and he said ten!' The coach thought it over, and he said, 'Well, look, he was only off by one.' "

Whistler's shoulders shook as he laughed, shuffled his feet, slapped his hands together. But no one seemed to enjoy the joke as much as he did; the man in the black overcoat with the thick glasses didn't even seem to hear it. Whistler decided he was out of it, had problems, some damn thing. The redhead giggled and the nice lady smiled appreciatively, but the football player gave a short, deprecative grunt. Then he punched the alarm button again, with such force that it shook the car, and so frightened Josie Swift with its suddenness that she cried out and grabbed hold of Whistler.

He looked down at the fingers curled around his arm. What did it remind him of? He could not remember, but he was uncomfortable and impatient for her to let go of him.

When she did, she moved away from him, into the corner, near a stack of boxes which Whistler had not noticed there before. She perhaps sensed his feeling. He disliked himself for it; she was not much older than his daughter, and she was obviously frightened. He said to her, "It won't be long now," and then to the football player he said, "Take it easy, hmmm?"

"Yeah."

"If we'll just be patient and wait—"

"I knew there was something wrong with this, though,

19

even before I got on; it took so long, I knew something was wrong."

"If you knew, what'd you get on for?" But he was not having any of Whistler's gruff humor; his expression did not change; it was dour and frowning; his forehead was perspiring, and the space between his nose and his upper lip.

He persisted. "That was why we had to wait so long; there was something wrong with the car."

"We had to wait," said Whistler, "for them to load it with this freight," and pointed to the boxes stacked behind the redhead. "See?"

"Who's *them?*"

"Hmmm?"

"Them? Where are *they* now? If they loaded it up, why didn't they ride down with it? Why aren't *they* answering the alarm?"

Whistler didn't know. He said, "They never ride down with it; there are receivers in the basement. And they probably *have* heard the alarm; they're probably doing something about it right now. Relax, fellow: let's just wait patiently."

It was a good, fast answer, never mind that it had no basis in fact, as far as Whistler knew. But back on the twenty-second floor, Whistler had seen something of Ben in this fellow, enough to guess he was the same kind of hothead Ben was. What they could not use right now in this seven-by-eight area, some twenty plus floors above ground, was a hothead the size of a football player. So placate him, patronize him.

Whistler said, "What position do you play?"

"Quarterback."

"The best."

"Yes."

"What was your most exciting game?"

"They were all exciting," and he looked at his watch.

Silence.

Then Mrs. Graeff spoke. "This is what New York City must have been like on November ninth, nineteen-sixty-five."

"What happened then?" said Whistler.

"The power shortage, remember? The big blackout."

"Ah, yes. It threw the whole city off."

"I was in Pennsylvania," Josie Swift said. "I heard about it on the radio."

"It was quite a night for yours very truly, and *I* wasn't even in the city," said Mrs. Graeff.

"You should have seen it," Whistler said, "the bars and restaurants with candles flickering inside, people just pouring

20

out into the streets from office buildings, this bright moon, strangers directing traffic—yes, New York has never seen anything like it."

Mrs. Graeff said, "Were you in New York City, Mr. Cougar?"

"I was on the island. . . . My name is Blades." He took a handkerchief from his pocket and mopped his brow.

"Long Island?" Mrs. Graeff inquired, passing over his introduction. He nodded. He would always be Mr. Cougar to her; she was always naming people things, and once she did it aloud, the name stuck. She called her husband Mr. Best Friend, and her girl friend Sameday, because their birthdays were on the same day in June. Strange, wasn't it, that in seventeen years she had never been able to think of any other name for her son besides Douglas?

Mrs. Graeff looked at Owl Eyes beside her, but he gave no indication that he wanted to join the conversation. Still waters; they were familiar waters to Faith Graeff; both her husband and her son were that way, but as familiar as they were, they were also strange. Owl Eyes was no exception. He had not uttered a word, yet one would know he was the intense, deep, brooding sort, dressed in his black coat . . . that in itself. And she would let him be; she would not stir up still waters; she never had. If others did, then she was there to handle it, but she could let things be; however odd, accept them.

What she was bent on doing now was handling Mr. Cougar, by distracting him. Even this little mention of the blackout seemed to have a tranquilizing effect on him. He did not look any happier, but he had put away his handkerchief, he had stopped punching the buttons on the wall panel, and now he was leaning against the wall, his hands clasped in front of him, staring down at his overshoes.

So far, so good; follow through. "Shall I tell you all what happened to me that night?" she said. Without waiting for an answer, "I have to begin late that afternoon."

# 3

November 9, 1965, was a Tuesday. Raymond was always early on Tuesdays. He would leave the Fogg Institute, where he was a physicist, around four, drive the ten miles from Fogg Valley to Sneden's Landing, New York, then down the hill at the landing to the big yellow house overlooking the Hudson. Tuesday was cook's day off; cooking was Raymond Graeff's hobby, and his reason for cutting his work day short once a week was to prepare dinner.

That noon Raymond had put in his order with his wife, who had relayed it to the grocery in Piermont. A leg of lamb, boned; some fresh chopped tarragon; a tin of Boletus mushrooms.

Raymond was going to make fillet of lamb with cepes.

Faith brought up a bottle of Barolo from the winecellar. She thought it might be quite fun to eat in their breakfast nook, right there in the kitchen. She put a gay red-and-white-checked cotton cloth on the table, set three places, and got out an old Chianti bottle, forcing a red candle into its neck. Then, red paper napkins and a few white roses from her forcing house, arranged in a red-and-white eggcup, as a centerpiece.

It all looked very dear.

Faith Graeff—a handsome, gray-haired woman, the type one would always think of as having charged down the hockey field at Radcliffe some thirty-five years ago, erect, with a large bottom and generous bosom, fair-skinned and blue-eyed, with perfect white teeth and handsome slim-ankled legs—studied what she had done for a moment, then went along to the solarium. It was her favorite room. She was a woman who regularly walked through her house thinking of her favorite things, choosing, as she did then, a favorite symphony, a Mendelssohn—No. 4, in A minor—to listen to in her favorite room.

22

Just at the end of the horns of the trio, a moment before the dashing saltarello, she felt a hand on her shoulder. She looked up and saw Raymond looking down at her. He was a slender, nearly skinny, man, a tall man with streaks of silver in his thick, black hair, and silver sideburns; he just missed being handsome. One looked several times at his face to make sure he wasn't, he was that near to it: his eyes were just a fraction too close together, his ears very large. But he had big, solemn brown eyes and a sensitive, wide mouth, and his expression was usually so completely serious that it was almost sad, and enormously endearing.

This Tuesday evening it was not as sad as it was troubled.

He said, "Did I awaken you, Faith?"

"I wouldn't fall asleep on Mr. Wedding March."

"Who?"

"Now, dear, you remember that that's my favorite sobriquet for Mr. Mendelssohn. Aren't you *very* early tonight? It's not much after five, is it?"

"Five-twenty.... Yes, I'm early. I have something to tell you, Faith. It's going to be difficult."

"What is, dear?"

"What I'm going to say. Saying it, I mean."

"Wouldn't it be easier if you sat down? This is such a pleasant room. Difficult things should be less difficult in this nice, cozy room.... Is it something Douglas did again?"

"I'd rather stand.... No, it's nothing Doug did. Where is he?"

"He's with his serpents. In the basement. Where else?"

"I think I'll just plunge in. There isn't any other way."

"One for the money, two for the show, three to get ready, four you go."

"I know you won't believe this, Faith; I can't say that I blame you. But I've fallen in love."

"Have you? How extraordinary. It *is* hard to believe."

"I appreciate that. . . . You don't know her. . . . She's ten years younger than I am, Faith."

"Forty? She's not young. . . . Is *she* in love with *you?*"

"We're very much in love, yes."

"I see.... Listen to that, Raymond. What beautiful music! They say it was inspired by a carnival in Rome."

"Faith, I must have a divorce."

"Dear Raymond. You were always a very romantic man, deep down. Everyone thinks you're just gravitation and radiation and E equals MC squared. But you always appreciated a pretty face, didn't you?"

"Faith, please. Please treat *this* seriously."

"We're going to have our Tuesday feast in the kitchen this week. In the breakfast nook. Remember when we always had dinner there, way back when we first moved to the Landing? You said you thought we were *afraid* of the rest of the house. I always thought that was such an amusing remark."

"I want a divorce, Faith."

"*I* can probably adjust to the idea; it's very cruel to Douglas."

"Is it? I wonder. I'd see a lot of him, maybe even more than I do now."

"You aren't home very often at that, are you, Mr. Best Friend?"

"Our arrangement has been hard on both of us, Faith."

"Our *arrangement*?"

"The way things turned out."

"You knew when you went with the Institute that it would be demanding work; I knew it, too. It would have been hard on us if we hadn't known, but we knew, dear. We can't cry over spilt milk."

"Faith, that isn't what I mean. What I mean is, the way things turned out in our marriage. We really have been little more than friends since Douglas' birth."

"*Little more* than friends? I think that's quite a lot to be."

"Perhaps. Quite a lot. But not enough, dear. One needs love."

"The complexion of love takes on different hues, Raymond, as it grows older. *Love is indestructable, Its holy flame forever burneth; From heaven it came, to heaven returneth.* Robert Southey wrote those lines. He had a rather mediocre talent, but he *was* poet laureate at one time. Then, I think, he went crazy. But I always liked those lines."

"Flora is very important to me, Faith; very necessary."

"What a pretty name. It means 'flower,' you know. Of course you *know*; it's very obvious. When I was a girl, I had a playmate by that name. I called her Flo-Bud."

"Does what I've just said register with you at all, Faith? I've never been more serious, nor more set on anything in my life."

"I hope Douglas doesn't do anything terrible."

"I think he'll understand. He's an intelligent youngster, Faith. Flora and I would want him to think of our house as his second home."

"Snakes and all?" Mrs. Graeff tittered.

24

"You shouldn't put so much emphasis on what's to *your* mind the peculiarities of an interest in snakes. Doug wants to be a herpetologist; there's nothing strange about that. You just make it seem strange."

"Does this woman live nearby?"

"Yes. She works at Fogg too; she's also a physicist."

"How boring for you, Raymond. Never mind. This whole business will probably be over before it's started, and you'll be yourself again and wonder what you ever saw in her."

"No, Faith. It won't go away. This won't go away. We've got to face it."

"I'm strong enough. I suppose Douglas is too, though I don't know how he'll react. He could do anything. I never know about Douglas, even though he is my own flesh and blood. There's no sense worrying about it. Eloise Pedley says I'm nine worries every ten minutes. I hate to give that impression to anyone, because I don't think of myself as a worrywart. I don't think I am a worrywart; would you say I was?"

"I'm leaving you at the end of the month, Faith."

As Raymond Graeff said his wife's name, the lights in the solarium flickered, dimmed, went out.

She said, "If he's blown a fuse down there in that basement——"

Her husband interrupted, "It's not Doug. Look out the window."

"It's all over the Landing. How inconvenient!"

"Look across the river," said her husband. "Look down at the Tappan Zee Bridge and Tarrytown."

"It's just some temporary failure. We won't have to wait long. Better fetch a candle, though, Raymond. There's one in the kitchen, and there are——"

He said, "What makes you always so very sure?"

"I beg your pardon?"

"I said, what makes you *always* so very sure?"

"I *am* Faith, after all," and she chuckled at her own little joke.

It was five-twenty-eight P.M.

An hour later, Sunyata was adjusted to the big blackout of 1965. Sunyata was Mrs. Graeff's name for the yellow house at the Landing; she had been inspired in her selection of a name by a lecture on Buddhism. "Sunyata" meant "that which exists absolutely and without predication." It had a positive ring to it, and Faith Graeff was a great believer in positive thinking. As much as she despised Douglas' pets—she thought of them always as "the hissers"—when they were

25

first introduced to Sunyata she had taken great pains to learn all that she could about them, if for no other reason than to protect herself in the event that one escaped. She devoured Ditmars' many books concerning reptiles, concentrating, of course, on the *Squamata* order and its suborder *Ophidia*. Snakes. . . . The information she gleaned from Ditmars did nothing to endear the creatures to her; she was somewhat fascinated by their scientific names, since they were based on Latin or Greek, but as melodious as *Agkistrodon piscivorus* sounded, as interesting as it was that the word was from the Greek *Agkistron,* meaning hook, and *odon,* or tooth, and *piscivorus,* from the Latin, fish-eating, it still came out to mean water moccasin.

Ugh.

But it *was* positive thinking, and even Raymond commended her for her attitude.

Although Sunyata was heated by gas, electricity was needed to ignite the gas, so that November evening the Graeffs depended on their living-room fireplace for warmth. While Raymond and Douglas carried logs in from the porch, Faith Graeff set up a little picnic on the rug, near the fire, and lighted candles, and fixed the transistor to WQXR, hopeful that the radio station of the New York *Times,* at least, might broadcast some music, instead of endless reportage on the emergency.

This was a vain hope, but one piece of information Mrs. Graeff heard was quite pertinent; when Raymond and Doug unloaded the last of the logs and began removing their coats, Mrs. Graeff wagged a warning finger at them and said, "Not yet. There's something we've forgotten."

"What's that, Mother?"

"Both the Bronx and the Central Park zoos seem to think more of their creatures than you do of yours, Douglas."

"Why do you say that?"

"We don't have any heat in the basement now, you know."

"That's right! I never thought of that! Dad? That's right. They can't survive the cold down there."

"And I can't survive *them* up here, where it's warm," said Mrs. Graeff, "so I think you boys had better fetch the little propane-gas heater from the garage. Put it in the basement."

"Gee, *thanks,* Mom!"

As Raymond turned to follow Douglas out to the garage, he paused a moment and said to his wife, "Just when I think I have you figured out, I realize that I don't have you figured out at all, Faith."

26

He was smiling, pleased by her gesture; he knew full well her antipathy for the hissers.

She answered, "Don't be silly, dear. I'm a very uncomplicated person."

But it took them so long to come back! Faith had forgotten that the garage door worked on electric motors. This necessitated breaking a window and then forcing the window loose from the paint applied during the summer; there was much broken glass; they were working by flashlight, and it dragged on and on.

Faith refused to allow her thoughts to dwell on the news which Raymond had announced earlier; she *refused*. She told herself it would all amount to a hill of beans, in the long run, just as so many other little incidents had; there was no point in letting it grow out of proportion in her mind, no point in taking a negative attitude. Men were so impulsive, weren't they? Far more impulsive than women. They never seemed to stop and think things through. Take Douglas and his failure to consider the temperature in the basement; if he had only stopped to think, he would not have wasted so much time running around the Landing to confer with this neighbor and that one, caught up in the excitement of the crisis. He would have tended to his hissers; it would have all been taken care of, and the three of them would be picnicking before the fire now.

She had always done the thinking for all three of them; yet they were so quick to imagine that they did not need her. Douglas thought more of his hissers; it was the truth, wasn't it? And now Raymond with this woman, this grown woman.

Well, she was not going to sit there pitying herself; she supposed the only way to carry on was to carry on, go down there in the basement and assist them.

She carried a candle to the steps leading from the kitchen downstairs.

"Hoo-hoo!" she called. "How are we coming, boys?"

There was no answer. They were probably still out in the garage.

She went on down; it was already quite chilly, and the thought occurred that the hissers might have pneumonia by now. They caught cold very, very easily. By tomorrow, they might all be dead.

But the satisfaction derived from this possibility was fleeting. Douglas would only get others. She had no doubt of that, even though she appreciated how devoted he was to

27

these, particularly the triumvirate—the rattler, the copperhead, and the blacksnake.

If Mrs. Graeff had had to choose one from all Douglas' hissers (if someone were to hold a gun at her head and make her choose one), she would have picked the king, not only because she liked black and yellow in combination, but also because Ditmars claimed the king almost never hurt people. She suspected that this fact was the reason Douglas was not so taken with his king; she suspected that Douglas admired the crueler, more deadly specimens. She was not sure why she had such a suspicion; her son had such an angelic face, the same solemn brown eyes which Raymond had, but soft, golden hair, and a small snub nose. He looked younger than fifteen; he was very well-mannered; he only occasionally got into trouble, and then it was not really his fault. He was just a loner. Oh, he had friends—some—three or four bespectacled types who liked snakes, too, but he usually went places alone, which made people uneasy. He liked to take walks. Was anything wrong in that? Not to Mrs. Graeff's mind, no matter what people said. Mrs. Graeff would much prefer Douglas' habit of taking walks by himself than his habit of watching his snakes eat. Live things. They swallowed them whole.

She set the candle on the ledge above the cages and looked down at the king.

"Hissssssssss!"

The snake ignored her noise; he was curled up by himself, in a cage beside the holy triumvirate. There was a partition separating the cages; if you pulled a cord, the partition raised and made one cage of the two.

Mrs. Graeff pulled the cord.

She rapped on the side of the king's cage with her gold wedding ring.

The king began to unfurl; the other snakes were all wrapped around one another.

Ditmars wrote that he had often seen bevies of heads of rattlers, copperheads, and blacksnakes peering from crevices in spring, when the creatures were contemplating leaving their hibernating lair. Those three species were tolerant of one another, and they would wind themselves into great coils, looping through one another, curling and intertwining.

It gave Faith Graeff goosebumps. So did watching them, after a little while. She was not frightened of them; she knew far too much about their habits for that. But the sight of them eventually made her squirm.

She supposed she was needed out in the garage.

She went back upstairs to get a coat and to exchange the candle she was carrying for a flashlight.

As she was fumbling for a scarf in the hall closet, she heard the boys below her in the basement. So she removed her coat, and in her mind she was visualizing the three of them before the fire, enjoying their little picnic. She had taken the red-and-white-checked tablecloth from the breakfast nook and spread it out on the rug in the living room; she had even carried in the eggcup containing the white roses. It *was* going to be a lot of fun, very like the old days when Douglas was a tiny child and they would all go on a picnic to Bear Mountain.

Then the shouting began. Douglas, mostly—in that high, nearly hysterical tone of his; then Raymond, trying to calm him.

They never got around to their little picnic. Faith Graeff tried to explain to Douglas that she had only meant for the king snake to warm himself with the others, until the heater was set up near the cages. Again and again she apologized to her son. She even admitted that she hadn't liked the hissers one bit, there was no point in denying it—but she had never meant for the king to kill the others. Never!

"How would I know he'd kill them?" she insisted tearfully. "Now, *how would I know that?*"

But Douglas remained unforgiving, inconsolable.

"It was my idea to get the heater for them, remember?" she insisted.

But Douglas would not even give her that.

"Won't *you* picnic with me, Mr. Best Friend? Must the whole evening be spoiled because of this?"

"They were the boy's proudest possessions, Faith."

"I know he fussed with them a lot, Raymond. But——"

"You knew they were his proudest possessions as well as you know most of what there is to know about snakes."

"Because of him! I learned because of him! But his interest wasn't natural!"

"What *is*, Faith?"

"I'd say a cozy campfire picnic, on such a night as this."

"I've lost my appetite."

"Because of the snakes? I'm going to get him some new ones, you know. I'm going to replace them. . . . And I *do* feel badly, Raymond, about my mistake. But a mistake is a mistake. We all make them."

"I'm going up to Doug's room to be with him. This isn't easy for him. Then again, what's ever been easy for Doug?"

"It *was* my idea to get the heater for them."

29

"Yes. It was."

"Then why am I being punished?"

"The only one being punished is Doug, and he's being punished for something *I* did; he's being punished because I told you about Flora!"

"I don't understand that, Raymond. I'm sorry about my mistake. I said I was and I am. Oh, I guess I'm not as efficient as I think. I don't blame you for leaving me."

"You're every bit as efficient as you think you are, Faith," Raymond Graeff had answered, "which is precisely the reason I'm not leaving you."

"You don't want a divorce?"

"I'm not leaving you. For Doug's sake."

So something good came out of that very black evening, after all, and like the rainbow after the storm, the lights went on right at that moment in Sneden's Landing, although in the distance it was still very, very dark.

# 4

Someone once said that a wise man, like the moon, only shows his bright side to the world. So it was that Mrs. Graeff's version of the blackout night at Sunyata was the story of a family picnic in the living room, which did not come off because of a mishap causing the death of her son's pets.

She had never told anyone that Raymond had asked her for a divorce, not even Eloise Pedley. In that way Faith Graeff was superstitious: what you admitted was fact; what you did not, was not. Even though Raymond had said it, he had not really meant it. Telling someone about it would have marked it on the record; there was no such mark, only a hazy memory of a confused moment in their marriage.

By the same token, Mrs. Graeff did not suggest that Mr. Cougar and Owl Eyes put out their cigarettes. It had occurred to her to mention the fire laws, yet saying anything about it avowed the possibility of fire. She held her tongue.

Midway in her recitation, Charlie Latham had begun to come around; things were sliding more into focus. He had reached into his coat pocket for his cigarettes, found three left in the package, and lighted one. The redhead still attracted him, but as he watched her, he felt his practical side fight its way through the vodka. It was best to concentrate on what action to take concerning his student's sudden appearance in New York. His original plan, Before Vodka, was to go to his apartment, get a good bag on, and sack out early; to ignore Lorine Spring's urgent request to call her at her hotel. That was the reason he had purposely skipped by the name of the hotel as he had read the wire. But, After Vodka, he had thought: why not? Now, too, why not?

The redhead would be trouble; dear God knows he didn't need any more. He had come very close to calamity on twenty-three; even though he had not done anything, she looked damned scared. Look at that look. He could not suppress the smile that came to his lips. She would not show she knew that he was watching her, but she knew.

Skip it!

Plan of action: when we get going, get off at the next floor. Take the elevator back up to twenty-three, pick up the telegram, proceed from there.

He thought of Lorine Spring's novel in his attaché case, of the tempestuous love scenes between the heroine and the minister, one Reverend Smoke. So he'd call her at her hotel, see, say, "Hello, Lorine, this is Reverend Smoke. Where there's smoke, my dear, there's fire—ha ha," and listen to her laugh back, uh-huh, and pace it that way: low key, strictly laughs, you like New York?, see much of the city yet?, feel like having dinner?, drinks before?, we could go over your manuscript, *I* better come to *you*, in *this* weather.

Uh-huh; casual, no sweat. . . . Charlie Latham lighted another cigarette from the one he was smoking, stepped on the butt, took the redhead in from top to bottom.

Mrs. Graeff was now launched on an explanation of the work of the Fogg Institute and her husband's position there.

Whistler liked her; she was made of strong stuff, like an Eleanor Roosevelt. He sensed that she played down the melodrama of life, that like Mrs. Roosevelt, whom Whistler had always greatly admired, she was not self-pitying; she was purposeful, and practical, and not without a sense of humor.

Whistler remembered that once Mrs. Roosevelt had remarked that an essential point in campaign behavior for politicians' wives to remember was not to get fat, because one had to sit three in the back seat. He could see this woman making the same sort of remark.

"I'm talking far too much," said Mrs. Graeff, "but there is one thing more about the Institute—the surroundings, the beautiful acres of well-manicured bright-green grass, and these enormous pines that—"

And he was grateful that she rattled on that way; the football player now seemed subdued; the man in the thick glasses, relaxed enough to turn his attaché case up on its side, sit on the edge, and smoke; the redhead rested her elbows on the top of the boxes and stayed quiet.

Quiet, but smelling—reeking—of a thick, sweet perfume. That was beginning to get to Whistler. She wore too much, and the wrong kind; it was the odor of gardenias—awful! It made Whistler sneeze.

"God bless you," Mrs. Graeff paused long enough to say, and then as she was about to resume her description of the Fogg Institute's landscape, a voice came over the speaker above the control panel.

"Hello? Can you hear me?"

T. T. Blades came alert. "Hello! Yes, we can hear you."

"Is everyone all right?"

"Yes, but what the devil's going on?"

"My name is Lou Gillespie. I'm an architect. I work in this building, so I'm not acting in any official capacity. It's just that I was here, leaving for the day, when the alarm sounded. How many of you are there?"

"Three men and two women. Can you tell us what happened?"

"We don't know yet. I took a look. I don't think it's anything *very* serious, but it's wise to take precautions. Don't try to get out; don't try to force open the doors. Be as calm and still as possible. I've called Skidmore Elevator; a crew is on the way."

"Is it that serious?"

"Probably not. But there's only one maintenance man on duty. Someone has to come from the outside; it may as well be Skidmore—it's their baby."

"Do you have any idea what the trouble is?"

"Something to do with the hoist."

"The hoist?"

"The cable. But there's no need to panic."

"Isn't there an automatic manual device?"

"Not in this case. Look, I'm not in any position to explain it. That's for the experts. But if you just stay calm—"

"We'll be here for a while, then?"

"Yes."

"*Damn!*"

"I'm sorry. If any of you would like to get word out to people who might be worried about you, I'll be glad to do what I can."

"Yes. Yes, I guess we'd all like to notify someone."

"I'll have to get something to write on, and I'll have to let my own wife know what I'm up to. It'll take me a while, but have your messages ready. Who'm I speaking to, anyway?"

"My name is Blades. T. T. Blades."

"You're kidding! The Cougar quarterback?"

"That's right."

"Well, you be captain, T. T. Okay? Keep things calm up there. There's no reason things shouldn't be calm; there's nothing to worry about. But don't try to extricate yourselves; don't force open the doors or the hatch. Will you take care of it, T. T.?"

"Yes."

"I'm a fan of yours from way back."

"Thanks."

"Okay—the next voice you hear will be yours truly with pad and pencil. Signing off for now."

T. T. turned around and faced the others. "That's that," he said. It was six-fifty-five P.M.

The only good thing about this day, so far, was that someone had finally recognized him.

# 5

Stanley Ryan, the Gart Building's maintenance man, was discouraged about getting ahead. The idea of advancement had come to him belatedly, after a discussion with the maintenance man across the street in 43 West. If *he* could get a better job, so could Stanley, or so Stanley had thought, until his perusal of an Arco career book, with the questions and answers from an examination for housing caretaker.

He was all right when it came to Municipal Geography,

Numerical Relations, Tables and Charts, even Following Written Instructions and Vocabulary, but the time it took him to figure out the answers to Judgment and Reasoning was the time allotted for the entire test. Furthermore, the questions put his stomach in knots; they were just not his dish of tea; he was not a man who ever thought that way, nor was he able to believe that being able to think that way was a logical prerequisite to the position of housing caretaker.

By six-fifteen that night he had spent exactly twenty-five minutes brooding over question 47.

"Distant firewood is good firewood."
Of the following, this proverb means most nearly:
(A) "Forbidden fruit is sweet."
(B) "The higher the tree, the sweeter the plum."
(C) "The fire which warms us at a distance will burn us when near."
(D) "Friends agree best at a distance."
(E) "The early bird catches the worm."

He didn't know what A, B, C, D, or E had to do with firewood; he didn't even know why distant firewood *was* good firewood; he told himself if Clancy over at 43 West knew, he'd eat his hat, and that was where he was when the elevator alarm sounded, across the street.

When he returned (Clancy said C, because they both had to do with fire), Stanley found a stranger fooling with the main-floor control board. Stanley was about to reprimand him, even call the police, certainly threaten to, when as luck would always have it, the man did to Stanley exactly what Stanley had considered doing to him.

He was Mr. Louis Gillespie of Gillespie, Goddard & Ross, the architectural firm which occupied the sixth and seventh floors of the Gart Building. He was fortyish, tall, silver-haired, blue-eyed, good-looking; he wore an expensive black coat with one of those fancy gray-fur collars. Stanley knew his type, and did not like him on sight. He was the type who had been handed life on a silver platter.

When Gillespie demanded an explanation for his absence, Stanley said that he was helping an old woman who had slipped on the sidewalk. Stanley said there was no excuse for touching the control board, whether or not the maintenance man was available, that it was against building regulations, and that Stanley just hoped there was no damage done, because Stanley would have to hold Mr. Gillespie responsible, tenant of two full floors of the Gart Building or not!

34

"I'm trying to re-establish communication with the middle elevator of the left bank. There's———"

Stanley did not hear the "re-establish." He said, "The only one that can work the speaker is the building superintendent. That's rules, and I'm in no position to change the rules. Anyway, why———"

"Now you listen to me, buddy," Mr. Gillespie said, "and listen very carefully. The hoist on the middle elevator of the left bank has snapped. Unless I'm terribly wrong, it whipped around and jammed in the brake mechanism, preventing it from fully engaging the brake shoes. There are five———"

More distant firewood is good firewood, Stanley thought as the man rattled on; brake shoes, engaging the brake shoes; big words do not a big man make; neither does calling someone "buddy"!

Stanley cut him off, indicating by his tone of voice that his patience was being severely tried. "I don't touch the elevators, see? The elevators aren't my province at all. I'll take a look, but———"

Gillespie placed his hands firmly on Ryan's shoulders, held him.

"Listen to me! *Listen!*" speaking very clearly, and very slowly, emphasizing every word. "The elevator is between the twentieth and twenty-first floors. There are five people in the elevator. The cable is broken. I do *not* think there are any brakes holding it secure.

Plain English, Stanley Ryan understood. He was suddenly speechless.

"I've already called the police and alerted Skidmore," Gillespie continued, "and I've established communication with the five inside. Help is on the way. But now I'm having trouble with the speaker. I just finished talking to them and signed off; now I can't get them back."

Suddenly this large, handsome man deserved his handsomeness, his position, his two floors.

Stanley Ryan said, "What are we going to do?"

# 6

"As you know, I'm T. T. Blades. I think we all ought to introduce ourselves."

"I do, too. I'm Faith Graeff, Mrs. Raymond Graeff."

"Josie Swift."

"Whistler, here. William Whistler."

"My name is Reverend Smoke."

T. T. said, "Good! Now everybody knows everybody. How about you fellows getting down two of those boxes for the ladies to sit on? Then I think we'll be more comfortable if we take off our coats."

T. T. made certain to register the names with the faces. He used a system of association he had counted on to remember the names of rookies, and before his pro football days, as a Marine, to remember the names of boots.

Mrs. Graeff, autograph. He had been certain while he was waiting for the elevator that she was going to ask him for his autograph. Before she had spoken he had thought of her as the tearoom type, but now both her demeanor and her looks reminded him of Ethel Barrymore in old films like *None but the Lonely Heart.*

Josie Swift: Joe (Joe Swan, the Cougars' most renowned cocksman) would be swift to make it with this little piece. What was it about them that you could always spot them? Not her clothes, she was *well* dressed, T. could tell that. But she had an aura about her; she was the kind of girl you'd see hanging around the stadium after the game, in cities like Buffalo or Green Bay, always in a little knot of others like her; too much makeup, huge mounds of lacquered hair, shoulder bags, tight sweaters, smoking cigarettes, and dallying, all bursting into giggles if you looked back over your shoulder at them.

William Whistler: Will William whistle next? So far for entertainment he had come up with a joke about a football coach who was as stupid as a moronic rookie. His type was

36

as familiar to T. as pigskin—the Businessman who viewed sports as nothing more than games, and sports stars as thick-pated oafs who couldn't even do simple arithmetic. . . . But in Shor's or P. J.'s it was always someone like Whistler who pounded you on the back and called you "pal"— someone like Gib's boss, Hockaday, with his rules about how his employees ought to dress, cut their hair, who the hell knows what else!

Reverend Smoke: Holy Smoke! Who'd ever take Mr. Magoo for a minister? But then what T. knew about the clergy, besides their firm handshakes on the church steps Sunday mornings, T. could fit in a bottle cap.

"Why don't you all give your coats to me?" said Whistler. "I'll stack them on these boxes." The perfume made him sneeze again. He remembered something his wife had told him about sneezing. Mariam was fond of taking courses at the New School; she would come home and tell him Max Lerner thinks this, Margaret Mead thinks that, then in time drop the credits and preface the information with: "*I* think . . ." Once she had said, "*I* think there's something *to* Aristotle's belief that a sneeze is the brain's way of expelling offensive thoughts. I know it *sounds* absurd, but in a majority of cultures it's connected with evil spirits escaping, or Satan hovering overhead—some kind of omen." She usually held forth after her classes, in their bedroom; Whistler had nicknamed it "the University."

Mrs. Graeff passed her coat back to him and sat down on the box he had fetched for her. "Two Semper Fidelises and a curate," she said. "If one had to get in a situation like this, one couldn't ask for better company. . . . Are you a Methodist, by any chance, Reverend?"

"No. I'm an Episcopalian." Charlie Latham gave his coat to Whistler, too. He was wearing a gray suit, white shirt, striped tie. He watched the redhead remove her coat. She didn't disappoint him. Thirty-six C, he figured. Might even be D. And a filmy white blouse cut low, showing a faint scattering of freckles near the V of her breasts.

Mrs. Graeff said, "I thought that Episcopalian ministers wore collars like the Romans?"

"They do," Josie Swift said flatly. She sat down on a box beside Mrs. Graeff, avoiding the eyes of *Reverend* Smoke.

Yes, she had spirit; Charlie Latham grinned. "Some do," he said, "some don't."

"Perhaps you're a low Episcopalian," said Mrs. Graeff.

"Yes, I am low."

"I *bet*," Josie Swift said. . . . Maybe this was always hap-

37

pening to her because of something about *her*. It was not a new thought; it occurred to her nearly every time·one of them slithered out of the crowd and sidled up to her. Did they think there was something about her that gave them the right? . . . Everyone had strange thoughts at times, strange feelings, didn't they? Was that a reason you had to be followed whole city blocks by some nut with drool on his lips?

She ought to just tell everyone right here and now what had happened a while ago up on twenty-three! But what *had* happened? He had said, "Hello. How do you like the snow?" and she had run. Now he knew her name; she was sure she didn't know his, and neither did the other three.

She folded her arms in front of her; her right hand, balled to a fist under her breast, received the pounding beats of alarm from her heart.

"Well, there's nothing wrong with low Episcopalians," Mrs. Graeff was saying. "I rather imagine I'd prefer them. Our own little Methodist service is quite plain, and our Reverend Sussmann often wears sport jackets. Not in the pulpit, of course."

Charlie Latham lighted his last cigarette. "Do you go to church every Sunday, Miss—Miss Swift? He had almost slipped and called her Miss Spring. In Lorine Spring's novel, Reverend Smoke was a Baptist, but Charlie chose to be an Episcopalian because the last legitimate school to employ him, a little junior college in Virginia, had been Episcopalian. He had been required to attend chapel so often there that he could probably officiate at the altar of an Episcopal church wearing a blindfold.

"No, I don't. But I'm an Episcopalian." In Doylestown, Pennsylvania, where she and Irene had gone to church all through their teens, she had been in the choir at St. James's. She had liked wearing the white silk robe and the floppy black hat, marching down the aisle Sunday mornings, holding the hymnal in front of her, singing "O Happy Band of Pilgrims" and "Forward! Be Our Watchword." Numbers 536 and 531, from *Processionals*. . . . Most everybody in the St. James choir was a high-school graduate now, some even college. Irene used to kid her after Sunday services, say, "Well, Miss Chic, can you bear to eat Sunday dinner with someone from the less-educated classes who don't know a salad fork from a dessert spoon?" Josie'd say, "It's *sheek* not *chick*." "Chick chick," Irene would say, "I'm nothing but a hen from the barnyard," and they would always collapse with laughter, because over in Doylestown it was really the two of

38

them against the world, never mind the St. James choir. . . .
Josie was still a Lahaska Swift.

Charlie Latham said, "Why don't you go to church every Sunday?"

"I just *don't*," she said.

"I see."

"*My* conscience is clear."

Mrs. Graeff turned slowly and frowned at her. She said, "That isn't really the reason one should attend church, to clear one's conscience."

"It's a start," said Charlie Latham. "There's an old saying that there is no pillow so soft as a clear conscience."

"Yes," Mrs. Graeff agreed, "going to church would be a very good start if one has a bad conscience."

Which meant *what?* Josie said, "Now, *look!* I don't want to talk about church or conscience or this that and the other thing!"

"Well, my dear, *you* brought it up," said Mrs. Graeff.

T. T. interceded. "Gillespie should be contacting us any minute. We better be thinking who it is we'll want him to call. I'll relay the messages. That way we can all keep our positions; there'll be less moving around." He was standing by the control panel. Mrs. Graeff and Josie Swift were sitting by the wall to his right. On the left side, back in the corner, was Whistler; next to him, directly opposite Josie, Charlie Latham.

Whistler said, "Find out if there's any way they can lower some food down to us."

"I'll do that."

"I had a Danish and coffee for breakfast and a can of Metrecal for lunch."

"I'll check on it, Whistler."

Now T. T. knew who the redhead looked like: Shirley MacLaine. He was worse than his wife who was never satisfied when she met someone until she could think of a movie or TV star the person resembled. She was starstruck; one of the worst fights they had ever had was in Danny's Hideaway one night. She wanted him to go up to the bar, where Jack E. Leonard was having a drink, and get his autograph for her. She couldn't understand why T. didn't want to do it. T. had even been reduced to saying, "For God's sake, *I'm* a bigger celebrity than he is; don't you know that?" Shirley had answered, "My eye! Were you ever on the Johnny Carson Show? *No!*"

Right now Shirley MacLaine and Ethel Barrymore had their daggers drawn.

39

T. T. said, "Will you all give me your attention for a minute? Now, we're an intelligent group, right? We're not going to fly off the handle and——"

"There's only one of us who did," Mrs. Graeff interrupted.

"No!" T. T. answered. "I almost did, earlier, and——"

"You had a boat to catch, Mr. Cougar; it was understandable."

"Maybe I'm just not intelligent enough for the group," Josie Swift said; "I mean, some people know about snakes and Mendelssohn and lamb with crepes and this that and the other thing——"

"Lamb with cepes. At *least* get it right, Miss Swift!"

T. T. snapped, "Cut it out! Gillespie says I'm your captain, so that's just what I'm going to be until we get this baby on solid ground! Every single one of us is inconvenienced by this—not one of us more than the other. Now, we're going to make it easy on ourselves by staying calm, the way Gillespie said. I'll do everything I can for you, but you have to cooperate. Okay?"

Charlie Latham said, "Can you do anything about the fact that I'm out of cigarettes?"

"Reach back in the pocket of my coat. I have an extra package of Kools there. They're yours, Reverend."

"Thanks."

"I think what we ought to do here is have one person talk at a time. We were at our best when Mrs. Graeff was telling us her experiences the night of the blackout. How about someone else volunteering to do the same now?"

Mrs. Graeff said, "How about you, Mr. Cougar?"

"Okay. Fine." But it took T. off guard; he remembered that night very well, everything he was thinking. He wondered how much of it he should tell them. He stalled; he said, "Meanwhile, if there's anything you want me to ask Gillespie about this fix we're in, keep it in mind. He should be back any minute now."

Maybe he wouldn't have time to describe the whole feeling of that evening to them; he was surprised to realize suddenly that he hoped Gillespie wouldn't interrupt him. Because he wanted to talk about it. Hell, he was dying to. Ever since it had all started happening to him, he had wanted to tell someone about it.

"It wasn't a lot different than most days," he started, when William Whistler broke in.

"Before you get started, Blades——"

"What is it, Whistler?"

"I don't think you ought to smoke. I didn't mind it in the beginning, but now we're going to be here awhile. We've got cigarette smoke and perfume—it'll get very close in here."

Blades said, "Gillespie didn't say anything about smoking."

"Who's Gillespie? He works in this building like myself."

"He's an architect. He knows about buildings like this, these elevators."

"Then he knows it's against the law to smoke in these elevators."

"Whistler, I know the hazards. But I think if we're careful——"

"And who's 'we'? You and the Reverend. The rest of us aren't smoking."

"I *know* that, Whistler. All right, maybe *I* need to smoke, to keep myself calm, and the Reverend probably——"

"I didn't think athletes smoked," Whistler cut in.

"They do, Whistler. They smoke and they drink and they eat; you'd be surprised how much like other people they are."

"Reverend?" Whistler said, "what's your opinion?"

For an answer, the snap of a Zippo, a flick of fire; Charlie Latham drew in deeply on the Kool. "I think if we're careful there isn't any harm in it."

Incredulously, Whistler faced him. "Just like that, hmmm?"

Latham smiled sheepishly at him. He answered, "A minister, but also a man."

"It'd be nice if you were the kind of man who waited for other people to say what they think. Three of us don't smoke, you know. I thought majority ruled: there's three against two."

Mrs. Graeff said, "Majority does rule. . . . I vote with Mr. Cougar and Reverend Smoke. If they'll be very careful, I want them to smoke. A little permissivity is due our situation here. Mr. Cougar's right; we've got to make this situation easy on ourselves."

Whistler punctuated her sentiments with a sneeze.

"God bless you, Mr. Whistle. . . . Now, Mr. Cougar has the floor."

It was not a lot different than most days; four of them were watching an old film of the Cougar-Trojan game—T. T.; Shirley; his father-in-law; and Artie Bold, the Cougar's flanker-back.

T. T. and Artie had seen the film several times, but looking at movies was a way of preparing for a new game. The films were shot with a pair of cameras: there was a sideline shot and an end-zone shot. Even if they watched movies all day at the stadium, T. T. and Artie usually brought one back to the Dunes, where many of the Cougars lived during the season. They ran it off on a projector, and Gib and Shirley watched it with them.

When T. T. was a rookie, Gib was his idol. Gib had been a fullback with the Chicago Bears, and he had coached the Cougars until doctors warned him that his heart could not stand the pace any longer. T. T. was drafted by the Cougars in 1955; Shirley was just sixteen. She had played with footballs instead of dolls as a youngster. T. would go for dinner at Gib's, and Shirley would sit there discussing football. She would say something like, "That boy is the best flanker in the field; he catches the ball well, he runs well, he blocks beautifully, and his patterns are good"; and Gib would take it up and answer, "He's got one weakness, Shirl: he places catching and running on a simultaneous level. The primary work is to catch, then run if he can." T. T. would smile to himself; the girl amused him and enchanted him, and if Gib thought there was nothing incongruous about a small, blue-eyed, golden-haired girl who favored floppy-bowed blouses and pleated skirts, talking like a combination of Red Smith and Jimmy Cannon, T. T. did. T. T. fell in love with the incongruity; he married her in 1961. He took his notebook with the game plans along on his honeymoon, and they studied it together.

He could not believe his luck; he tried to explain it to

himself with the rationale that Fate was making it up to him for the lonely childhood he had spent, being shuttled from one foster home to another. Like T.'s mother, Shirley's had died in childbirth; as badly as T. wanted a child, he could not help Shirley overcome her fear of having one. T. T. became resigned to that fact. In 1964, after another heart attack, Gib came to live with them; that was family enough; T. T. told himself that, and that he had everything he wanted.

T. began to believe this so stringently that when something happened to shake this belief, he refused to acknowledge what it was. Who it was. Instead of thinking of the change as having been brought about by another woman, he searched for reasons for the change in other areas. He believed that one big reason was that there were too many evenings like that one in November, where a day of thinking football was followed by a night of thinking football.

Wasn't that valid?

T. T. was stretched out on the floor, his head resting against a leather hassock; he was considering the idea, weighing its validity. He was listening to the sound of the ocean banging against the deserted beach outside the windows of the Dunes, and he was telling himself he should think of some way to relieve the monotony of perpetual shop talk; that was a big thing wrong with all of them; not Artie, so much—he was new in pro ball—but T. and Gib and Shirley worried the game day and night, week after week, month after month; yes, and year after year. Yes. Listen.

"I'm no sprinter," Artie was saying as he watched himself on the screen.

"You're going at a good clip here, Artie," said Shirley.

"No, not very fast."

"It sure looks it."

"The fastest I ever ran the one hundred in college was ten-one. I'm just not a fast runner. That's why ninety percent of my patterns are short."

T. T. felt like getting up and walking across and turning off the projector. He supposed he might do it, if it weren't for Gib; he thought it would hurt Gib's feelings. These nightly sessions were the high points in Gib's day; what did the old man have left but football? Then T. T. felt the same edge of panic that had been coming and going since the beginning of his discontent; felt what would he have besides football when he was Gib's age, not even a daughter, as Gib had; told himself *that* was the crux of this unexpected and irritating problem, *that* was the root of this new sensation of decline—a fear about there not being more to life than the

43

sport. . . . No woman was involved, no person; and as though something proved him to be on the right track, the projector just plain stopped, right while T. was thinking all this.

But she was there and she was not going to go away, and any belief to the contrary was a mistake.

It was as much of a mistake as T.'s belief was that he could relieve the monotony of all the football talk, for it was monotonous only to T.; he saw that clearly, and supposed he had known it all along. The blackout only served to dramatize it; they sat there, after an hour of concern over what was happening, unwilling to be victimized any longer by another world, and in the candlelight slipped back, a little distance at a time, their voices faint at first, their statements tentative, until they had recaptured again their microcosm, full circle finally, with Gib's voice bursting above the noise of the news on the transistor: Gib starting in on things he had said six, seven, eight times before, and would say again, his audience no less appreciative than they were the first time; Shirley's eyes shining in the light dancing across her face, Artie leaning forward in a posture of eagerness. Gib said, "The only man I was ever really afraid of was Clark Hinkle of the Packers. In thirty-three we had ourselves a head-on collision. I'd worked out a rather peculiar defensive technique; instead of tackling a runner, I'd use a body block that could knock him———"

Shirley said, "T.? Where you going?"

"Walk."

"Take a flashlight."

"It's bright enough."

"—a body block that could knock him back a couple of yards," Gib continued, "and often caused him to fumble. Well, Hinkle—"

The Dunes was a large apartment house on Long Island; summers the apartments rented for fifteen hundred dollars a month. Off-season, which was football season, they could be had for two hundred a month. They were furnished, and in the basement there was a steam room. Many of the Cougars stayed there from September until the Bowl games. T. T. always used to look forward to coming here from training camp. Most of the players brought their families with them if their children were pre-school age. The wives would get to know one another; the kids would play together; it was like one big family, and T. T., who had never had a real family, reveled in it.

This season started out that way; even Gib's spirits seemed to soar once they settled in at the Dunes. Gib had been ailing

44

in Florida, and was short-tempered as a result. When he had first come to live with them, he had had to sublet an apartment he kept in Manhattan. The lease still had two years to run. At the start of this season, his tenant was complaining that something was damaged on the terrace. She called the Dunes four times before Shirley finally made T. go in and attend to it; Gib had put it off because his disposition was never improved by a visit to the 57th Street place. He had made a lot of money in his day; he had never thought then that the time would come when he could not afford to keep that apartment.

It was a hot day when T. went in; he was expecting the tenant to be middle-aged, dowdy—he didn't know why. But Lois Cadwallader was in her twenties, and this threw him, this and her face, and for a moment after she opened the door and invited him in, he didn't go in; when he did go in he had a strange immediate physical pull toward her, something T. had never experienced before, only read about and disbelieved in.

He was not the type who could ever make up his mind about what was a beautiful woman and what was not, but he did know a good many women judged as beauties by his colleagues were not at all interesting to him; he did know, though he did not know why this was, that it was always the face first for him, that it was always a certain type of face. He had seen it as a young man working in the yards of the rich, watching the daughters of his employers tool up in convertibles fresh from tennis or swimming at the country club; their complexions seemed fairer, softer; they were unmolested by the liquid makeup other girls wore which showed up crudely in daylight. There was a way that these young women had of speaking, too, and standing, walking, a whole aura to them which enthralled T. He used to think of them then as being like little old ladies who had never aged, but had learned through years of practice just how to be and do and handle anything. As he grew older, they became the unobtainables, available only to the privileged. Occasionally they would show up before or after a game on the arm of some prestigious soul bent on dazzling them whatever way he could, and T. would always watch them, always wondering as he did if in bed they knew things to do that were very different from the average; subtle, wonderful ways to please a man. The thought excited him, for he believed it had to be, since they went other women one better in everything you'd think to name; it *had* to be. And sometimes T. would dream of such a woman; she would always appear all in white,

45

holding out her hand to him with an amused little smile, and he would go toward her all grins and very sure of ·himself, and wake up from the dream as intrigued as though it had been real.

T. never told anyone about the dream. For one thing, it was too fleeting; he sometimes found himself unable to distinguish whether he had been awake or sleeping when it came. For another, he was not one to talk about his feelings; he didn't know how to, and neither did most of the people he spent his time with. As for love, he left the verbal expression of that pretty much to the Hallmark people, and Shirley did, too.

The duckboards on the terrace were rotting; that was what it was all about. He stood out on the terrace with the girl, examining the duckboards, admiring the view of the East River, breathing in the fresh-air scent, and her scent, commenting on the fragrance of Abelia.

"How do you know its name?"

"When I was a kid I was a gardener's assistant one summer."

As they made idle conversation, T. realized it had been a very long time since he had had any interest in flowers or plants. He never bought Shirley flowers; they made her wheeze. She said she was allergic. "To all kinds?" T. had asked once early in their courtship. "All I know is, my lungs get stuffed up around flowers," she told him. There were never any in their house; there were never even any green plants. T. hadn't thought much about that, but he did suddenly, and he thought of other things; why he had never in the very beginning felt the physical pull toward Shirley he felt now; why Shirley never wore any perfume; why Shirley's hair was so curly, why it didn't fall in a soft, sweeping wave to her shoulders; then—this girl did something to her eyes, used some sort of liner; why had Shirley never bothered to learn any of those tricks?

He came away after several hours with her unable to remember very much of what they had talked about; he could still smell her scent and recall the soft tone of her voice, a very precise way she had of saying words: "you" was never "yah"—she didn't slur her words—she had a way, he could not forget this, of bringing her arm up and out to point at something in the distance, and her arm would rub the side of her breast as she did it, and it seemed like a very intimate gesture. In her hand she had carried a thin chiffon scarf— yellow; it was such a feminine thing to do; his mind kept probing his memory for more details of the interlude, and

46

they came—these strange glimpses of her, saying this word, standing in that posture, touching a table edge so, turning a certain way, and he was surprised at himself for being able to recapture so much about her, such a variety of her ways; that struck him as unusual, too. He had no way of knowing it was very usual for someone who had fallen very deeply in love, all at once, as it happens occasionally.

Two weeks later, after he had checked into the Cleveland Sheraton the night before a game, as he was watching *Gunsmoke* with Artie Bold, the telephone rang.

"Good luck, T."

"Who's this?"

But he knew who it was.

"I'm sorry," she began, "it's—" and they both said her name together.

That was all; he was too flustered to ask her what she was doing in Cleveland, if she would see the game next day, anything. She hung up after wishing him good luck again. He called the lobby and asked the clerk if she were registered, but she was not.

"What's the matter with you?" Artie asked. "You look mad."

"Mad?" He was still too shaken to concentrate much on a conversation with Artie.

"Your face is all red. Who's the Lois Caterpillar you thought might be registered here?" Artie always twisted a person's last name.

"It's a friend of Shirley's and mine."

"I never heard you mention her."

Artie had a right to sound a little skeptical; after all, didn't he know all their business, everyone they knew, every single detail of their lives?

For the first time, T. T. resented it; got a taste, for the first time, of the *disadvantages* of one big family.

The Cougars won 45 to 17. It was a particularly good game because at the end of the first half there was a 10-10 tie; the second half was exciting football, two touchdowns in the third quarter and three more in the fourth.

T. was receiving congratulations in the dressing room after the game; the doors for the newspapermen had just been opened, when Artie came across to T. and said, "The caterpillar is outside; she wants to see you."

That was the second time, and the last time, he had seen her.

He had missed the bus carrying the Cougars to the airport; they had spent the evening together, most of it at a restaurant called Scott's, where the help waited patiently with the chairs atop the surrounding tables, they had lingered so long over their steaks and the bottle of burgundy. He had not touched her once that whole evening, and yet the intensity of the intimacy he had felt simply sitting there with her, and later walking her back to her hotel, was something he had never experienced before, not even when it was very good in bed, in the beginning days with Shirley. He compared it with the thrill of winning a tough game, with the feeling there was then of excelling at something, for it was not only the high sensation of tension and euphoria, but also threaded through it the wonder at its existence, coupled with the fear of its demise.

What T. T. remembered about the night of the blackout was walking by himself down the beach at the edge of the waves, under a very bright moon, thinking something was wrong with Shirley because she did not like perfume, thinking Artie mooched too many meals off of them, thinking Gib repeated the same stories too often lately, thinking every single kind of silly thought he could think, as he often did in games before he threw the ball, so not a part of him would point the real play.

# 8

Although William Whistler usually read only the newspapers and *Business Week,* in fifteen years he had pored through thirty-one studies of Nazi concentration camps.

His grandfather, David Wiesel, had been gassed at Chelmno in 1942. He had never met him; he had heard long stories about him from his father, a frightened invalid who spent most of his adult life in pajamas. "Billy, the only time your grandfather ever laid a hand on me I was already twenty-three, home on a visit, six years he hadn't seen me. I told him things were a lot better over here, but different, too. Now, I told him, I was Whistler, not Wiesel. The *alter cocker* hit me so hard I fell down."

There was a photograph of David Wiesel in a gold frame on the mantelpiece in their living room while Whistler was growing up. He looked dignified, competent, zealous, formidable—everything Whistler's parents were not.

He was a doctor. The point of every story Whistler's father told about him was his integrity, his honor, his strength of character, his pride. The family was on welfare then; this reflected glory was all there was.

On Whistler's sixteenth birthday he left school with the express purpose of removing the Whistler name from the relief rolls. He became an assembly man in an aircraft factory.

By the time Whistler had completed his six weeks at Parris Island, three years later, both his parents were dead. His only living relative, Dr. David Wiesel, was being transported from Germany to Poland so that his corpse, like those of his two thousand traveling companions, would not poison German soil as the Nazis worked out a solution to the Jewish problem.

The question Whistler sought an answer to in the thirty-one books was always the same: *how* could it have happened? He couldn't see the Jews letting it happen; he couldn't believe there was no way for them to fight back, mutiny, escape.

Whistler was not a religious Jew. He observed the big holidays to please his in-laws; he gave money to U.J.A. and bought bonds for Israel, but he thought of himself mainly as a delicatessen Jew. His heartfelt allegiance was to the food. He would rather eat at the Stage, Rappaport's, or the Tip Toe Inn than at the Forum of the Twelve Caesars.

But he was also a man who loved his own, even though he could not believe with them; there was no censure of the Jews in his question, only astonishment, and there was always the other question: what would *I* have done?

As he listened to T. T. Blades, he thought of what it would be like if their number were multiplied by ten, if they were all squeezed into the area as the Jews had been packed into cattle cars and then transported to camps.

It was an exercise in self-control, typical of William Whistler: think how much worse things could be; think how much worse they had been for others.

But it did nothing to decrease the odor of gardenia and tobacco, nor to ventilate the stuffy car, nor to ease the craving for food. Now he had the beginnings of a headache. He had spread his coat on the floor beside Miss Swift; he was

49

sitting on it with his knees up, keeping the first finger of his right hand near his nose to stifle the sneezing.

Blades's vignette did not touch him in the slightest. He suspected that Blades enjoyed describing his involvement with the girl, as Ben always liked talking about his conquests. Blades was just finishing up and his face had an almost jocund expression, which had not been there before he had told his little story.

Mrs. Graeff was the first to speak. "Yes, when there are no children in a marriage, that marriage can be a very weak country, vulnerable to all sorts of interference from outside forces."

"We're back together now. That's one reason this trip was so important. It was going to be a second honeymoon."

"Have a child, Mr. Cougar."

"She still doesn't want one."

"Adopt one."

"She says she wouldn't raise another woman's child."

"She's making a mistake, Mr. Cougar."

Charlie Latham said, "My lighter's out of fluid. Who's got a match?"

"Reverend *Smoke,* indeed. You smoke too much, Reverend."

"I know I do, Mrs. Graeff. I'm trying to quit."

"The way to quit is to just stop it," said Whistler. The night *he* did it was his wife's birthday, two years ago. Mariam had been begging him to give it up; he was a two-, two-and-a-half-pack-a-day man. They had gone to Café Nicholson for dinner, then walked down to Billy's for Irish coffee. At quarter to twelve, Whistler had lighted up a cigarette and said, "I have another birthday gift for you. This is the last cigarette I'll ever smoke."

That was the way to quit.

"I can't quit anything cold," Charlie Latham said.

Blades passed him some matches; he pulled out another Kool and stuck it between his lips. "I'm trying to cut down."

Whistler said, "You don't seem to be tonight."

"He's nervous," said Mrs. Graeff. "Aren't you a little nervous, Reverend?"

"Yes, now that you mention it."

"Yes, of course you are. Every one of us is."

"I'd be just as nervous about getting lung cancer," said Whistler.

"Thing is, we all die; no advantage to longevity."

"*Reverend* Smoke! Naughty, naughty, naughty! *Naugh-ty!*"

said Mrs. Graeff. "That must be heresy! I'll have to report you to your bishop!"

He laughed. He answered in falsetto: "Is this the bishop? Oh, it is? This is the Flying Nun, and I'd like to report a very *low* Episcopalian."

This made Mrs. Graeff giggle uncontrollably, her face radiant as a schoolgirl's.

Josie Swift said, "You'd better get your ash, *Reverend.*"

"What, dear?"

"The ash from your cigarette just fell into the top box."

With the bodily efficiency of a trained athlete, T. T. moved rapidly, ripped open the box with his hands. "I see it!"

"You've got it?"

"Yes."

"Good!"

"Oh, my!" Mrs. Graeff exclaimed. "I thought you boys were going to be careful."

"Hey, here's the answer!" T. T. said. "Look!"

He held up a round glass ashtray.

He said, "You should see the stuff in here: water glass, gum erasers, pencils, paper, glue, stapler, paper clips, envelopes; we can set up an office."

Mrs. Graeff said, "Some little secretary must have emptied out her desk in there."

"Look at all the stuff!"

Josie Swift felt herself blush at the description "some little secretary." While the other three were busy exploring the open box, she said in a low voice to Whistler, "I don't think they should smoke either. I mean, it makes me all the more nervous."

"Tell them."

"They won't listen to me."

"Why not?"

"You know they won't. Not to me."

"A turtle doesn't get anywhere unless he sticks his neck out."

"Hey, that's groovy."

"Hmmm?"

"Like, I never heard that before."

She smiled at him.

*She* was easy to please.

But Whistler was not; he could feel his impatience gathering force away from his little exercises in self-control. Mrs. Graeff's gushing over Reverend Smoke ruined the image Whistler had had of her; she was the only one besides himself whom he had counted on to add some balance to the group.

51

Now he felt totally at the mercy of the fatuous, the naïve, the self-solicitous.

He leaned his head back against the wall and shut his eyes. He wished he were having shad roe at Whyte's, or beef flanken at Lou Siegel's, or the short ribs there; he could eat a couple of orders of butterfly shrimp over at Bill Chan's.

Something else he had learned, reading those thirty-one books: in concentration camps food was the favorite topic of conversation. A Dutch psychiatrist named Rümke had labeled this habit "culinary dry screwing," which was like a shrinker, to make a perfectly human reaction sound like something depraved. Listen to one of them, there wasn't anyone without sex on the brain.

Charlie Latham was back opposite Josie Swift, perched precariously on his upturned attaché case. "You must have been watching out for me, Miss Swift."

He put one hand back against the wall to steady himself; was he weaving, or did she imagine it?

"I was watching out for *me*."

"You must have been watching out for me, too, to notice my ash dropping."

"I just happened to see it."

"I just happen to be in your debt."

"No, thanks."

"Yes, I am."

"Never mind my debt."

Mrs. Graeff said, "Good heavens, Miss Swift! Reverend Smoke is merely being polite. Your answer to any common courtesy seems to be sass."

"Mrs. Graeff, I don't know what your big hang-up is, but I just want to be left alone *period!* Like, I'm not *asking* for any common courtesy!"

Mr. Gillespie's voice came over the speaker, saving the moment.

Josie Swift had been dreading this. It would be just a matter of minutes before T. T. Blades would turn to her and ask her who she wanted to send a message to. She was going to come off like a real zero.

It was now eight-fifteen P.M.

# 9

During dinner one evening, when Bob and she were guests of friends of his in Georgetown, Josie was confronted for the first time with an artichoke.

From the other guests she picked up the knack of eating it very quickly, tearing off each leaf, dipping it in the vinaigrette sauce, nibbling just the tip, depositing the remains on the plate provided.

Groovy.

What a gas.

The whole scene for a few inches of cooked leaf.

But then . . . *then*, a certain p-elegant Mrs. Margaret Van Something or Other, who resembled Tony Bennett in drag, leaned forward from across the table and said, "Tell me, dear, did you like the heart?"

"Ma'm?"

"The artichoke heart; the *pièce de résistance;* the *raison d'être?*"

"I certainly did. It was extremely tasty."

"I thought you didn't like it, dear . . . because you didn't eat it."

There were embarrassed noises; a few titters from the other ladies present. The Senator, at the far end of the table, was engrossed in conversation with the hostess.

Josie knew her face was very red. She said, "I guess I didn't know it had a heart."

"I suppose you'll learn these things," said p-elegant, her lips slanting in a nasty smile.

Later, to help Josie calm down, Bob put a coat around her shoulders and took her for a walk.

"I'm sorry."

"Nobody knew you were upset, Jo; you held up fine."

"Not about that. I'm just not knowledgeable."

"What you don't know now, you'll learn."

"There's too much to learn. You have to start with basics. I don't even know the basics."

"Do you think I care?"

"You may not now, but it'll get to you."

"Do you think I'd rather wake up beside Mrs. Van Pelten mornings?"

"You see, I don't like that; I don't like being a sex object."

"That's too bad, Jo, because that's part of it."

"All of it."

"No."

"But people think it. They think you're an old man after me."

"I am."

"*You* know what I mean."

"Jo, Mrs. Van Pelten is jealous of your youth, your charm, and your ability to attract one of Washington's best catches. Now, let's not pay more attention to the incident than it warrants."

A columnist wrote it up under the headline:

ARTICHOKES HAVE HEARTS: DOES MAGGIE VAN PELTEN?

A certain poor young thing who's been dragged hither and thither by a certain rich old and we once thought, oh, far too wise to find himself involved in a May-September liaison, Washington personality, was put down by Maggie VIP, as only she can spew it; seems little Miss Moppit didn't know there's a heart in an artichoke, as well as a Senator. Maggie pointed out the obvious to the obvious displeasure of the old man's darling. No fool like an old fool, and you guess whether or not I mean him or Maggie. . . . I don't mean po' Offan Any; she's not up on her vegetables, but she knows her animal: the aging male one; feed ego dust daily.

Bob rode back with Jo to New York on the plane; he usually didn't. She knew he was doing it for her; it was his way of saying he did not care what a gossip columnist said about them.

But he did care; Josie knew this. He was very quiet; if a passenger on the plane passing by in the aisle seemed even slightly to hesitate near their seats, Bob looked up with a scowl. At Kennedy, before they got off, Bob asked the stewardess to be sure there were no photographers hovering nearby.

54

He said to Josie, "I'd rather have us photographed after we've announced our engagement. That's all."

It was one of those moments when Josie wondered if Irene was right; Irene said wait and see, there wasn't going to be any wedding.

"Then what does he want with me?"

"Maybe he gets his kicks looking at you. You sure he never tries anything?"

"No. He doesn't."

"Maybe he can't get it up."

"Don't talk that way about him, Irene. I don't like it."

"Listen, Doll, he's like any other mother in pants, and don't try to make out that he isn't. His thing might not be able to stand up anymore, but he's got one, dear."

That day in the plane, Josie finally said to Bob, "I'll get off and go on without you. What do you think about that?"

It hurt her very much when he said that sounded like a good idea.

It was a recurrent memory; times like this, when it came right down to using his name in connection with her, Josie would not.

Even though Josie knew that Bob was probably next door at the Algonquin, frantic with worry at what could be keeping her, she told T. T. Blades she had no message for anybody.

# 10

Blades said, "The last message is to Mrs. William Whistler. The telephone number is six-eight-seven-eight-one-oh-six. Tell her that her husband has been delayed at the office and——"

"Not at the office!" Whistler said.

"Where, then?"

Whistler stepped in front of him. "Gillespie? William Whistler here."

"Go ahead."

"Just tell her I've been delayed."

"Got it. Aren't there two other passengers with messages?"

"They have no messages."

"I better have their names anyway."

"Reverend Smoke and Miss Josie Swift."

"Smoke. Swift. . . . All right. I'm sorry we can't get any refreshments in to you. I can't do anything until Skidmore gets here. But I'll deliver these messages, and then I'll be back to man the phone until someone can relieve me."

"How long will it take you to get back to us this time?"

"I told you that wasn't my fault; we had to get new batteries."

"Can we have a few more details, Gillespie?"

"I thought T. T. Blades was my relay man."

Blades walked over beside Whistler. "You heard him."

"I heard what? You haven't asked him anything about our situation."

Gillespie said, "Blades? It's better to keep just one man in charge."

"I just want a few details," said Whistler. "For instance, exactly where are we?"

"Okay. . . . The car is between the twentieth and twenty-first floors."

Blades went back over and leaned against the wall.

"Which floor are we nearest?"

"It's a toss-up."

"Are we midway, then?"

"I'd say so."

"How many feet from either floor?"

"Mr. Whistler?"

"What?"

"I'm here on my own time. I'm not acting in any official capacity."

"I appreciate that, Gillespie. Is there anything wrong with letting me know what we're up against here?"

Blades said behind Whistler, "He's told us everything he knows."

"How the hell do you know that?"

Blades shrugged. "He has, that's all. What do you want from him?"

"Facts, Blades. Facts!"

"Hello, Whistler?"

"What?"

"Blades is right, you know. You have the facts."

"What's wrong with the hoist, Gillespie?"

"Whistler, I'm an architect, not an engineer, not an authority on——"

Whistler cut in. "I'm in the food business, Gillespie, but common sense tells me there's a reason that this car can't run on manual. If the hoist is broken, the car is being held by brakes, and the job ahead is to reattach the cable. Isn't that right?"

"You know more about it than I do, Whistler."

"That's becoming obvious."

"Just stay calm, Mr. Whistler; there'll be a crew here very soon."

"How soon, in this weather?"

"They'll get here as fast as they can."

"They've had two hours already."

"I won't bother asking you if you know what the streets are like outside; you don't. But they'll get here. You just be patient. Now, that's all I can say, Mr. Whistler. I don't like being stuck here myself."

"We appreciate it."

"Thanks for that, anyway."

"It's just this: isn't there anybody down there in an official capacity?"

"The maintenance man is alerting the building superintendent; when he's free, I'll put him on."

"Right. Thanks, Gillespie."

"Signing off."

Mrs. Graeff said, "If we're going to be here awhile, I'd like to move across to the other side."

Whistler said, "What for?"

"I simply don't like the sitting arrangement."

She stood up and Josie Swift gave the box she had been sitting on a little shove with her foot. She said, "Be my guest."

While Charlie Latham reached over and slid the box up beside him, Whistler said in a whisper to Josie, "Don't start anything."

"She's the one with the mouth on her."

"There we go now, Mrs. Graeff." Charlie Latham was fussing over her, while she smiled gratefully and began whispering to him.

Whistler said to Josie, "You have on a lot of perfume."

"It's Miss Blanc. I've made it my trademark."

"You've got on too much."

"The thing is: you can't smell it on yourself. That's why."

"I suppose."

"Do you hate it?"

"Oh, well."

"So you do."

"Not particularly." He sneezed.

"God bless you!" Josie said triumphantly, before Mrs. Graeff could bless him.

She smiled at Whistler; for the first time he noticed her eyes. They were very green. Mariam and Kathy, his daughter, both had brown eyes; so did most of the women Whistler had ever known.

He said, "There's no sense blessing me every time. I can't stop."

"You got a cold?"

"No."

"Maybe there's dust in here."

"There's everything else." Then, damn it, he realized he had not asked Gillespie about the smoking.

Josie Swift whispered, "Oh, wow. I wish I could tell you something."

"What?"

"Tell all of us," said Charlie Latham.

"Nothing," Josie said to Whistler.

Mrs. Graeff said, "Let them have their little secrets. We'll have our own."

Blades had shut up. What was eating Blades, Whistler realized, was the fact Whistler had taken over with Gillespie. Blades was standing against the wall sulking. He was exactly what you could expect of a professional athlete. They were all overgrown adolescents, used to being fawned over and spoon-fed.

He must have been some Marine! Well, necessity is the mother of invention: limited wars turn out limited warriors; he probably just squeaked by in Korea, but if Whistler had had his ilk along on February 19, 1945, at oh-nine-hundred, lotsa luck!

It was some day, that one, the sun coming up just as they went up on deck and from the line of debarkation, several miles out at sea, Iwo Jima was visible; and on Suribachi, at the south end of the island, there were bursts of fire and smoke from naval shelling; everybody was waiting by the ladder nets, dressed in green combat blouses and trousers, with the pistol belts strapped on, the long knives, ammunition, bandage rolls, canteens; everyone had checked his carbine, put on his helmet with its camouflage cover; now they were poised to go over the side, for the big invasion of Iwo Jima.

It was a tense moment; any second they would make their

58

descent through the maze of nets, down the Jacob's ladder, onto the bouncing gangways and into the lurching boats. Not a few men were killed on these descents.

As they were waiting for the signal to go, Whistler had said to his lieutenant, "The wind's running in our favor; sea's calmer too."

"Fuck what's in your favor," the fellow answered. "Mind what isn't."

A Blades would not have understood the officer, but Whistler had; he had appreciated that the lieutenant was right: there wasn't anything good about a war; there wasn't anything good about a wind in a war, or a sea in a war; there wasn't anything good about thinking there was.

It was a fast sermon on survival, tough and true.

Still was.

But there did not seem to be anything in Whistler's favor now, not on the surface. . . . Give him time; first, get a new raconteur to divert everyone's mind again; that's the only obvious asset; then look for the hidden assets.

Like your own ingenuity.

Like those boxes that one on top of the other reach halfway to the roof of the car.

Like the removable hatch on the roof of the car.

Start to put it together, Will; no one's going to if you don't.

Mrs. Graeff was still bending Latham's ear.

Whistler murmured to Josie Swift, "Hey?"

"What?"

"Why don't you ask the Reverend what *he* was doing blackout night?"

"I don't care what he was doing."

"He was probably saving souls."

She looked at Whistler; he winked.

She laughed. She said, "Yeah. His Holiness."

"I dare you. Ask him."

"You could double-dare me; I wouldn't ask him."

"You won't have to," Charlie Latham said, "I'll tell you."

"Oh, wow. Little pitchers."

"So tell us," said Whistler.

"Yes, Reverend. Take the floor," Mrs. Graeff said.

Charlie Latham got to his feet, holding to the wall. He said, "All right by you, Blades?"

"Well, you got it cleared with Whistler, didn't you?"

"*You're* our captain, Mr. Cougar."

So they were teams now: Whistler and Swift versus

59

Blades, Smoke, and Graeff. Whistler looked down into her green eyes. He remembered an old song called *Green Eyes*. He was a young man when it was popular. He had not even met Mariam yet. Sometimes he remembered those few years before he married at nineteen, and he wondered what he had been doing with himself that he was a virgin when he married. Maybe he didn't wonder as much what he had been doing, he knew that: he had been working; maybe what he wondered was what he had missed.

## 11

He stood with the attaché case at his feet. "That day," he began, "my wife and I were leaving for Vermont. We were not going on a vacation, but going there to live for an indeterminate time. You see, my wife was ill with alcoholism."

Inside the attaché case there was a piece of paper stapled to the title page of Lorine Spring's novel:

PROFESSIONAL WRITERS' SCHOOL
Reader's Report
File #3409. Spring, Lorine Fillmore
Reader: Charlie Latham, Instructor
Title: THE WORST MISTAKE

Comment:
This concerns the tragedy that befell Reverend Martin Luther Smoke, when he turned down a more lucrative and prestigious position with his diocese to spare his dipsomaniac, D-cup wife the rigors and temptations of mingling with an upper-crust congregation.

Smoke takes a leave of absence and flees with his voluptuous package to a remote village in Vermont, there to lead a pastoral life watching cows and blizzards and the contents of whiskey bottles bubbling down his beloved's throat.

What did this noble sacrifice come to?

Wife Salena eventually crawls out of the bottle forever.

But not for Martin Luther's sake; she does this, instead, for a ne'er-do-well postman who has a drinking problem of his own, and to whom she is sexually beholden, to put the whole thing in a far less prurient and perspiratory way than Miss Spring socks it to us.

Salena gives up everything (presumably that means the good Reverend along with the sauce) to stay in Vermont and live with the mailman.

Thus, she repeats the mistake her husband made, marries for sex and ends up with a souse.

There is a bed under every man in this book and a bottle under every bed, and you can become very thirsty reading it.

Recommendation: Further encouragement, of course. Form letter #24, on revising, plus form letter #26 on showing great promise.

Additional comments: Miss Spring reacts to any praise with fabulous enthusiasm; I think she will be a sure bet for all sixteen of our courses.


"—so I remember the night of the blackout quite vividly," Charlie Latham persevered with the masquerade. "And because she had started drinking so early that day, I remember also the afternoon of the blackout, when I came home from the rectory to find Salena in the parlor, very, very intoxicated."


# 12


At four that afternoon, Charlie Latham emerged from the subway at 181st Street in Washington Heights. Although he lived only a block away, on Overlook Terrace, three doors from a small neighborhood grocery, Charlie went three blocks in the opposite direction, until he spotted the new delicatessen which he had noticed yesterday, en route from an afternoon movie.

Its name was Zooky's. Two stores down there was a Gristede's; next to that, a Spotless Cleaners.

Charlie crossed the street and walked down so he would not have to pass in front of Gristede's or Spotless. Washington Heights was not the fanciest part of New York, and this fact was reflected by the caliber of clerk employed by the chains in this neighborhood. Last week one had come right out into the street to hail Charlie; he had called after Charlie, "Hey, Latham"—*Latham*. No Mister. Charlie had gone right on about his business, composing in his mind a letter to the Gristede's people, as he walked along, advising them that goodwill was not yet anachronous.

When Charlie was opposite Zooky's, he recrossed Broadway, straightened his five-year-old Countess Mara tie, fixed his hat from a jaunty angle to one more serious, and entered the delicatessen.

He left the delicatessen at four-forty, carrying two huge bags of groceries. He crossed and recrossed Broadway again, walked back the three blocks, and arrived at his apartment building with a big smile for the doorman.

"*Good* evening, Jerry."

"Hi, Mr. Latham . . . Mr. Latham?"

"I'm in a rush now, Jerry."

"I'm supposed to talk to you about the rent, Mr.——"

"Check's in the mail, Jerry; how's the family?"

He passed the row of mailboxes without bothering to open his own. He took the elevator to three and walked down to 3-F, where he rang the bell.

His eight-year-old son's voice called out, "Who is it?"

"It's Chawee, Fwank. Can you come pway wif me?"

There was the rattle of a lock, and the door opened, and his son stood there shaking his head with an exasperated smile on his round face. "Oh, *Daddy!*"

"Hi, Fwank!"

"I don't talk like that anymore."

"Whaf wong wif the way I talk?"

"You talk like a baby; I don't talk that way anymore."

"It wasn't too long ago that you did, Bigshot."

"Where'd you get all *that* stuff?"

"At the grocery. C'mon, help me unload it. Where's Mommy?"

Frank followed him into the kitchen. "She's in lying down."

"I've got roast beef here. What do you know about that?"

"Cooked?"

"Do you want to eat it raw?"

"I like it when Mom cooks it, when there's gravy and potatoes and everything."

"Start putting things away while I hang up my coat."

"How much did all this stuff cost?"

"A fortune. We're wiped out."

"How much?"

"What do you care? It's not coming out of *your* allowance."

"What allowance? You missed two weeks in a row."

"You've got all my I.O.U.'s, haven't you?"

"This stuff must have cost ten dollars or more!"

"Just put it away. The Milky Ways are yours."

"Oh, boy!"

Charlie went into the foyer to hang up his coat.

"Charlie? You didn't buy more candy for him?"

His wife wore a light-blue robe. She was barefoot and sleepy-eyed. She stood in the doorway of their bedroom. She was a very nice-looking woman, young without looking too young or fragile. She looked the way Charlie felt a wife should look—substantial, very feminine, wholesome. He was glad she had put on some ten pounds since he had married her; he liked her a little plump, not fat, but just a trifle overweight. He liked it that she did not cut her hair; when it was undone, as it was now, it reached nearly to her waist, soft, brown hair, that he never tired of stroking; and when it was done up in a bun, he felt that it gave her a very strong, very sure look, one he admired, as he admired so much about Gwen.

"Sure, I bought him some candy; is it a felony or a misdemeanor?"

"His *teeth*, Charlie."

"Come here, Sweetheart."

She never wore any makeup. He liked that about her, too, and the fact she worried about ordinary things like Frank getting cavities. While he kissed her he thought of what a good woman she was. He didn't know any who could even come close. Most were sluts, teases, deserving of anything they got, not that he ever wished any of them ill.

"Charlie, take it easy."

"I'm sorry."

"Said he . . . three broken bones later."

"I bought us some caviar," he said while his lips brushed her hair. "Not the red kind, either; the real thing."

She touched his cheek with her fingers and sighed.

63

"What's the sigh for?"

"It's just a sigh. I'm going to get dressed."

He went into the living room. Should he have a drink? One? He opened a chest where he kept liquor. Remember when there was anything anyone wanted? *Anything;* he never let anyone down, whether they drank Scotch or tequila, gin or campari, rye or blackberry brandy. His bar was the most well-stocked one on the university campus, and he did not buy house brands, either; he bought the best. He always afforded the best. It was the same with his wardrobe, with the furnishings in his and Gwen's home, and her wardrobe and the jewelry he bought for her. It was all the best, and he never offered anyone else less than the best; that was his conceit. He made no more than the other young professors; he simply sacrificed any savings. No one would ever call him cheap or ungenerous; he had a heart as big as all outdoors, did Charlie Latham, and everyone liked him, admired him; he had earned his Ph.D. by the time he was twenty-three, yet no one ever thought of Charlie Latham as a grind. No one did. He was an example, really, of what a modern teacher should be: he was brilliant, fun-loving, good-looking, a devoted husband, a father . . . and he did not have a single enemy. Not at the university, not at Georgon College, not at Yansetti Junior College either.

That it all could have gone to seed with such miraculous swiftness still caused him to wake up mornings thinking none of it had happened; it *could not have happened,* was all. Faced inevitably with the fact that it had happened, he could not seriously worry the matter. They would all realize their mistake. It was very possible they regretted their actions but could not rescind them once they were invoked; it was highly likely that his name was mentioned with deep remorse at the injustices he suffered. Surely there were some among them who had pointed out that old Charlie was *always* horsing around; you can't really believe he *meant* to do anything to those girls? Haven't any of you ever seen Charlie's wife? *Come on!*

One drink? Charlie debated the idea as he stood in the living room with a bottle of Old Taylor already in his hand. How would *one* hurt? But he put the bottle back; he was the type who felt incredibly virtuous having made such a decision, as he felt all but canonized when he could count back a week and know he had been totally dry.

On the other hand, his mood could swing the other way, and he would scorn his own self-righteousness; oh, a drink is *sinful,* Charlie; creepers, Charlie Latham, a drink could lead

64

to two, and two could lead to three, four, five, and, sakes alive, you'd have a little buzz on, dear.

Never mind that under the umbrella of the buzz he went crashing into walls, went whirling headlong into doors and furniture and rungs of stairs; his mind could minimize anything, such as when he would ask himself: now, *honestly*, what was so g. d. f---ing awful about paying a young lady the compliment of showing you were attracted to her? If it was such a g. d. f---ing awful thing to do, somebody tell old Charlie Latham why the little c's had marched themselves into his classrooms smelling like roses, with their boobs ready to put one of your eyes out.

Okay, keep the faith, baby; he did not have a drink. He went over and stretched out on the couch, thinking about the movie he had seen that afternoon, reminding himself not to slip and say anything about it, since he was still supposed to be working—can you believe it—as a substitute teacher at Food & Maritime Trades Vocational High School. A Ph.D. teaching Chocolate Cake II.

This will hand you another laugh: he *was* offered a full-time job that morning. A teacher's placement bureau advised him of an opening in a school for underachievers. He could feel the color in his face when he was told that; he hated it when the low blows showed, when the purse-mouthed personnel could divine the humiliation spreading through him as he sat breathless, while an uncomfortable warmth flooded his stomach and seeped into his bowels, while he fought it: smiling, shrugging, affecting a nonchalance: "What a moronic idea," while Purse-Lips scribbled something across his application blank with furious force.

What did she write with such conviction?

Smart ass! Unfit to associate with underachievers!

Gwen came into the room, saying, "Where's the mail, Charlie?"

"We didn't get any."

"We get *Time* on Tuesdays, Charlie."

"It wasn't there."

"We get bills the first of the month too, Charlie."

"Empty box, Sweetheart."

"They don't go away if you ignore them." She sat down on the hassock near the couch. "How was school?"

"Okay. We made alphabet soup out of a dictionary."

"Did you get paid or something?"

"Umm hmm."

"What did you buy for dinner? I heard Frank exclaiming when you came in."

"First course—caviar with onion chopped up in it and lemon sprinkled over it. Followed by roast beef, blood rare; artichoke hearts, one hothouse tomato as big as my fist, and a crisp head of fresh Boston lettuce. For dessert, rum cake with mocha frosting, *or* Creme Danica on thin crackers, *or* both! There. Do you love me?"

"Charlie, you *didn't* get paid, did you?"

"No. I robbed a bank. Was it on television?"

"No. You went and opened a charge at that new delicatessen on Broadway. . . . Didn't you?"

"What new delicatessen?"

"That's what you did, didn't you? If you had been paid, you would have gone to the A & P and bought some meat."

"I *did* buy meat!"

"*Real* meat!"

"Where do you and Frank get the idea meat isn't real unless it's raw?"

"Charlie, you went to a delicatessen. There isn't one within five miles of here that would give you credit. You *had* to go to that new one."

"Velly cwevah, Chawee Chan."

"Why do you do these things, Charlie? Why?"

Frank's voice said, "What did Daddy do now?"

"Frank, don't eat the candy before dinner," said Gwen.

"Did Daddy spend all our money?"

"Daddy didn't do anything," Gwen said.

"Oh, yes, Daddy did, too," Charlie said. "Daddy was really awful today, Frank. He drowned a sack of kittens in the Hudson River, and he tripped an old lady on the I.R.T., and he spit in a baby's eye, and he frugged in St. Patrick's——"

At that point the lights failed.

By eight o'clock Gwen was across in 3-H helping Mrs. Paulson feed and put to bed her three children, and Frank was distributing candles Gwen had found in a kitchen drawer. Charlie had walked up to the subway with a flashlight; he had seen several people home, guiding some up as many as ten flights of stairs.

When he returned to the apartment building, he remembered Mrs. Carroll in 1-A. He did not exactly remember her; she had been on his mind since early afternoon; since leaving the employment bureau, he had thought of going to visit her, but he did not want to spoil his mood now. He felt euphoric. He had begun to feel so down, just before everything had blacked out, so wearied by the sound of his own voice answering Gwen with wisecracks, so uncertain as to how long he could contain the façade he had managed ever since things had begun to go wrong for him. Say a lot of things about the control he supposedly did not have, but don't say Charlie Latham didn't have any. He had more than enough, and he could feel it coming back in the flurry of activity: helping Gwen make sandwiches for the neighbors, seeing those people home safely, sending Frank around with the candles; that was the old Charlie; nobody was going to convince him it wasn't.

What if he just visited Mrs. Carroll long enough to see that she was all right, never mind getting involved in the rest of it? She was an old woman, and she was a widow, and she was probably all by herself in there, afraid, and they *were* friends; there was no reason he could not just check up on her as a friend, then go on his way.

He went down to her door and knocked on it, promising himself ten minutes and that was it.

"Go away!" Mrs. Carroll called out. "Who is it?"

"It's God, Mrs. Carroll."

"*Who?*"

"The Holy Ghost, Mrs. Carroll."

"You'll blaspheme your way into hell, Charlie Latham."

"Do you have a candle?"

"Frank already gave me one."

"Are you going to let me in, or are we going to talk with the door between us."

"I don't need company."

"This is Judgment Day, Mrs. Carroll. Misery enjoys company."

"This is power failure. This is Con Ed on the blink."

He heard her chuckle; then she opened the door, smiling, holding a candle, dressed in an old white-flannel nightgown and a red sweater and stocking shoes. "You should be with your wife; let an old hen like me sit in the dark."

"My wife is helping Mrs. Paulson with the kids."

"I go to bed this hour anyway."

"Let's have some tea, Mrs. Carroll; pick your spirits up."

"You know what I thought: what if it's the Chinese?"

"They'll rape you in your bed. What do they care that you go to church every Sunday?"

"You think that's funny, but it's truthful."

She made tea by candlelight, and Charlie sat at the kitchen table with her while they listened for a while to the radio. Then she snapped it off and said, "Same thing over and over; some broken record."

Then she looked at Charlie, leaning forward, making it

obvious she was scrutinizing him, and she said, "You got a job yet?"

"I've got some leads."

"Leads! I've heard that one."

"I'm weighing some offers."

"Your wife know you don't have work?"

"No."

"You can't go on the way you're going, Charlie Latham. I know a way you could help yourself. My cousin——"

"Mrs. Carroll, I'm a *teacher*."

Mrs. Carroll went on undaunted. "My cousin is in the shoe manufacturing business down on——"

Charlie began to sing, "I do not ask, O Lord, that life may be a pleasant road."

Mrs. Carroll joined in, "I do not ask that Thou wouldst take from me aught of its load."

Yansetti Junior College had been an Episcopal institution; Charlie had come to know most of the hymns by heart. They sang: *My Soul Be on Thy Guard; Dear Lord and Father of Mankind; We Sing the Glorious Conquest; Eternal Light, Eternal Light; Softly Now the Light of Day; Earth Has Many a Noble City;* and *Purer Yet and Purer.*

Then Charlie said, "The last one reminds me of a soap commercial."

"Make fun, but just the same, you know the words to all of them."

"It's your influence, Mrs. Carroll."

She got up from the table. She said, "Go on, now, go back upstairs. You don't have to sit with an old lady."

"I was glad to."

He stood up; he hesitated.

She said, "It was nice of you."

Then he began. "Mrs. Fulton, my horse died and it's going to cost an arm and a leg to get another. Without my horse, I've got no way to earn a living here on the range."

She sighed.

Instantly he wanted to take it back; he was ashamed when he heard himself continue, "No way at all, ma'm."

She said, "I knew better than to think you came down here out of the kindness of your heart."

"Sorry, ma'm. Real, real sorry."

She said, "Just once, why don't you ask for it like a normal human being? Just once, why don't you say you need to borrow some money? Can you tell me the answer to that one, Charlie Latham?"

68

Charlie said, "I rode out to Hogtown and got me an estimate, and you know——"

"Stop it! I don't want to be put through all that. Just tell me. Ten?"

"Times three, ma'm."

"No. Not thirty. No. You owe me two hundred and fifty dollars, Charlie Latham. Not thirty more. Ten is what you get, and it's all you get."

She reached up in the cupboard for her bag.

"Ma'm, I'm mighty indebted——"

"Stop it! I hate that cowboy voice the worst. I hate them all, but that one I hate the worst. Here. Here's two fives. Go. If your wife knew how you beg, she'd move right out of this building; you think she could face me if she knew?"

"Much obliged, ma'm." And he went out of the apartment as fast as he could.

On the landing between the second and third floors he stopped and leaned back against the wall and shut his eyes. He could feel the beginning of a headache. He turned off his flashlight and stood there for several minutes.

Then he took hold.

Why the fit because he borrowed a little money from an old woman with money to spare?

A two-hundred-and-sixty-dollar debt; big deal!

When he had it, he had *given* that much away; he had been known for being a soft touch.

Why the sweat, why the sweat?

He smiled to himself; poor, old, solemn Charlie, make a federal case out of *everything*.

Hell-git! Git goin', pard'ner!

He took the stairs by twos and sailed into his apartment, calling out, "Where's my brood?"

There was no answer. He walked into the bedroom, which was dark, but he was right, Gwen *was* there.

"I thought I heard you. What are you doing in the dark, Sweetheart?"

"Charlie, Jerry says the rent isn't paid for October."

"Jerry said that to you in the middle of this business? That's what he said? Couldn't he see you helping everybody, rushing around to see that everybody was all right?"

"Charlie, it isn't Jerry's fault; the landlord gets after him to speak to us."

"At a time like this? When you're helping everyone?"

"We could redecorate the lobby, Charlie; we'd still owe the rent. I thought you paid October, Charlie. Now we owe two months."

"I'm going to pay it tomorrow, Sweetheart."

"I don't believe you anymore, Charlie. You told me you'd paid October."

"Sweetheart! Sweetheart!" He went over and sat down on the bed in the darkness beside her. He took her hand. "I kiss your hand, madam."

"I don't feel like joking, Charlie."

"Look how we helped people tonight, Sweetheart. Not many folks bestirred themselves to do anything for their fellow man: but the Lathams were in there pitching."

"Let's not pat ourselves on the backs, Charlie."

"Why the deuce not? You tell me, why the deuce not? I think we've got a right to toot our own horn."

"Oh, Charlie, everything's not so simple."

"Why the sweat, why the sweat? You want to make a federal case out of everything! I'll pay the rent. We've given away more than that measley sum!"

"Charlie? Do you know what Frank did with the candles I gave him to give to the neighbors?"

"Mrs. Carroll got hers. I looked in on her, Sweetheart, sang a few hymns with her."

"He sold the rest for a dollar apiece."

"He what?"

"He sold them, Charlie—a dollar apiece."

Charlie did not say anything for a moment; for a moment Charlie could not speak. When he could, what came out was, "Ah so, Ah so," in his best Japanese voice.

# 13

"What you really did, Reverend, by taking her away like that, was facilitate her drinking."

"You're right, Mrs. Graeff."

"I don't mean to blame you."

"I know."

"You had good intentions."

"The road to hell is paved——"

70

"With good intentions, yes."

"Maugham wrote something in *The Moon and Sixpence* about——"

"Somerset Maugham!"

"Yes."

"What was it he wrote in *The Moon and Sixpence?*"

"He said that a woman will forgive a man any harm he does her, but she will never forgive him for the sacrifices he makes on her account."

Part of drinking for Charlie was the talking, always had been. Sit on a bar stool, talk to the fellow next to you about H-bombs changing the weather; get into a big discussion of Ravi Shankar at some party; Charlie had even enjoyed those nights he'd wander down to Mrs. Carroll's with half a bag on and talk to her. And he'd enlarge on things, sure, that went with it; he'd do a little inventing, create some original fiction about his life, yes. And always, always for a while right after, he'd feel so damn euphoric, as he was feeling now.

Mrs. Graeff said, "We're inclined to imagine that in making a sacrifice for someone, we're doing them a service; perhaps that's what's wrong about self-sacrifice. It's really a form of bargaining: I'll do this for you, because you're going to do that for me."

"Maugham wrote something else I like: 'Conscience is the guardian in the individual, of the rules which the community has evolved for its own preservation.' "

"That's a difficult one, Reverend; would you mind repeating it?"

"Before you do, Reverend," said Whistler, "I'd like to make a suggestion."

"Ah, so! Rilliam Ristler rishes speak to humble audience."

"Seriously."

"Sewiously."

"Okay, Reverend, you're probably the life of the Sunday-night box-lunch parties in the church basement, but——"

"Mr. Whistler, I, for one, strenuously object to your rudeness. It is forgivable, perhaps, in a young girl who has obviously never been taught any manners, but you know better."

"I know this, Mrs. Graeff: we're still here, and it's now fifteen minutes after nine."

"It *is?*" She looked down at her wristwatch.

"It is," said Whistler. "Gillespie said he was returning as soon as he made the phone calls, and we haven't heard from him; he's had enough time to make three times that many calls; where is he?"

T. T. Blades was now sitting on the floor by the control panel, his legs crossed Indian style in front of him. "What do you want *her* to do about it, Whistler?"

"I'm not just talking to Mrs. Graeff. I'm talking to everyone. I suggest we take a look at our situation from the roof of the car."

"Oh, that's good thinking, Whistler. That's the one thing Gillespie warned us against doing; he said don't open the doors, don't open the roof hatch."

"You're used to taking orders, aren't you, Blades?"

"I'm used to giving them."

"Really?"

"What do you think a quarterback does?" What does an ex-quarterback do? He gets used to guys like this; these are the kind of guys he'll have to hang around with—the briefcase-and-ulcer set.

"Do you give orders to your coach?" Whistler asked.

"No."

"No, you don't. *He* gives *you* orders."

"What's your point, Whistler?"

"We're programmed differently, Blades. I'm not used to taking orders, and I don't like anyone else sizing up my situation for me."

Charlie Latham said, "I thought *I* had the floor."

"And you're the damnedest minister I've ever met, Smoke."

"If he is one," said Josie Swift.

"I beg your pardon, Miss Swift, but would you *dare* to repeat what you just said? For I believe that I would then have a perfectly valid excuse for slapping your face."

Charlie Latham said, "Why, Mrs. Graeff, don't you know that I could be the devil masquerading?"

"Exactly!" She laughed. "Oh, it's fortunate you have a sense of humor, Reverend."

"What's number thirty-two in *The Hymnal*, Reverend?" Josie Swift said.

He imitated Woody Woodpecker. "The, the, the, the, that's all folks."

"Why should he know the hymns by number?" T. T. Blades said.

"He should know most of them; I do. I only sang in the choir."

"He's not a computer, Miss Swift; he's a minister."

72

"Any Episcopalian minister would know that thirty-two is *From Every Stormy Wind That Blows!*"

"From every swelling tide of woes," Charlie Latham sang softly; he didn't know the numbers, but he knew the words; he had to keep from laughing aloud; she had almost outfoxed him; and he felt good now, just loaded enough for a nice glow. He had always wondered if you stopped right at the peak, would you stay up there; if you didn't go over it with another drink, would it hold? Affirmative, mates; nirvana! "There is a calm, a sure retreat; 'Tis found beneath the mercy-seat. There, there, on eagles' wings we soar; And time and sense seem all no more; And heaven comes down, our souls to greet; And glory crowns the mercy-seat."

Mrs. Graeff applauded when he had finished singing, and T. T. Blades joined in the applause.

Then, "Lou Gillespie here."

Blades got to his feet. "T. T. Blades."

"Okay. First. Tell Mrs. Graeff that her husband already knew about it from Roger. There's a bad storm at Sneden's Landing, too; he can't get the car out, but he's kept the reservation for her at the Dorset. He wants her to call him when she checks in there. Got that?"

Mrs. Graeff nodded. "Got it," said T. T.

"Blades? Your father-in-law isn't home yet."

"Did you try calling him at Hockaday? He stays late at the office sometimes."

"There's no answer. Just about everybody's left the building by now. We've kept this situation from them as much as possible. We don't want a crowd jamming the lobby. But I called the Cunard Line. They'll get a message to your wife on the *Franconia*."

"Thanks, Gillespie."

"Incidentally, I didn't describe the situation. I said you couldn't get through traffic because of the weather. It's feasible."

"Right."

"Mr. Whistler's wife wanted to know if it was business; I said it was. I hope that's okay with him. She asked me outright; I couldn't think of anything else to tell her."

Whistler walked up to the control panel. "What's the situation now, Gillespie?"

"Hello, Whistler."

"Thanks for calling my wife; it's best if she thinks it business."

"I don't know how long she'll accept that, if she has her radio on."

"Are we news?"

"Well, someone from WINS was here. You know, they're the twenty-four-hour news station. They do on-the-spot coverage of stalled automobiles, anything that happens; they'll probably put it on the air."

"My wife stays with television . . . What *is* the situation now, Gillespie?"

"Status quo. The crew from Skidmore isn't here yet."

"Where the hell do they have to come from?"

"They'll be here any minute, Whistler."

"That's what you told me an hour ago. . . . And how come it took you so long? Don't misunderstand me, Gillespie, I'm not on your back; I just can't figure out why everything's moving in slow motion."

"We've only got one phone booth in the lobby, Whistler. Before we cleared the lobby, people were lined up for it."

"There still isn't any chance of getting us some hot coffee, something to eat?"

"How would we do that, Whistler? If we could do that, we could probably get you out."

"Can't you lower someone through the roof hatch?"

"Whistler, no one here has the authority to get anywhere near that shaft. The car has to stay intact until Skidmore gets here."

Beside Whistler, Blades said, "You see?"

"Gillespie?"

"What, Whistler?"

"You say no one there has the authority."

"Right."

"Isn't there anyone with any authority there?"

"Right here, right now, Whistler, there's only the maintenance man."

"I'd like to have a word with him."

"Gladly. You want to hang on?"

Whistler turned to the others. "I can see why Gillespie doesn't want to get involved; he *doesn't* have the authority, but the maintenance man is an employee of the building. If there's no other representative, he should be responsible."

"Why can't you just relax, Whistler?"

"Blades, when I know I've done everything I can, then I will relax."

Gillespie said, "You there, Whistler? I have the maintenance man."

They could hear Gillespie telling someone to take over, and a man's voice protesting.

Then, "Hello?"

74

"Who *is* this?" Whistler demanded.

"It's Stanley."

"Look, Mr. Stanley——"

"Mr. Ryan. Stanley Ryan. I'm just a maintenance man here."

"Look, Mr. Ryan, if we're midway between twenty and twenty-one, would it be too much to ask of someone to open the doors on twenty-one and lower some food and hot coffee to us through the roof hatch?"

"I don't have anything to do with the elevators. That's not my province."

"You're the maintenance man, aren't you? What exactly do you maintain?"

"The elevators aren't my province. I don't do anything with the elevators unless the building superintendent okays it."

"*Mr. Ryan!* You're not in charge of the sidewalks, either, but if someone were to fall down in front of the Gart Building, would you wait until the building superintendent okayed it to help him up?"

"This isn't my job."

"We need help, Ryan."

"Help's on the way, and that's all I can tell you. I'm not even supposed to carry on a conversation over this thing; that's the building superintendent's province."

"Well, where is he?"

"He lives out in Queens. He's coming. He doesn't like it if things are done he didn't okay, and I've got my job to think about. When the Skidmore people say it's okay to open any doors or hatches, that's when we'll do it."

Gillespie's voice again. "Whistler?"

"What?"

"Sit tight. You've only been there a little over three hours; you can't be starving."

"Can't I?"

"Don't make waves, Whistler, okay? Everybody should stay still. There shouldn't be any moving around."

Whistler said, "When that crew finally gets here, I'd like to talk to its head."

"Sure. We'll arrange it. . . . All right, I'm signing off now; if there's something important, press the alarm and I'll come to the speaker."

"Why don't you just leave it on?"

"We don't want to run down the batteries. . . . But I'll be here; I'll hear you if you ring the bell."

Across from Whistler, Charlie Latham was lighting another cigarette.

"Hey, wait a minute, Gillespie!"

"What now?"

"Should there be cigarette smoking?"

"Are you kidding? Absolutely no smoking."

Whistler said to Latham, "Did you hear that?"

But the Reverend wasn't easy to fathom, for he was giving Whistler this silly grin now, and he was moving his shoulder and working his body as though he were winding up for something.

Charlie Latham was; he was winding up for his Jimmy Cagney impersonation; he was about to do Cagney saying, "You dir-ty rat!" but all he managed before he lost his balance and smashed face-first into the elevator doors was, "You dir-ty—"; then he hit; his glasses fell from his head to the floor, where they were found and crushed to pieces by his left black-calf Florsheim, size 11½.

# 14

"You didn't tell them we were here, did you, Gillespie?"

"How could I? Then they'd want to talk to you. *He* would, anyway; Whistler would."

"Well, I haven't got a *damn* thing to say to them. I couldn't look a one of them in the eye," said Milton Farley. He was the head of the Skidmore crew; he had arrived forty-five minutes ago, studied the situation, then huddled with Lieutenant Scholz of the Emergency Service Division of the New York City Police. He had told Scholz this was not anything he could handle, and it was not anything the division could handle, either. The only man he knew who could even guess about how to attack this problem was a fellow named Gil Holland, Skidmore's prime troubleshooter.

Scholz, Farley, Gillespie and Stanley Ryan stood in the lobby of the Gart Building going over things.

"There's no way we can get them anything to eat?" Gillespie asked again.

"Not a chance," Farley said.

Scholz said, "Once more. Describe the problem."

"Here it is, Lieutenant: she's got a broken cable. Now, normally when a cable breaks, four brake shoes automatically engage the vertical rails. The car is then held secure by two pairs of brakes on both sides. We reattach the cable, and that's it. But—this one was a fluke. When the cable broke, it whipped around and caught in the linkage; it jammed the safety-brake mechanism. The brake shoes aren't fully engaged; the car is being held, but not held fast. It could slip. It could go all the way."

"They're lucky there're not more of them," Gillespie said.

"Gillespie, anyway you look at it, they're not lucky."

Scholz said, "Gillespie, why haven't you told them what their situation is?"

"I'm afraid of panic."

"I'd *want* to know," said Scholz.

"I would, too, Lieutenant. But if I were up there with them, I wouldn't want the women to know, and I wouldn't want that hothead Whistler to know."

"He the one that's hungry all the time?"

"Yes. He's the head of Whistler Foods; they have offices on the twenty-third floor here."

Scholz said, "My kids are always singing their commercial: 'Whistle While We Work.' "

"If I could get food in to him," said Gillespie, "I think I could quiet him down."

"Forget the food!" Farley snapped.

Then he realized his nerves were getting the better of him; he said, "I'm sorry, Gillespie. I guess I'm hungry myself."

Gillespie said, "There's a coffee shop right across the street."

Stanley Ryan was standing behind the three men. His brow was furrowed in thought. His wife said that whenever Stanley thought very hard about something, his face always looked as though he were sitting on the can with his pants down, grunting. So much for her opinion of his thinking processes; so much for everyone's opinion of what a great thinker he wasn't, including present company. But something was coming to him, slowly, something he remembered from his infantry days in the mountains of Tunisia; cripes, must have been twenty-five years ago . . . this big platform loaded with artil-

77

lery, halfway up the ledge, hanging by ropes, and one rope beginning to give.

Scholz said, "What can we do while we're waiting for Holland?"

"That's just it," said Farley. "I don't know. I've never seen one like this."

Scholz said, "There are more elevators in New York City than anywhere in the world, but I've never seen one like this either, and I've seen my share of stalled elevators."

"Let's get some food sent in," said Farley. "We're just going to have to wait for Gil."

"Stanley?" Gillespie said. "You're not doing anything; will you run across and get some food for them?"

But Stanley Ryan did not hear Gillespie. Stanley was hard at work on the problem; his thoughts were far away in time and space—Africa, circa 1943.

# 15

"Do you have a pencil, Mr. Whistler?"

"I have a pen, Miss Swift."

"Can I borrow it a sec?"

He took it from the inside pocket of his suit and passed it to her. He was back sitting on his coat, on the floor beside her. He was watching Mrs. Graeff administer smelling salts to the minister. Smoke was also sitting on the floor, his shoulders leaning against the elevator doors. Blades was standing next to him; he was holding the black frame of Smoke's glasses, with their shattered panes.

Whistler was remembering what the minister had started to say. You dir-ty . . . what? You dirty Jew?

How would Smoke know that Whistler was a Jew; Whistler wasn't making any secret of it, but how would Smoke know?

"Jew-baiters know," Mariam always said. "They have special built-in antennae, and they just know."

Whistler remembered something else: the way Smoke had

78

flipped open his lighter and lit his cigarette before Whistler had even been able to finish what he was saying about smoking in the elevator.

It was a suspicion he had not entertained in a long time—that he was being treated in a certain way because he was a Jew; it was ironical that it would be a minister who would revive the feeling, but this fellow was a far cry from Norman Vincent Peale.

Mrs. Graeff said, "Breathe deeply, Reverend. . . . I never have fainting spells myself, but I've always carried my little bottle of Yardley."

"Boy! He hit those doors like Cassius Clay had swung at him," said Blades.

"He shouldn't have gone into all that upleasantness with his wife. It upset him. I don't think he realized how much it was going to affect him."

"Be all right," Charlie Latham murmured. "Just dizzy."

"Don't try to talk, dear."

"Glasses."

"They're broken, Reverend," said T. T. Blades.

Josie Swift looked in her bag and found the small pad she carried for writing down things she wanted to remember. Across the top sheet was written: "Tanqueray gin—pronounced tanker-ray. Everett M. Dirksen is Senate *Minority Leader!*"

She tore that sheet off and stuck it at the back of the pad. Then she wrote: "I think he's drunk and is not a minister at all. Before I got on this elevator I met him on the twenty-third floor and he—"

How was she going to put it?

T. T. Blades said, "Let's move you away from the doors, Reverend. It's not a very safe spot, right in front of the doors."

"You're absolutely right," said Mrs. Graeff.

Latham made the move himself. He pushed himself across so that he was now beside Josie Swift.

"—acted funny," she scribbled. She crossed out "funny" and wrote "very strange. He stood in front of the door and he—"

"You keeping a diary of what's happening, Miss Swift?" Latham said.

"Of what happened."

"Of what happened when?"

"Don't try to talk, dear," Mrs. Graeff said again.

"Somebody should," he said. "Somebody."

"Yes. Yes, he's right," said Mrs. Graeff. "Who hasn't had a turn?"

"Count me out," said Whistler. "I've said what I had to say. If you're all willing to act like sheep, there's not much I can do about it. If I were to open the roof hatch and take a look, I'd make one-sixth as much commotion as he just made, and none of us would be any the worse for it. We might be a lot better off because of it, too."

"—wasn't going to let me get by," Josie wrote.

"Then it's Miss Swift's turn, if Whistler is passing," said Charlie Latham.

"How about it, Miss Swift?" T. T. Blades said. "Will you tell us where you were the night of the blackout?"

"What *are* you writing?" Whistler asked.

Now everyone was looking at her; she couldn't tell Whistler she was writing him a note.

"Something I want to remember."

She folded what she had written and kept it in her palm, while she put the pad back in her bag. When she returned Whistler's pen, she would pass the note with it; she would pick just the right time.

"You have the floor," said Charlie Latham.

And she knew what he was trying to do; he knew what she was trying to do.

But he could not see very well without his glasses, could he?

So she'd play along with him: begin at the beginning with the Franchers' party, and before she reached the end of her little story, there would be two people wise to the Reverend Smoke.

# 16

... go melt back into the night Babe
everything is made of stone
there's nothing in here moving
and anyway I'm not alone—

"Bob Dylan here," said Josie Swift.

She snapped her fingers and did a few frug steps; she was in the crowded barn by herself. Irene had disappeared with Lake Francher.

With *the* Lake Francher of New Hope, Pennsylvania; a $winger; daddy owned $ome kind of big company.

This was The End of the World Party put together by Lake Francher and his brother, Harlan, around six on the evening of the power failure.

Pennsylvania was not affected, but shortly after news of the blackout came over the radio, Ted Plant and some fellows Irene and Josie hardly knew stopped by the Delaware Inn and said come out to Franchers' barn, the Chinese were going to drop the bomb, and everybody was going to drink the Franchers dry before they did.

Irene waited table at the Delaware; she only worked a half day on Tuesdays, and she was just finishing up. Tuesdays Josie sat with Mrs. Larsen's parrot, while Mrs. Larsen bought groceries for the week. The parrot was thirty-three years old and ill, and Mrs. Larsen never left the house unless there was someone there to watch after it. The Larsen house was on Canal Street, and when Josie was finished she would walk down to the Inn for a ride home with Irene.

On the way out to the Franchers' in Irene's seven-year-old Buick, she said, "How's this for fancy? Do I get you asked to nice places, or don't I?"

Irene was twenty-three, six years older than Josie; she was a Clairol redhead; she always smelled of Juicy Fruit and Chantilly, and she loved anything with a leopard motif. The car had leopard slip covers she had sent away for, and she was wearing a fake fur with a leopard pattern. Both parents had been dead since Josie was twelve, and Irene had been mother and sister to Jo. They rented the top half of a double house on the Acquetong Road near Lahaska; they did all right, with color TV and wall-to-wall carpeting, and the whole living room slip-covered in leopard velveteen.

"We won't know anybody there," Josie said.

"If you think I don't know Lake Francher, you've got another think coming. Whenever he comes into the place, he tries for my table. Sometimes he waits until one is free. I seen him do it half a dozen times."

"*I* don't know anyone in that crowd."

"You know Harlan."

"No, I don't. Just because we went to the same school?

81

Him and his crowd act like they never laid eyes on me, I meet them anyplace."

"What *crowd?*" Irene said angrily. "You talk as though it was some kind of fancy click. They're just people live around here same as we do."

"How come they're having a party in a barn? I thought they was rich."

"You don't think there's going to be any hay in the barn?" Irene laughed and squeezed Josie's knee. "Don't be so burshwa, honey."

"What's that supposed to mean?"

"Burshwa means you don't have class. A customer taught it to me. He wants to buy me a drink once, see, and I says a beer would do nicely, and that's when I first heard 'burshwa.' 'Order a *drink,*' he says. 'Beer is burshwa.' "

Irene was right. There was no hay in the barn. It was the fanciest barn Josie Swift had ever seen, with wooden floors and beamed ceiling, and a bar with leather-seat stools; studio couches and marble-top coffee tables and modern paintings; and a hi-fi with loudspeakers at opposite ends of the barn.

Josie wasn't much of a drinker; she accepted a whiskey and soda, but it tasted strong, so she nursed it. Irene stayed with her for a while; they sort of hung together near the bar, holding their glasses, doing slow little steps to the music, singing snatches of the songs they knew, checking in with one another every few minutes.

"There's Billy Inman; father owns a horse-riding stable."

"It's real nice here, isn't it, Irene?"

"S'okay, honey. . . . That's Fred Wolfe, honey."

"Who's he?"

"The Wolfe family own the place on Burnt Hill Road; they're rolling in dough."

Then Lake Francher himself walked up to Irene, and Josie had to hand it to Irene, she knew how to handle herself. Heck. She introduced Josie to Lake Francher, then started right in with a conversation: "How's the world treating you?"

"Just fine. How's it treating you?"

"Can't complain, Lake, can't complain."

Very cool. Before Josie knew it, her sister was out there dancing with Lake, then neither one of them was anywhere in view.

Josie had an inferiority complex, so it was doubly hard being left by herself in that crowd, but she knew anything by Bob Dylan and that was what was playing, so she jigged around and sang to the record, as though she could not ask for anything more to make the evening perfect.

> You walk into the room
> with your pencil in your hand
> you see somebody naked and you say
> who is that man?
> something is happening here
> you don't know what it is
> do you Mister Jones?

Over in one corner of the barn a group was gathered around a radio, and periodically someone would shout out the latest: "Sabotage feared!"

"The President is talking directly to Hoover!"

"SAC is on the alert!"

But the whole crisis didn't amount to a hill of beans where Josie was concerned, because even if it was the end of the world, being at the Franchers' would still be more exciting. More terrifying, too. She doubted she'd ever be in a class with Irene; how did you *like* that sister of hers? Can't complain, Lake, can't complain, she says.

"Hi!" said a voice behind Josie.

She turned around, and there stood Harlan Francher with his hair combed so neatly and parted on the side. What was it about rich men's hair? It was always straighter and longer, and it shone; Harlan's was coal black; he had very dark-brown eyes and fine features and good skin. He wore a navy blazer with gold buttons, and gray flannels, loafers, and bright-red socks. Freshman year he was president of the drama club at high; any year he was most handsome in his class. It was Lake who had the style, Harlan who had the looks. And, of course, Harlan was younger, seventeen, same as Josie.

Josie said, "Hello, Harlan. I didn't think you remembered me."

"What would I have toddled over here with my drink for?"

"Search me."

"I wouldn't mind."

"Well, I don't mean that the way it sounds."

"Where'd you learn to dance like that? Howie Waterhouse?"

"*Howie Waterhouse!* You're around the bend if you think that. Howie don't dance; he's a farmer."

83

"Do you go with him?"

"Who said that? You really are around the bend if you think that. Heck. Howie *Waterhouse?* He's stuck on his cows."

"You've never been out here before, have you?"

"I was never asked before. I see you and your crowd, you look through me like you didn't know I was alive."

*"Tiens. Tiens."*

"Huh?"

"I said well, well."

"Well, you do. I says, if they want to be stuck up, that's *their* problem."

"I want to be friendly."

"I'm glad to hear it, Harlan, because I'm not a snob or this, that, and the other thing, but if people don't treat me nice, I don't treat them nice back."

"May I take you home?"

*"Now?"*

"When you want to go. Lake's taken your sister home."

"My *eye!"*

"He did. She made me promise to see you home."

"She's got the car; they didn't go in her car?"

"They took two cars."

"Oh."

"His and hers. Like on the bath towels?"

"You sure, Harlan?"

"Positive, Ducky."

"Well. Heck. I don't know what to say."

"What say we drive over to the Centerbridge Inn and have some drinks, and then I'll drive you home?"

As much as she wanted to stay, she wanted everyone to see her leave with Harlan. She didn't have anything to worry about; he made a production out of the exit. He was calling out that he would see everyone later, *maybe*, and then he made a big deal of her waiting while he backed his Sting Ray up to the barn door, honking the horn as he pulled up, and, get this, actually getting out and coming up the walk to lead her out to the car!

"I'm glad you're such a gentleman, Harlan," she said.

"Isn't Howie Waterhouse a gentleman?"

"I wish you wouldn't bring *him* up all the time. I don't like our names linked together."

He laughed. Then he said, "You sit with Lizzie Larsen, don't you?"

"Tuesdays."

84

"I don't know." He laughed again. "It strikes me funny."

"Well. I understand that. I think it is unusual."

"*Unusual?* To baby-sit for a thirty-three-year-old parrot?" He was hardly able to talk, he was laughing so hard. "Well—I—don't—know; that all depends on your—haw-w-ah—view, view, viewpoint."

She looked across at him thoughtfully; she tried to discover if there were any ridicule of her intended. She ventured, "She's a real nice bird. You know she sings arias from operas."

"She—she-she-what?"

"Harlan?"

"Wha-wha-what?"

"Are you laughing at me or at the bird or what all?"

"At—the—whole—whole—thing," he managed.

She said, "You must think I'm awful dumb!"

"Why?"

"The way you laugh at me. How would you like it? Har-de-*har, har, har.*"

"Oh, bullshit, it's nothing to get worked up over."

"And I don't like that word, either, Harlan Francher. You better show me some respect!"

"*Merde!*"

"Huh?"

"I said anything you say, missy."

Then suddenly he swung the car off the road and cut the motor.

"Hunt-uh, buster! Oh, no you don't!" she said.

"I'm not going to touch you."

"You're doggone tooting."

"Do you let Howie?"

"*Let—him—what?*"

"Oh, come off it, Josie. Come *off* it."

"Well *what?*"

"Bang you!"

"Take me home this minute. *This minute!*"

"I can't oblige, Ducky. My brother and your sister aren't going to be finished until midnight. Now. That's what they said, that's the time they said."

"You're lying."

"I'm not lying."

"I don't believe you."

"I happen to be telling you the truth."

"Irene doesn't even know him," said Josie. "He tries to get her table when he goes to the Inn, and I suppose they've held

85

conversations, but she doesn't know him well. Even if she did——"

"She doesn't know half of them."

"Don't you talk like that, Harlan!"

"Well, admit it. You know your own sister. Don't act so dumb!"

"Harlan, take me home. This minute."

He put his hand on the dashboard and flipped on the headlights. He turned and looked into her eyes. "Do you really want to go home, see for yourself?" There was a long pause. "Do you, Josie?"

"No," she said.

He turned the lights off.

He lighted a cigarette.

Jose said, "She's been in love with him for a long time."

"Bullshit!"

"Secretly."

"*Bull*shit!"

"Well, I was the only one who *knew!* She didn't tell anyone but me!"

"She's catting, Josie! Don't clean it up!"

Josie Swift didn't say anything. He sat there smoking his cigarette, staring out the window. Finally he said, "How would you like to be seen with me a lot?"

"What for, Harlan?"

"For your ego and for mine."

"Huh?"

"You don't often get seen with a guy like me, and I don't often get seen with a girl like you. It'd do us both good, where it counts."

"Oh, wow. I must be D-U-M-B. I don't make head nor tail of what you mean, Harlan."

"In plain English, you need to look like you've got some class, and I need to look like I've got some ass."

She felt a sudden sensation of pain inside her, as though her innards had fallen; she stiffened and could not seem to let her muscles loose again. She sat there saying nothing, waiting for what he would say next. It was as though she were being punished for admitting about Irene to herself; now all of reality was going to be revealed, like a penalty for wrong-doing.

"Don't get me wrong," he said.

"I heard you, Harlan," she was able to get out.

"What I mean is, I won't touch you."

"Huh?"

"I won't touch you."

86

"What are you *talking* about? Will you just let me know what you're talking about? I think I understand you, and then I don't, but I wish you would just make it clear what you mean!" There were tears in her eyes; she could not be more confused. She held on—like holding on to a feather—to the wild hope he would crush her against him suddenly and say he wanted to marry her or something else crazy and impossible, anything but this muddle which was exposing truths so hurtful she was not sure she could stand or walk once he did get her to where she was going.

He said, "I'll take you around, that's all."

"Oh, sure. I'll believe that one."

He sighed and rolled his window down and tossed away his cigarette.

He said, "Well, what do you think?"

"I think it's very sweet of you, but I don't understand. I mean, if you're too much of a gentleman to touch me, why would you want me to have a reputation? You know? Because if people think that, I'll get a bad reputation, Harlan. Even if you are a Francher."

"Josie," he said, "it's not sweet of me. You already have a reputation, and I want some of it to rub off on me."

"Huh?"

"They come in from Lambertville to get at your sister. They drive down from Upper Black Eddy, from Frenchtown, to get at her; you know that? You say you don't know that and I'll say you're a second Helen Keller, Josie Swift, because anyone in the county over twelve years old knows that. They come from as far away as Trenton; they journey———"

"Shut up, Harlan."

"I'd take you places."

"I don't understand why you want to."

"I'm not going to explain it."

"Well, you must care about me. You must."

"Nope. I don't. We sit here, and I'm not even tempted. You'll be safe as the gold in Fort Knox, Josie."

She said, "Hey! . . . You're not a—you're not a fairy boy?"

He looked at her, a grin tipping his lips.

She felt as though maggots were attached to her; she felt as though red ants were crawling up her legs; nothing gave her the creeps the way that kind of thing did. She wanted to feel sorry for him, but he wouldn't even let her do that, because he was laughing now like he was proud of it.

"Harlan, I don't ever want to see you again," she said.

"What?"

"I don't. You're not a very nice person, if you ask me."

He let out a hoot. "If I ask you? Oh, my God! Oh, that's beautiful! I love it!" He turned to look at her. "Why, don't you know what you are? Don't you *know?* Don't you know that Mrs. Larsen wouldn't ask anyone but you to sit with her parrot, no more than somebody with kids would ask you to baby-sit? You and your sister are trash, jokes; don't you *know* that?"

She didn't answer him.

"Ted Plant and Lake flipped a coin for your sister tonight; Lake got tails, and tails is your sister."

She didn't feel any pain in her stomach then; she felt numb.

## 17

She knew Mr. Whistler was jumpy, but how jumpy surprised her. While she was talking she had let her hand dangle and brush his knee. His pen was between her fingers, and the note was clutched in her palm. His body had jerked as though he had been touched with a hot poker. At the end of her story, she still had the pen and the note.

She had edited her story. The Senator had taught her that word; he had told her once to edit the truth when circumstances called for it, not to lie, but to withhold unpleasant facts.

The only way she mentioned Harlan was to say that the party was at his house; she did not mention sitting with Lizzie Larsen, either.

Charlie Latham was the first to speak. "I remember parties like that when I was a kid."

He seemed much younger without his glasses; without his glasses, Josie was not frightened of him, perhaps because he could not see her very well and was no longer staring at her. His eyes were blue; he had quite white skin, as though he spent most of his time indoors. Unspectacled, it was a weak face. Josie no longer felt any urgency about passing the note to Whistler. She dropped it down into her boot.

He reminded her of Harlan, too. Not Harlan the night of the Franchers' party, but Harlan as she had seen him those few times last summer: thin, like this man, pale as he was. Harlan with the wind out of his sails, with nothing much to say anymore, even though she would pretend she had forgotten all about that other thing.

"I missed the partying," said T. T. Blades. "I was always in training. No liquor, eleven o'clock curfew, even in college. I was pinned to this Tri Delt, and it used to burn her up that I couldn't take her to the parties."

"Instead of Bob Dylan," said Latham, "we had Johnny Ray, Les Paul and Mary Ford—and I remember one song in particular, *Come on-a My House;* Rosemary Clooney." There was a girl that year who was crazy about him. One night at a party she sang that to Charlie. She did an exaggerated bump and grind to the music, zeroing in on him, pretending to strip; everyone was laughing, egging her on; she leaned over him and she was going to kiss him. He was sitting there holding a Dr. Pepper, watching her breasts come closer and closer to his face. Next thing, he was standing in a corner, doubled over. "Charlie just tossed his cookies!" someone was explaining to the room. "He couldn't even make the can. He just barfed."

T. T. Blades said, "I'd tell this Tri Delt: 'Do you want to go with a football player or a party boy, because, honey, I can't be both.' "

"We didn't have sororities at Radcliffe," said Mrs. Graeff. "I never approved of them, either. Nothing against you, Mr. Cougar."

T. T. laughed. "That's okay, Mrs. G. I didn't belong to a sorority. Boy, I'd give anything for a cigarette."

"So would I!" said Latham.

Whistler sat silently. Jackass; all she had wanted to do was return the pen. But your actions will find you out; he had been thinking about her just at the moment her hand had brushed his knee. He had known someone like her, so briefly, once, years ago. He never allowed himself to remember it; it was pointless to, it was destructive. He would not even review the circumstances now, but in the same way one feels on a certain day nostalgia for another time, because of the look of the day, the smell and feel of the air, so could Whistler remember his impression of that girl—the sickly sweetness of her perfume, nearly as overwhelming as this gardenia odor; then, standing beside her, or sitting near her,

89

not even looking at her, just something about the way she moved and made you aware of her movement, you felt the rhythm of her body as though you were intimately involved with her.

Then he had turned it off, instantly, the second she touched him; he was disgusted by himself. He realized he had not only learned to accommodate the heady aroma of her perfume—he had stopped sneezing; he was also apparently accommodating this whole situation.

He remembered a sentence his grandfather had always used to close his letters: *wie es kommt, wird es gefressen*—as things come, we'll eat them. When he was a boy, it had seemed a stalwart statement; years later, when he began reading about Nazi Germany, he understood how this fatalism had helped destroy men like David Wiesel.

Blades's voice broke in on his thoughts, "Well, what do you say, Whistler?"

"To what?"

"Mrs. Graeff just said she didn't see why we couldn't have an occasional cigarette."

"I know how my own husband is, Mr. Whistle. It can be one in the morning, but if he's out of cigarettes, he gets in the car and drives seven miles down the road to a gas station for a pack."

"You're all convinced this isn't very serious, is that it?"

"Nobody said *that*, Mr. Whistle."

"But if you thought it was really serious, you wouldn't take *any* chances, would you?"

"It seems like such a small chance."

"Mrs. Graeff, the fact is, we don't know how serious it is, isn't that right?"

"Yes. Mr. Gillespie did assure us that everything would be all right, though."

"What do you think Mr. Gillespie would say if I rang the alarm and asked if smoking should be permitted?"

Blades said, "Okay, Whistler; have things *your* way."

"No, not my way, and not your way. Our way, Blades. I'm all for compromise. You want to smoke, and I want to go up on the roof and have a look."

"That's a little different, Mr. Whistle. That could endanger our lives!"

"Take a good look at me, Mrs. Graeff; would you take me for a suicidal type?"

"The fact is, none of us knows anything about you. You're the only one who's refused to play our little blackout game."

"Believe me, I'm not the suicidal type. I'm not going to endanger anyone's life, including my own. This car is locked in position; if it could go up or down, we'd be able to get off at twenty or twenty-one on manual."

"What do you think you'll see up on the roof?" said Blades.

"How far we are from twenty-one, for one thing."

"Oh, who *cares* how far we are from twenty-one, Mr. Whistle!"

"We could be stuck here all night," said Whistler. "There's one hell of a storm outside. The Skidmore crew isn't even here yet! We could——"

Mrs. Graeff said, "They'll be here any minute; I *feel* that."

"They should have been here before this," Blades said.

"But what can you *do*, Mr. Whistle; what can you do besides go up and see what's wrong?"

"Mrs. Graeff, I'm not a minister, I'm not an athlete. I'm a very practical, efficient, logical businessman. I've been around machinery all my life. I've supervised the extrication of goods from more broken-down warehouse elevators than you can shake a stick at. If I sound like a man who takes chances, forget it; I don't. But I'm not a 'yes' man, either. If the lights go out, I don't send for someone else to check the fuse box. I check it. If something is wrong with my car, I don't drive it into a gas station to find out what the trouble is. I find that out myself, and then I tell the gas station what I want done.

"You heard them downstairs. You all heard them. There's an architect who'd make a dandy Western Union boy, and there's a maintenance man who's afraid to tie his shoes until the building superintendent okays it. We could sit here all night. We might have to anyway, but if we have to, I'd like to know that we have to because there's no alternative. I never have been the type to just sit and accept my fate without questioning whether or not it really *is* my fate.... All I want is a look. And I might be able to do something for all of us, if I get that look. I might be able to give Gillespie a few ideas. . . . Look, we're not sheep, let's not act like sheep!"

Josie Swift applauded.

If she had not applauded, Mrs. Graeff would have said, "Oh, *very well*," for it was on the tip of her tongue. But the child's applause put her off; she was such an unpleasant child, really very common. Mrs. Graeff was reluctant to join with her in anything.

"I think we ought to wait a little longer," said Mrs. Graeff. "I *do* feel the Skidmore crew is practically in the lobby."

But she realized, too, that she was punishing her poor Reverend Smoke, and Mr. Cougar; oh, she knew what they were going through; Raymond without cigarettes was Raymond without human feelings.

Drat that damned little hoyden for clapping!

"Mrs. Graeff? How does this strike you? Blades and Reverend Smoke can light up now. While they're smoking, I'll tell you what I was doing the night of the blackout. When they're finished smoking, and I'm finished talking, if we haven't heard from the Skidmore crew, I'll get my chance to size up our situation."

"Eminently fair," said Charlie Latham, reaching for a Kool.

# 18

At the Hotel Biltmore, waiters moved among the tables with candles guttering on their trays. At the table next to Whistler and Ben Hyde, a transistor was broadcasting the latest news about the power failure.

Ben said, "Have a peanut, Will."

He laughed. Whistler had finished an entire bowl of salted peanuts in the time it had taken them to drink a martini apiece.

"Do you know what your first reaction is in any emergency, Will?"

"No. But I'll bet you do."

"Will, you eat. You eat anything. Do you remember that buyer in Dallas, years ago. Elkhart, Elkman, some name like that—the one we could never get anywhere with?"

"George Eckhart."

"And right after we'd call on him, every single time, we'd go down the road to that Plaza Burger, and you'd order cheeseburgers like there was no tomorrow." Ben paused to light a cigarette from the candle between them; he was smiling. He could imitate Robert Kennedy so well that people did double takes. It was one of his favorite stunts when he called on buyers. Some men sold the product; some sold themselves. Ben was in the latter category; he performed for his clients. He knew his routines and his audiences like a night-club entertainer knew his. . . . At least he used to; lately he seemed less enthusiastic.

"Well, it's natural," Ben continued. "You don't smoke; you're not much of a drinker. So you eat. Oral gratification."

"What's the emergency, Ben?"

"Hmmm?"

"I said, what's the emergency that makes it necessary for me to have oral gratification?"

"What's the emergency?" Ben laughed again. "Oh, I don't know. Maybe A. T. and T. hit a new low. . . . Maybe your daughter's just told you she wants to be analyzed."

"Fat chance."

"You tell me, then."

"I'm serious, Ben."

"What do you mean, you're serious? You sound like a Con Ed lackey."

"You're supposed to be an enlightened follower of Freud and other theorists of human behavior; why'd I eat the peanuts? You say it's my reaction in any emergency, oral gratification. Okay, Ben, but you know me pretty well. Well enough to know that this thing hasn't inconvenienced me personally. I don't have a bad heart, so it didn't hurt me to walk down twenty-two flights; it won't hurt me to walk home, either, which I'll be doing shortly. I'm what? About ten blocks away from my place. My wife and daughter are there, safe and sound. What's the emergency?"

"When something like this happens," Ben said, "there's a sort of contagious feeling of foreboding."

"Do you feel it?"

"To some extent, I suppose."

"I think you're having a damn good time. You've got a good excuse this time, for not going home to Fran, for getting oiled. You don't want to come to my place. I don't think you plan to volunteer at a local hospital or report at a civil-defense office. The whole thing is an excuse for you to goof off. What's the emergency?"

Ben sighed and gave Whistler one of his long-suffering smiles. "You just hate it when I point out anything to you that might tell you what makes you tick. This whole conver-

93

sation started with a little remark about oral gratification, and pow! I'm an unfaithful husband who drinks and fiddles while Rome burns."

"No," Whistler said, "You're just a bad psychologist. I never met a good one; I never held hot snow in my hand, either. . . . If you can get the waiter's eye, tell him we'll have another round. . . . Ben, I ate all the peanuts because I'm worried. I eat when I'm worried. I ate the cheeseburgers in Dallas because I was worried. Isn't that a simple enough explanation? Call it oral gratification if you want to, but it doesn't explain what I'm worried about. If I were to leave it up to you to figure out what it is worrying me, you'd probably tell me I was breast-fed or I wasn't breast-fed, and this emergency was reactivating a lot of old anxieties. Well, Ben, this does happen to be an emergency, but you haven't figured out the reason. There aren't any old anxieties being reactivated, but there are a lot of new ones being activated."

"Go on, Will. I'll get the waiter's eye when I'm able."

"In two words, Ben—Vesey Street."

"The warehouse. What about the warehouse?"

"If this keeps up, the freezers are going to defrost."

"Will, the thing is going to be over by midnight."

"If it isn't?"

"What the hell can we do?"

"I haven't thought about anything else since we got here. You know what really bothers me?"

"Sure. We'll be out a lot of money if this keeps up. But, Will, it'll be over by midnight, at the latest."

"What really bothers me is that Spartan warehouse down the block."

"I don't get it."

"Ben, we're small potatoes. But Spartan is big. If this develops into a real crisis, if the freezers do defrost, and if I know a damn thing about the Health Department, an inspector will head for Spartan first thing, soon as the power goes back on. Thawed goods will be dumped, Ben. Since we're right next door, the inspector's going to drop by our place too."

"Like I said, what the hell can we do?"

"If it wasn't for Spartan, we could get our stuff refrozen before they got around to us, if they did; my guess is they wouldn't bother with us."

"You'd take the chance of refreezing?"

"Damn right!"

"Even if it was a complete thaw?"

"Not if it went on for a week and the stuff was high. But, Ben, we can't afford such a loss."

"If you ask me, we can't afford to move anything the Health Department says we shouldn't."

"That's why I'm sitting here thinking of some way to move it before the Health Department says anything . . . if it comes to that."

"Okay, I've got the waiter's eye."

"Well, what do you think?"

"I think you're crazy."

"You're the one going to the funny doctor, Ben."

Ben Hyde said, "Cranberry jelly. Seaside Tuna. Duvall Tomato Paste. Fairlea Mayonnaise . . . Familiar names, Will?"

"What do you want us to do, take the loss without a fight?"

"Fran won't touch anything made of cranberries. How many years ago was it that there was a cancer scare tied in with canned cranberries? It was all cleared up, but she remembers it; she won't even buy fresh cranberries. The same with Seaside and Duvall and Fairlea; they had one bad shipment apiece, but it got into the newspapers, and as far as some housewives are concerned, all the shipments since then are bad. . . . Will, we'd take a very little loss, compared to what we'd take if some bad stuff got through."

"I wouldn't ship anything that was spoiled."

"You're taking a chance with anything thawed; you know it."

"Ben," said Whistler, "I'm going to sit here and have another martini, and another bowl of oral gratification, if the waiter will put one down in front of me, but by the time I leave, I'm going to have an answer to the question: 'What happens if this goes on through the night?' Because we're going to be in trouble unless I come up with something."

When Whistler got home, the apartment was candlelit; the smell of coffee and bacon came in from the kitchen.

"Is that you, Will?" Mariam called in.

"No. It's the Boston Strangler."

"I hope you're hungry."

"I am. But I have to make some phone calls."

"Can't you make them after you eat?"

"No. They're important."

"You might have to wait to get a dial tone."

He carried one of the candle holders into his den, set it on his desk, then picked up the phone. He got a dial tone immediately. Then he called the plant in New Jersey and alerted the night watchman to the fact there could be shipments leaving before morning. After that he called the plant manager in Clifton and explained what he wanted done. It was a simple maneuver; he wanted four refrigerated trucks to load up immediately, and be ready to travel at the word; each truck was to carry four loaders, employees of Whistle who wanted to work at overtime prices. The job was to deposit the frozen load, and pick up the thawed or partially frozen goods on Vesey, and return them to the plant, where they would be refrozen.

"Do you want to refreeze the lot if it's thawed, Mr. Whistler?"

"Right. . . . And time is of the essence," said Whistler in a good-natured, practical tone, trying to make the whole operation sound like an ordinary exigency. "Oh, and another thing."

"Yes?"

"I don't know when the power will be restored, naturally, or how people will function after it. There might be an inspection, the Health Department."

"Yes, sir."

"If you're ready to roll the minute you get the word from our end that traffic is moving, you should have the whole operation over with before an inspector shows up. In case you don't, keep the truck temperatures low; not so low things will thaw completely, but low enough for the lot to look as though it had been there all night at a minimum temperature. Do you get it?"

"Yes, Mr. Whistler."

"That's it, then," said Whistler. Then a folksy touch thrown in to dispel the possibility of wrongdoing: "Up in Vermont, on a night like this, we'd bundle; we'd call it a Godsend."

"Yes, sir." The plant manager laughed.

Whistler sat at the table in the dining room while Mariam brought in an asbestos place mat and set it on the table. "It's almost ready," she said.

He said, "Where's Kathy?"

"In her room; I got tired of hearing her transistor."

"She eat?"

"We both did, honey."

She went to the kitchen and came back with a lacquered tray containing coffee, scrambled eggs and bacon, toast, and a bottle of Raffetto Chut-Nut.

He said, "Where's the curry?"

96

"Try it on your toast; it's good."

"Boy, I feel like a privileged character," he said.

"I thought Ben would come back with you."

"No. He'd rather get drunk."

She stood and watched him as he ate; she had a long dress on, royal blue, made of velvet, silver slippers, the silver necklace he had given her for their anniversary last winter.

He said, "Did you dress up for Ben?"

"Yes."

"Sorry to disappoint you."

"Maybe he'll change his mind and show up yet."

"No. He's three sheets to the wind by now. We had a little fight."

She always dressed for Whistler's arrival in the evening, even if they were going to drive out to Thwaite's on City Island for lobster, before taking their cruiser for a ride; she would be wearing something similar to what she had on, and she would keep it on while they had cocktails, then change if it was a City Island night or they were going somewhere else. Otherwise she would stay dressed, though Will would usually change to old clothes. Will loved her dressed that way; he liked to call her "Duchess," because she did look a little like Wally Windsor used to look back in the days when the Duke was king.

They had been married since December 8, 1941; Will married her the same day he joined the Marines.

Mariam said, "What did you and Ben fight about this time?"

"The usual thing."

"Not his psychoanalysis again."

"No. Business."

"Because I think you tease him too much about his psychoanalysis, honey."

"He's the one brings it up. I mind my own business, and the next thing I hear out of his mouth is oral gratification."

"You fought about business? The whole town in darkness, and you two sat at the Biltmore fighting about business?"

"Something came up. I don't feel like going into it. It has to do with one of our warehouses."

"Then don't go into it. Relax, Will."

"You know me, Mariam, better than anyone. You know I'm a responsible person, and a careful person. And you know about Ben—the mess he's made of his marriage, and

97

the way he drinks. If you were going to put yourself in one of our hands, who would you pick?"

"I made that choice twenty-four years ago."

"Don't be cute, now; I mean, this is a serious question."

"*Your* hands, Will. You know that."

"Not just because you married me? I want an objective answer."

"Ben is very human. I like him. But I trust you."

"This is good chutney."

"Why do you ask that question, Will?"

"Oh, I don't know. Since Ben's been going to this head nut, he's gotten all sorts of guilt and he's trying to fill everyone with it. You get a simple business idea, and he makes something negative out of it."

"Well, that's rather typical of analysands."

"Is it, Mariam?"

"I think it is. Pam Burnside was one of our most industrious volunteers at Lenox Hill; then she had herself analyzed and found all sorts of pejorative reasons for what she was doing; she never volunteered after that."

"What do you mean pejorative reasons?"

"You know, Will; she said the reason she was trying to help out was because her mother died in childbirth and as a little girl she felt she'd killed her, so volunteer hospital work was her way of paying penance. She said, why should she pay penance when she hadn't killed her mother. I said, 'Pam, for heaven's sake, we need volunteers, and it's something to do that's very helpful.' I said, 'What else would you do on Thursdays and Tuesdays?' She said, 'Maybe I'll screw.' "

Whistler laughed. "That's the first sensible thing I ever heard happen as a result of head shrinking."

"But to have to pay so much money, Will, to come to that decision."

Then they both began laughing, and Whistler pushed his chair back and held out his arms.

Mariam came across to him. "Who cares about Ben Hyde right now? I have a surprise for you in the bedroom. It's made of Belgium lace, and it cost an arm and a big toe, so you'd better enjoy it."

"Who *cares* about Ben Hyde!" Whistler chuckled.

But he did care that Ben had raged against his idea for saving the lot at Vesey; he did care that Ben, after his third martini, tried to lord it over him, with his holier-than-thou histrionics about all the people who were going to drop dead if Whistler refroze the lot. Ben knew better, knew Will would never take such a chance for any amount of money.... So William Whistler cared very much, and he had a sneaking suspicion that what had happened between them at the Biltmore was not simply another business disagreement, but something which had been showing itself slowly of late, the beginning of something as irrevocable as a landslide after the ground has begun to shift.

# 19

"Do you want Mr. Skidmore to call you at the Algonquin?"

"Yes, if I'm still here by the time you locate him!" Senator Robert Anderson slammed the phone's arm down on its hook and stepped out of the phone booth. Opposite the telephone was the newsstand; he glanced in that direction, on his way back to the bar, and stopped short. He went over and clapped his arm around the shoulder of a short, balding man who was buying a paper.

"Hello, Roger."

"Bob! What are you doing in town on a night like this?"

"I almost didn't get here. There weren't any planes leaving Washington, trains are all knocked off schedule. That's not bad enough, the person I had an appointment with is stuck next door in an elevator."

Roger laughed. "So is one of my clients."

"I hope it's a laughing matter. It's been a couple of hours now. I just called Hillman Skidmore at his home, and he's not at his home."

"You called Skidmore?"

"Who'm I going to call? There's no Mr. Gart. Somebody's got to be responsible."

"I don't think it's very serious."

"Who'd you talk to over there? They sent me packing."

"They sent me packing, too. But I talked to Lou Gillespie —he's an architect, has offices in the building. He said it wasn't anything too serious; they have to reattach a cable. The snow's holding up the Skidmore crew."

"I spoke with Lieutenant Scholz. He didn't say it wasn't serious; he just made it plain he didn't need me butting in. So I've been running back and forth, getting nowhere. Can't even get in the door anymore. New York's Finest aren't very impressed with Washington's Finest."

"Ryan, the maintenance man, is going to come over and get me when they start rescue operations; you can come back with me. He'll get us in. Until then, there's not much we can do but sit it out. How about the bar?"

"Yes, I'm already ensconced in the front bar. C'mon, buy you a drink."

Robert Anderson had roomed with Roger Tyson at 433 Fayerweather, his freshman and sophomore years at Yale. After their graduation in 1927, Roger went on to study law at Columbia; Bob entered Harvard Law. They saw each other infrequently, but they were close enough friends to ask each other favors from time to time. After Millie Anderson's death, Roger arranged a few weekends where it was understood that the Senator was the escort of Roger's sister-in-law; apparently Roger thought of it as a favor to the Senator. Bob Anderson viewed it as a favor to Roger.

The Senator had a certain rapport with Maggie Van Pelten—she knew a lot of Hill gossip, she was a good raconteur, she liked people and usually had a lot of them around her, but over a long weekend in the quiet of the country, it could wear very thin. Maggie didn't play tennis, she didn't swim, she didn't like to take long walks, she had very light skin which did not take to the sun; you entertained Maggie indoors to the click of ice cubes against crystal, solo, because Roger and Phyllis Tyson believed in letting their houseguests be by themselves.

But the thought had been well-intentioned; Maggie lived in Washington, so did Bob; Maggie was divorced. Bob was widowed; it wasn't an inconceivable idea, matching the two of them.

It simply hadn't taken.

One favor Roger *had* done for the Senator was to find a place in his office for Jo.

While they sat down in the small bar near the entrance of the Algonquin, Bob Anderson said, "It's odd meeting you like this, because earlier I was beginning to get hopping mad at you."

"For what?"

100

"Before I heard the elevator was stuck, I thought *you* were to blame for keeping Miss Swift."

"Who's Miss Swift?"

"The young lady I asked you to help out with a job."

"Oh. Her. No. The *young* ones never work late. They have to be over thirty for that."

"If I had someone like her on my staff, I'd *see to it* she worked late."

An uncertain expression crossed Roger Tyson's face; abruptly Roger changed the subject from anything personal to the most general kind of political discussion, all of it a rehashing of recent newspaper columns and stale gossip. Tyson stayed on that key while he ordered and slowly sipped a Dewars and soda and while Anderson finished his Tanqueray martini.

Increasingly, Robert Anderson was bored with these conversations. He supposed they had always been boring, but his threshold of boredom had been much higher before Millie's death; he had gone through the ordinary motions of living effortlessly. If there had been a surfeit of these conversations, he hadn't realized it at the time. The Senator and Millie had spent an enormous amount of time off hunting or fishing or camping by themselves. About forty-two years of it, whenever they could get away. Doing those things alone was unrewarding. His appreciation of this fact resulted in a certain panic which had compelled him to act like the old fool there was no fool like. He had gone on one of those desperate cruises where eager social directors pushed bravely smiling widows at him. He had spent weekends trekking to New York discotheques, joined a tennis club, accepted a lecture tour of various colleges where he had ogled the co-eds; he had even attended a few Pairs and Spares suppers sponsored by his church. Then, after he had been thrown together with Maggie, she had been hostess for him to a series of noisy parties; Maggie called them "scout meetings."

She said, "You scout around for what appeals to your appetite, and I'll scout around for what appeals to mine," which was very Maggie: to want nothing more than to possess you, but to hammer in an impression completely to the contrary. What else was very Maggie was her way of describing a search for somebody, for Maggie was indeed hungry. So many of the women the Senator met during that phase were, and their hunger made them hard, cunning, and driven. A simple date for a movie, or a game of tennis, or a

101

Sunday afternoon drive, triggered off a series of invitations from people whose names were completely unknown, friends of that simple date who were ready now to begin the elaborate procedure of matchmaking.

Anderson had just about given up the idea of female companionship; he could get laid or, more ceremoniously, let himself be paired off at everything from sit-down dinners to patio-and-pool parties with women who basked in the reflected glory of having a senator as an escort, while hawking their assets as partners in marriage, like street vendors chanting praise of their wares.

Then one weekend the Senator had accepted an invitation to relax at the farm of his old law partner, in Bucks County, Pennsylvania. On their way back from a revival of *The Odd Couple* at the Bucks County Playhouse, they had stopped in at a roadhouse-discotheque for drinks, and the Senator, feeling his, had struck up a conversation with a redheaded dancer forty-three years his junior, who was not even sure that the United States Senate was a part of Congress.

Talk about the odd couple.

He was sure there would be plenty of talk. But he didn't expect that there would be much surprise involved in it; just: look what the damn fool has gone and done now. For anyone who knew Senator Robert Anderson was aware that he had always enjoyed the oddities of life more than the bromides. Before he had married Millie Davidson, she had been a professional astrologist. In the Senate, Bob Anderson had always relished punching holes in the deep-hued conservatives of both parties, and he was one of the most amusing and guttiest infighters on either side of the Senate aisle.

He was up to handling the talk, *and* the girl; in fact, he was looking forward to doing both.

Roger Tyson's voice brought Anderson back to the present. "Bob, are you listening to me?"

"Not very hard, Roger."

"I didn't think so. . . . Do you mind if I ask you something?"

"Try me and see."

"This girl we hired. Do you mean to say you're waiting for *her?*"

"That's what I mean to say, Roger."

"That's what I thought you said earlier. My ears heard it and registered it; my intelligence couldn't."

"I'm going to marry her, Roger."

"On that note, I'll have another."

"So will I."

"I think you've had too much already."

"Who'd you think I'd marry? Maggie?"

"You could do a lot worse. Apparently you're hell bent on doing a lot worse."

"I think I'm doing a lot better, but that's what makes horse races."

"I really thought you weren't the type to remarry; I used to tell Maggie that."

"I was much too happily married to stay a widower, Roger."

"Uh-huh. Well, your choice is a great tribute to Mildred."

"Millie doesn't need any posthumous tributes. She's resting comfortably."

"Mike's dead; I'm alive."

"Hmmm?"

"I was just remembering Liz Taylor's remark after Mike Todd's death. . . . Before she ran off with Eddie Fisher."

"I'd forgotten how starstruck you always were."

"I'd forgotten what an exhibitionist *you* always were."

"Remember when you made the Yale band? You couldn't talk about anyone but Hubert Prior Vallee."

"I liked Rudy; he was a lot more levelheaded than you ever were."

"Oh, didn't I know it! Rudy this, Rudy that; Rudy played at the Savoy Hotel in London, Rudy, Rudy, Rudy. I was glad when I moved from Fayerweather to McClellan, I can tell you that."

Tyson laughed. Bob Anderson signaled to the waiter that they wanted another round. Then he said, "What is it about poor Eddie Fisher, anyway?"

"What do you mean?"

"Remember back when Bill Manchester was in all that hot water with the Kennedy book? Remember Mrs. Kennedy supposedly made some remark to the effect that short of her running off with Eddie Fisher, the American public would never think ill of her?"

Roger Tyson smiled. Then he said, "You're sorry you announced it, aren't you, Bob? Is that why you're straying from the subject?"

"Not at all."

"You don't seem very prepared to defend it."

"I didn't know you were prosecuting, Roger."

"You knew I would. I won't be the first, either. I hope you don't want to be re-elected, Bob."

"Short of *my* running off with Eddie Fisher," said Robert

103

Anderson, "I'll take my chances with the American public, too."

"Jackie's prettier than you are, Senator. . . . Watch my drink while I check in with the wife, all right?"

# 20

Stanley Ryan's boss, the superintendent of the Gart Building, was fond of saying, "When anything goes wrong, people don't want to listen to you, they want to blame you."

He was the third superintendent to work for the Gart Building in four years, so maybe he had good reason to fear the management. He called them "the lickpennies"; if something minor went wrong in any system like the air-conditioning or the intercom, he would say, "An ounce of prevention isn't a pound of cure where 'the lickpennies' are concerned; it's just money out of their pockets, and they don't want to pay it. They don't think the machinery's at fault, they think the super is!"

Very little was reported wrong under his tenure.

Sometimes Stanley was glad he didn't have the knack for getting ahead. This was one of those times. He would not be in the super's shoes for anything. He felt a perverse satisfaction at the fact he was in the center of things, but in no way about to receive the blame.

Yet, if nobody was going to blame him, nobody was going to listen to him, either, and he had this idea. Try to tell them anything; they responded by sending him on another errand.

"My idea," he kept beginning over and over again, "goes back to Tunisia—" until finally, exasperated, Gillespie had berated him. "I wasn't in Tunisia during World War Two, Stanley, but I can imagine what those mountains were like, and how hard it was to move heavy equipment! Okay? Now, for once and for all, tell me exactly what the hell that has to do with this?"

"I've been trying to tell you. We had this wooden platform, loaded with artillery, halfway up the mountain. I bet that platform was easily as heavy as the elevator car. Then the rope holding it began to give. Well, we cut these heavy timbers, and we made a wedge underneath. You see what I mean? Why couldn't we go through the floor below and——"

But midway in his sentence, Stanley Ryan's words were arrested by the grating sound of steel on steel, a great, grinding roar, and women screaming.

# 21

"The old fool!" said Phyllis Tyson. "Maggie's well rid of him!"

"The girl's the one I told you about," Roger said. "Remember? The one who wore that awful gardenia fragrance? I had to ask her to cease and desist."

"Are you sure he isn't drinking?"

"He's drinking. But he's sober."

"Millie will roll over in her grave."

"Well, Millie was a bit offbeat herself, remember."

"To tell you the truth, I'm glad, for Maggie's sake. He's too eccentric. Maggie wouldn't have been happy with him—I don't care if he is a senator."

"I don't believe a word of it, but you keep telling yourself that, and maybe you'll convince yourself. Anyway, I'll be here a while; don't wait up for me."

"What's going on next door, Roger?"

"Everything's held up by the weather; they haven't even started rescue operations."

"Raymond keeps calling here; I don't know what to tell him."

"Tell him not to get his hopes up. It doesn't look serious."

"As a matter of fact, he sounds quite concerned."

"I'd understand a lot better if it were Raymond bent on marrying this Eliza Doolittle of Bob's. Raymond could show

105

just cause for insanity, after years of cohabitation with Faith."

"She's been through a lot, Roger."

"*She* doesn't know it."

"Now, what does that mean?"

"That means she doesn't see any more to life than compost piles, Philharmonic concerts, and the lovely blue-black color of an evening sky in winter on the Hudson."

"I can see you've had too much of her today."

"Slightly overexposed, yes; it's like too much sun, it can poison your system."

"Don't get yourself worked up or you'll have too much to drink, and tomorrow you'll feel it."

"I'll feel it anyway. The only one getting any younger is Bob Anderson."

"I do hope Faith's all right; she means well."

"I suppose she does. . . . She'll be all right. Tell Raymond not to worry. I'll see her through it and then take her up to the Dorset."

Then Roger Tyson hung up and went back to join the Senator at the bar.

It was ten-thirty P.M.

# 22

"Why the hell didn't you explain their situation to them?" Gil Holland thundered.

"I thought they'd panic."

"I don't mean you, Gillespie. I mean *you*, Farley."

"Gillespie was in charge."

"I was in *charge*?"

"You were the only one who spoke to them."

"Don't pass me the buck!"

"Lieutenant Scholz said you ought to tell them!"

"None of this was my responsibility," said Gillespie. "I did what I thought was best, but it wasn't my responsibility."

"Shit, I'm so sick of hearing that it wasn't anybody's

responsibility!" said Holland. "Wasn't it anybody's impulse to use his head, either? To find out how much weight the car's carrying? To warn them not to move around? To get a repair man for that speaker, so communications could be kept open? To get extra batteries for that speaker? When that speaker first started going on the blink, why didn't you *do* something so it wouldn't happen again? Jesus! Shit!"

Gillespie said, "I did warn them not to move around! We did get extra batteries for the speaker! It's not the batteries; I don't know what it is, but it's probably connected with what just happened. . . . As for weight, I figure it to be under eight hundred pounds; that's not heavy."

"What'd you figure the freight weighed in at?"

"I didn't know anything about the freight!"

"A moving man tells Ryan that a car carrying office supplies went down without him, and nobody's curious about what happened to the stuff."

Gillespie said, "I didn't put it together. I didn't think it was on with them. Look, Holland, I'm——"

"I know. You're sick of the shit because you don't have to take it. Right?"

"Nobody in the elevator said there were moving cartons on it."

"Where did you and Ryan and Scholz think those cartons went?"

Ryan said, "The fellow from Ace Van didn't tell me about it until he was leaving. He said an elevator with odds and ends went down without him; he was in a hurry because of the weather. He'd come back for the things. That's all."

"Well, where did you think the *things* went?"

"To the basement, I don't know. I thought somebody down in the basement might have unloaded it."

"Nobody did, though, did they? And we've got no idea how much is on that car with them. . . . What'd they say, Gillespie? One more time."

"A woman's voice said, 'Look out for the cartons.' "

" 'Look out for the cartons.' That's all. First we heard this grinding noise and screaming; then I turned on the speaker, and the car must have slipped another couple of inches right then, and the woman said, 'Look out for the cartons,' and that was the last thing we heard before the speaker conked out."

Lieutenant Scholz came around the corner, heading toward Holland, Ryan, Farley, and Gillespie. There were half a dozen

Division policemen at the other end of the lobby, near the elevators, more up on the eighteenth floor. There was an ambulance from Roosevelt Hospital waiting outside; the driver and an intern were across the street in the coffee shop. In front of the Gart building, more police had erected a barricade of sawhorses in the snow; a crew was shoveling and putting down salt.

Scholz said, "We've got inhalators, oxygen cylinders, portolights, gas masks, acetylene tanks, flooring saws, horse belts, and you name it, in our truck, but we can't find a bullhorn! We've got to get hold of a bullhorn. My men tried shouting from sixteen, and from fifteen, but they can't hear us. If they can, we can't hear them."

"I didn't think so," said Holland.

"There's no way we can open the doors on sixteen?" Farley asked.

"If you want to chance killing five people."

"I just thought——"

"Jesus Christ, don't any of you get the picture? What the shit is the matter with all of you? We don't dare breathe near sixteen, see? We don't dare think near sixteen, see? *You* want to open doors! We don't dare drop a feather because WE DON'T KNOW WHAT THE HELL WE'VE GOT ON OUR HANDS BECAUSE NO ONE THOUGHT TO GET ANY INFORMATION FROM THEM, LIKE WHAT WEIGHT THEY'RE CARRYING!"

Holland stalked away; he went down toward the phone booth where the building superintendent, his face bathed in perspiration, was trying to locate some lumber and find a way of cutting it to size and transporting it. The snow was now three inches deep, still coming down.

Gillespie said to Farley, "Sure. Wait until good old Gil gets here, the man said; good old Gil knows what to do."

"I've never seen him like this," Farley said.

"He's a real cool troubleshooter. God, I hope he's always handy in an emergency. He's inspiring."

Scholz grunted. "Good ideas don't yell; he just hasn't got any good ideas for how to handle this."

"He's got a good idea," said Stanley Ryan, "and I gave it to him."

"Now, if you can just dream up a way for us to find some wood, Stanley," said Gillespie.

"Distant firewood is good firewood," said Stanley.

"What?"

108

"Something I was just thinking about earlier. Nothing," Stanley said.

But it set Louis Gillespie to thinking then, to remembering a townhouse the firm had designed on East 38th Street, complete with a garage, though the owner did not have an automobile. The owner was a pop sculptor. He used the garage space to cut out these huge, three-legged wooden figures, some of them ten and twelve feet tall. He had been shown at the Museum of Modern Art and at the Whitney, but the client was modest, self-effacing. My firewood, he always called his pieces.

# 23

Whistler had not counted on the spotlight shining from the top of the shaft. He looked up at it and was blinded by its brilliance. He shut his eyes; when he opened them, he saw the drop of twenty floors. The sudden, sickening sensation of giddiness was familiar from his dreams of falling, and he toppled over backward, down through the hatch onto the floor of the elevator.

The car moved.

Mrs. Graeff let out a piercing scream.

Whistler scrambled to his feet as the car moved again, and Josie Swift cried, "Look out for the cartons!" They knocked over T. T. Blades, who landed with his full weight on Mrs. Graeff.

For a split second there was silence, and during that silence all five became aware of an acrid odor permeating the car.

Then Mrs. Graeff moaned. "God, oh God."

Blades was kneeling beside her. "Don't move."

"What's that smell?" said Charlie Latham.

"Something spilled, something in that box we opened." Josie Swift leaned down and lifted a half-gallon tin. "This."

Latham took it from her. "What is it?" He squinted at the words on the side of the can.

"Rubber-cement thinner," said Whistler. "Oh, Jesus! That's petroleum naphtha! How much of it spilled?"

Charlie Latham said, "How is she, Blades?"

"She's hurt her leg."

Josie said, "Quite a lot spilled. It must have been open."

Whistler ripped off his coat, began unbuttoning his shirt, loosening his tie.

"I'll be all right," Mrs. Graeff murmured. "Won't I? Will we be all right, Mr. Cougar?"

"Stay still. Don't try to stand; don't move your leg. . . . Yes, we'll be all right."

"How do you know?"

Charlie Latham knelt beside her too. "We will be, Mrs. Graeff." Then he said, "What are you doing, Whistler?"

"What's he doing *now?*" Mrs. Graeff complained.

Whistler was removing his undershirt. "I'm going to mop this stuff up. It's flammable as gasoline, and the fumes are even more toxic."

"God, oh God"

"Would you feel better if I say a prayer?" said Charlie Latham.

"Oh, would you? Would you, Reverend?"

"Yes."

Whistler said, "Miss Swift, get those coats up so that stuff doesn't soak into them. Blades, can you help get the boxes stacked up where they were?"

"Can you use my T-shirt, Whistler?"

"Let's see how much this gets up first!"

"We fell again, didn't we?" said Mrs. Graeff, "I knew he'd do something like this. I wanted to wait for the Skid-more———"

"Shall we pray, Mrs. Graeff?"

She sat there with her legs stretched out in front of her, her back resting against the wall. Blades had removed the shoe from her right foot. She closed her eyes as Charlie Latham recited all of the Sixty-ninth Psalm that he could remember; at Yansetti Junior College, its recitation had been a standard opening at Evening Prayer.

" 'Hear me, O Lord, for thy loving-kindness is comfortable; turn thee unto me according to the multitudes of thy mercies. And hide not thy face from thy servant; for I am in trouble: O haste thee and hear me. Draw nigh unto———' "

Charlie Latham, when the elevator fell, thought only of last night's phone call; usual time, seven, eight o'clock; he would ring the number, maybe once or twice a month, and he would hear Gwen say, "Hello . . . Hello . . . Who is this?"

He would call the Virginia number station-to-station, dialing it direct. He would not answer her; he would just listen, hearing what he could of her life, whether or not the radio was on, the TV, if there were sounds in the background, as though there were company there, whatever.

Better, anyway, than the midnight and early-morning calls right after the divorce, when he would beg her to take him back, if he were very drunk; and if he were just slightly potted, say he loved her with a French accent, or in a Scottish dialect, or as an Irishman, or in Old English.

"I feel nothing for you but pity, Charlie." Then, "Charlie? Are you there?"

Tears streaming down his face, trying to talk without choking halfway through, he would manage, "Vas you dere, Charlie?"

"You're destroying yourself. It's a crime."

"The weed of crime bears bitter fruit. The Shadow knows— heh! heh! heh!"

And one night, so drunk he could remember it only vaguely the next morning, he had directed a cabdriver to take him home; he had forgotten and given the driver the old Overlook Terrace address. There was no doorman on duty there after nine; the new tenants had never changed the lock. Charlie had the old key on his keyring; in a short time he was being struck over the head by a big fellow in striped pajamas, whose wife, her head bedecked in rollers, cowered behind him screaming for help.

The police released him, but a photographer from the *Daily Mirror* lived nearby; he had photographed Charlie being escorted from the apartment building; it was there on page three the next day.

There were so many bad times after the divorce.

Last night, Frank had answered the phone.

"Hello . . . Hello . . . Who is it, please?"

In a year and a half, could a kid's voice grow so deep, sound so adult?

Whatever made Charlie speak to Frank? He wasn't drunk. God be his witness, he was stone sober.

He wanted so badly to talk with the boy; the only thing, though, that he found to say was, "Ha-woe, Fwank; ha-woe,

111

ha-woe"; then he pressed the buttons of the receiver down, sick.

When the elevator fell, he thought: that's the way my kid is going to remember his old man; a blithering idiot, speaking baby talk to him over the telephone. Ha-woe, Fwank.

If there was any way to survive this, well, he was going to, if for no other reason than to make some better last impression on his boy.

No big-deal, change-his-whole-life-around impression; Charlie did not kid himself about that anymore, but he was going to say something better to his boy, if he said it with his last breath, and thought of little more to say than, "I'm sorry, Frank."

If he were ever going to speak to Frank again, he was going to need more than his own determination to survive—luck; that went without saying, but something else, too: the cool of the other four trapped with him in the elevator.

" 'Thou hast known my reproach, my shame and my dishonor,' " he continued, " 'mine adversaries are all in thy sight. Reproach hath broken my heart, I looked for—' "

He saw Miss Swift pick up his attaché case and set it in the corner. THE WORST MISTAKE, by Lorine Spring. He remembered the afternoon the manuscript had appeared on his desk, the fatuous mood it had inspired; yes, the hero would have to be a minister succumbing to the prurient pull of the flesh; he had let out a whoop of laughter as he had read through the first chapter, and poured three fingers of vodka into a coffee cup.

Charlie thought of telling them that he was not a minister; they had always been at their best when someone was revealing something about himself. It would be no surprise to Josie Swift, and maybe not to Whistler, but he could not chance the effect it would have on Mrs. Graeff and T. T. Blades; it would probably produce hysteria in her and anger in him.

But somehow it was necessary to get that game going again, to replace the blackout with something else they had all been through.

Whistler was putting his shirt back on. "It still smells like hell in here. It's a good thing no one was smoking." He stuffed his undershirt into the open box. "We'd have gone up like a tinderbox."

"Well, I hope you're satisfied, Whistler," Blades said.

Josie Swift said, "It wasn't his fault. He was trying to help us!"

"Big help!"

"If I *did* cause the car to move by going up on the roof, we're in some fix here. I hope you realize that, Blades."

"What's the point of talking about it?"

"You started it!"

" '—that love his name shall dwell therein, Amen' " Latham finished quickly. He said, "We've got to make an effort to keep our heads! It's more important than ever now."

"Thanks to our logical, practical—what was the other adjective you used to describe the kind of businessman you are, Whistler?"

"Efficient, Blades!"

"Yes. Efficient. Your blackout story illustrated that."

"What do you mean?"

Blades gave him a sardonic smile and didn't answer.

"Do you mind telling me what you mean by that?"

"I pass," said Blades. He walked over and knelt down again beside Mrs. Graeff. "How does your leg feel?"

"Don't fight with him. He's dangerous."

"I'm *what?*"

"I won't," said Blades, ignoring Whistler. "Are you in much pain?"

"Not too much, thank you, Mr. Cougar."

He began massaging her ankle. He knew that it was probably broken; he knew, too, that the real pain would not begin for a while.

It was beginning to register with him that they were in serious danger, that this was the way a large animal must feel when he was held by a trap in a small area, that this mounting anger, focused on Whistler, was the trapped animal's rage. The fact that Whistler was such a zealous businessman did not help matters; T. could never see himself in that role, yet probably right now there was a letter in the mail to Hockaday setting it in motion.

"Does it feel better now?"

"Yes, thank you."

"Move it as little as possible, Mrs. Graeff."

"What if something else happens, and I'm helpless like this?"

"I'll take care of you."

"I don't think you could even lift me."

T. T. laughed. "I could lift two of you."

When he stood up and walked over to sit down on the box under the control panel, Charlie Latham said, "I have an idea."

113

He did not seem like the same person to Josie Swift; without his glasses, he looked bewildered and helpless. His voice had been so solemn, and he had seemed so sincere when he was praying by Mrs. Graeff; then, he had known all the words to *From Every Stormy Wind That Blows,* and the prayer had sounded authentic. . . . With his hang-ups, if he really was a minister, he was ready for Snap City.

"What's your idea?" Blades said.

"I want you to listen to this, too, Whistler."

"It's generous of you to include me, Reverend."

"Whistler, you don't have to use that tone; I'm not blaming you for anything. If the ash I dropped in that box a while ago had connected with the thinner, none of us would be here to talk about it."

"Well, that's honest."

"The fact is, Blades and I made a mistake when we smoked; you made a mistake when you went up on the roof. Probably the whole reason we're stuck here is that somebody made a mistake. But nobody meant to do harm. Somebody just made a whopping mistake."

"It makes a dandy epitaph," Whistler said. "Somebody goofed."

Josie Swift said, "Har-de-har, har, har, har!"

"What's your idea?" Blades asked again.

"Why don't we all try to think of the worst mistake each of us has ever made; then let's take turns telling about it."

"Mine was getting into this elevator." Whistler laughed. He was more nervous than he dared admit to himself; always, then, Whistler resorted to jokes. His father and mother had been the same way; while they watched their savings dwindle in the depression years, there was the constant *galgenhumor* orchestrating their feelings of panic; gallows humor; it was their protest, defense, and salvation.

And now Whistler was trying to put Blades in a better humor, for what the Reverend had said *was* true: there was no one here with malice. "I heard about a mistake a football player made one time," Whistler said. "He was filling out an application blank for a charge account; it was in this city where his team had gone to train before the season. He wrote in his name and his age and his address, and then he came to 'Length of residence.' He gave that some thought, and then he wrote 'forty feet.' " Whistler gave a huge guffaw.

Suddenly Blades moved. He lunged at Whistler, held him by the throat, and backed him into the wall. "Shut up!"

114

"Wait a minute!" Latham shouted. "He was making a joke!"

"*Shut up!*" Blades repeated.

Whistler uttered a gurgling sound, while Josie Swift tugged at Blades's coat.

"Let him go, Blades!" Latham commanded.

Blades did. He said, "I couldn't help it," turning his back on Whistler, who was visibly shaken.

"You asked for that, Mr. Whistle!" said Mrs. Graeff.

"I did?"

"You've been aggravating us from the beginning."

Whistler sat down heavily on the box at the rear of the elevator. He said nothing.

"Don't any of you have a sense of humor?" Josie went back and sat down near him. She said to him, "You okay?"

"I'm okay."

"Wow! Nice people!"

Charlie Latham said, "Will you all please listen. I meant it a few seconds ago when I said we all ought to think of the worst mistake each of us has ever made. We'll level with one another; we'll describe the circumstances. We don't have to name names, identify things too specifically."

Mrs. Graeff said, "Confession is good for the soul, is that it, Reverend?"

"Think of it as an extension of your blackout game, Mrs. Graeff."

T. T. Blades said, "We used to do something like this after we won a big game; we'd have a session the next day and go over the worst thing about the game. It kept us from getting big heads."

"I'd just as soon," Josie Swift said.

Then Whistler, forcing a smile, "I've been playing this game for years, with my partner, Ben Hyde. I call it parlor analysis. See, Ben's being psychoanalyzed, and he's an authority on mistakes. If he was here, believe me, he'd blame this whole thing on somebody's early toilet training."

Latham said, "We want to get our minds *off* who's to blame for anything. If we concentrate on our own errors, we won't have time to worry about the other fellow's; if we knock ourselves, maybe we won't knock each other."

"It's actually a game of survival," said T. T.

Mrs. Graeff said, "But don't make ladies go first!"

"I'll go first," said Charlie; "I'll start it off."

## 24

Brave man.

But what if he really told them?

He didn't, of course. He stuck closely to Lorine Spring's text, which was a further recital of Reverend Smoke's marriage to a woman with whom he had nothing more in common than physical rapport. But what if he had told them, described any ordinary time that it had happened, like that day in Old English I, a long time ago, at the university?

This student had come up to him after class and begun a conversation about the Cotton Gnomes; they were fairly common in Old English poems—sententious sayings, proverbial, aphoristic, figurative, moral.

She was going to do her paper on them, she said.

She said, "I just love them."

"I'm glad," Charlie said.

"Some of them are so heathen in character, Dr. Latham."

"Fate replaces God, that's all."

"But the Cotton Gnomes have a mixture, don't they?"

"Yes, there's a dual pagan and Christian character to them."

"Why is that?"

"Christianity was still a new religion when they were written; the pagan ideas didn't fade out overnight; there was a nostalgia for them, along with the interest in Christianity."

"You know, Dr. Latham, I didn't think I'd like this course at all, but it's fascinating."

"In the beginning, I didn't like anything about Old English."

"Really?"

"I'd confused it with Middle English. I wasn't prepared for all the work. I remember how I hated the dative case, nearly quit early on, when we came to it."

"The dative-instrumental." She laughed.

"Yes, for openers."

There was a place where he sometimes stopped in for a beer afternoons, on his way back to his and Gwen's apartment. It was not a student hangout; it was near the campus, though, a couple of blocks from the classroom where he was talking with the girl.

God be his witness, he had intended nothing more than a short conversation about the subject, over one beer, and it had begun that way, with an innocuous discussion of an elegiac poem called *The Wanderer.*

God be his witness.

Did she imagine that he lured her there to do that thing? Did she imagine that he would choose a place where he was known to do that thing?

Didn't she know that what he did surprised him more than it did her?

Why didn't they ever know?

"I shouldn't have another," he said.

"It's so much fun."

"Is it?"

"I'm so curious and all. About you."

"Why?"

"You're young, but you're so interested in this old stuff. Things like Wilfstand's *Sermon to the English,* and *Beowulf,* and all. I find that really fascinating."

But even if he had left after that beer, some other time, some other place, with some other girl, he would have, probably, he would have done, been compelled to do, the same.

There was no reason to think that if there had not been a young girl who wanted to do a paper on the Cotton Gnomes it never would have happened. No reason to dwell on it. No reason to call it all to mind again. That red-haired girl—to always remember her face out of all of them. . . . Certainly there was no reason to try and know, still, still to try and know why he wanted her to look at him, why she had to scream.

Why were they always so afraid, and he so vulnerable to the suppliant helplessness in their eyes?

# 25

Ben Hyde.

The name had registered with Josie Swift. Her thoughts returned to a party she had gone to with Bob a few weekends ago in Washington.

There was this man who could imitate Bobby Kennedy so well that after a while he seemed to resemble him.

Josie liked him immediately. He paid a lot of attention to her, too.

She could see Bob scowling at her across the room, and she was amused because she thought that Bob was jealous. He was, of younger men, although he tried to hide it.

Later, when she was coming from the bathroom, Bob took her aside.

"Stay away from Ben Hyde."

"Why? I like him."

"Jo, follow my advice. All right?"

"Are you jealous?"

"Nope. Not this time. He wants a favor from me, Jo."

"A political favor?"

"Something like that. He's with a plant in New Jersey that wants out of an investigation of air pollution. I'm heading up the subcommittee doing the investigating. I gave him a cold shoulder. He's buttering you up."

"Could you help him?"

"I *could*. I help him, I have to help the next fellow."

"Why don't you just tell him that? Then he won't butter me up."

"I can't tell him. He hasn't put his cards on the table."

"Oh, wow. Lots of intrigue."

"You'll learn all about this sort of thing eventually."

"Shall I tell him I can't talk to him because he's a Communist?"

Bob laughed. "Want another drink?"

After that, Bob got himself involved with a group of men. While Josie avoided Ben Hyde, she found herself wandering about alone, with no one to talk to.

She wandered into the library, not knowing it was the library, and there were no other people in there; the next thing, Ben Hyde had come in after her and closed the door behind him.

"It's proper. You're not married yet," he said.

"I think *you* are, though."

"Yes. Do I look so settled? Old married man?"

"No."

"Well, then. Do I have bad breath?"

"No."

"What's the matter with me, then?"

"Nothing, nothing is."

"Something, something is."

"No."

"Are you really going to marry Senator Anderson?"

"How did you know?"

"Everybody's talking about it."

"We haven't even announced it officially. What are they saying?"

"Saying robbing the cradle; saying it's a long, long, long, long time from May to September."

"No, *seriously*."

"They're shocked."

"Because I'm not good enough?"

"You look good to me."

"Is that why you're buttering me up?"

"Are you a piece of bread?"

"Search me."

"Buttering up is the Senator's phrase. That's what *he* says. . . . I suppose he told you I wanted him to do something about the pollution hearing? I suppose he said I was buttering you up so he would?"

"Are you?"

"I want to do *him* a favor."

"Har-de-har, har, har."

"You don't have to believe it; just relay the message."

"Tell him yourself."

"He won't stand still long enough. He's suspicious of my intentions. There's no subtle way for me to get his attention. I'm a subtle man."

"I don't know anything about air pollution, or factories, or

Senate hearings, or this, that, and the other thing, but I'm suspicious of your intentions, too."

"I have good intentions. The man I work for 'nas good intentions. There are good intentions all the hell over the place, and I could puke."

"Why work for him if you don't like it?"

"I work against him."

"Why don't you just change jobs?"

"One day I will, but for a while I just want to act out."

"Act out what?"

"Hostilities."

"Why is everyone so mixed up in intrigue and getting even, and this, that, and the other thing?"

"I worked for this son of a B for a long time, and I said yes, yes, yes, yes, yes. Then one night when I was as high as I am right now, I said no. Not to him, not to his face, but I said no. I went to the telephone and called the Health Department and reported a small infraction of the rules. They confiscated everything in our Vesey Street warehouse, and four truckloads coming in. They leveled a ten-thousand-dollar fine on Himself. The ability to do that cost *me* thirteen thousand dollars—that's what I'd paid my analyst until then. It was worth every nickel. That son of a B never knew it, but Ben Hyde had finally said no!"

"He never found out?"

"Never knew it."

"Why do you hate him so?"

"Because he's Mr. Perfect; he doesn't ever do anything wrong. Oh, the food they confiscated was safe, wasn't contaminated, anything like that. He's Mr. Perfect. Listen, once I was responsible for his losing a large amount of money. Pfffft-gone, and I was to blame. Know what he said? Said, 'Forget it.' "

"Heck. You hate him for that?"

"When I was a kid, I was a sissy. Every bully in the block was waiting for me after school. So my father met me after school and drove me home. He didn't bother to teach me how to fight; he liked the fact I was weak. That way I couldn't compete with him for my mother's love. I was no competition. He encouraged me to be a weak little nothing, grateful to him because he protected me. And I said, yes, yes, yes, yes, yes to him, too."

"Oh, wow. It's over my head."

Bob appeared in the doorway of the library then. "We're leaving, Jo. I'll meet you out front after I get the car."

120

Josie Swift said to Ben Hyde, "Well, good-bye."

"Tell the Senator to call me. I'll give him some real leads for his investigation. No strings, tell him."

"I liked you better when you were being Bobby Kennedy."

"You like fantasy better than reality. That's why you're marrying a father substitute and this, that, and the other thing."

On the drive home, she told Bob about it.

"Another nut!" he said. "Frank Lloyd Wright once said that the nation had been tipped on its side and they'd all slid into California, but I think a good many landed down here in Washington, too."

"Do you think he really wants to help you?"

"Do you think he really worried about the consumer when he reported whatever it was to the Health Department, or do you think what he wanted was revenge on his boss?"

"Imagine hating someone for not making you pay back money!"

"Santa Claus is only popular with children, Jo. Adults don't like him. I remember something Senator Ellender said once— he was complaining about the ingratitude of certain relief agencies. He said first they were given the surpluses; then they asked the government to pay the freight charges; then they asked the government to mill the grain and package it. The next thing, they'd ask the government to cook and serve it. . . . No good deed goes unpunished."

"Will you call Ben Hyde?"

"Not personally. One of my staff will. It might be very useful. The manufacturers stick together; they agree to exaggerate the cost of new incinerators and various antipollution devices, and they minimize their contribution to the air-pollution problem. We know that they've held meetings and prepared an elaborate defense. It isn't news to us. But we have to go to an awful lot of expense to prove it, and often we can't."

"It's news to me, though. I sure don't know much about your work."

"You're catching on fast. You did something very smart tonight, Jo."

"What?"

"You ignored my advice about talking with Ben Hyde. You'll always have my respect if you ignore my advice and come up with such good results."

Then they both burst out laughing.

Oh, wow. Small-world department.

# 26

"Strangers and pilgrims, abstain from fleshly lusts," said Mrs. Graeff when Charlie Latham finished talking. She glanced up at him and smiled. "From Peter's First Epistle . . . I know that the point of this game is not to go into long discussions of our mistakes, Reverend, but may I make an observation?"

"Feel free." He went across and sat down on a box beside Josie Swift. Sitting down brought a modicum of relief, but the pressure on his bladder was building.

"I think you're very fortunate to be rid of Salena."

"Yeah, I agree with her," said Whistler. "You didn't lose anything, you gained something."

When they were living in Washington Heights, some Sundays, Charlie would take Frank for a walk up near the Cloisters. Frank was the kind of kid who never complained, and invariably when he announced he had to go, he really had to go, then and there, wherever they were, because he had been holding it for a long time.

They would have to step to one side while Frank relieved himself, and some people would smile understandingly, but others would give them dirty looks. Once Charlie had really bawled him out about it, shouting at Frank as they went down a wooded path toward Fort Tryon Park: "When you first feel you have to go, *tell me,* so we can find a bathroom; do you *hear* me?" Frank had answered, "I'll try. But if I don't remember, don't stand with me, Daddy; then no one will think you're with me." There were tears in his eyes; Charlie had scooped him up and held him close and said, "Oh, Frank! Frank, you matter to me more than anyone."

It was one of the few times, maybe the only time, that Charlie had ever come right out and told Frank how he felt about him, without using baby talk, or someone else's voice. After that, for a long time, there was never a Sunday when

Frank didn't have to suddenly go. It had seemed as though he were deliberately defying Charlie, but Charlie never reprimanded him for it. Until this very moment, it had not occurred to Charlie that the kid might have been testing him, or waiting for Charlie to say something like that again.

"However," Mrs. Graeff continued, while she massaged her ankle, "I cannot in all honesty sanction divorce. I gather you can't, either, if you see it as your worst mistake."

The pose was hard to maintain on a full bladder; he didn't feel like talking at all. He managed: "I didn't mean my divorce was my worst mistake; I meant that marrying for the wrong reason was."

Whistler said, "You married a bad apple, that's all." He was sitting on the other side of Josie Swift. He pushed up his shirt sleeve and looked at his watch. He said, "It's eleven-thirty."

Mrs. Graeff said, "It *is?*"

"I don't know what the hell could be taking so long!"

Blades pressed the alarm again. There was still no sound. Blades said, "Maybe everyone's gone home."

"What *did* you see up on the roof, Mr. Whistle?"

"That's just it, Mrs. Graeff; I couldn't see anything but that damn light in my eyes."

"And we fell again; I could feel it. We fell twice."

"I think we only fell once," said Blades, "and then the boxes fell."

"No, Mr. Cougar, *we* fell again."

"We did fall twice," said Josie Swift. "The car moved twice after Mr. Whistler landed on the floor."

Whistler said, "Altogether, the car slipped three times. One of the brake shoes must be broken. Maybe more than one."

"Wouldn't we have hit the bottom of the shaft by now?" said Blades.

"No. There are four brakes. . . . You see, if that's our situation, we're like an airplane with an engine or two konked out."

Mrs. Graeff said, "Coming in on a wing and a prayer."

"Yeah, something like that," said Whistler.

Josie Swift said, "Mr. Whistler? If we were going to fall all the way, we would have by now, wouldn't we?"

"Yes." But once, in a Chicago hotel, Whistler had seen an elevator fall four times, a floor apiece, at spaced intervals, before it suddenly plummeted twenty floors to the bottom of the shaft. . . . None of the passengers had survived. . . . Whistler felt his heart hammering against his chest; he wondered if anyone besides him realized that these might be their last hours. It was just beginning to really reach him, not just his mind, but now his body: the beginning of terror—the knot in his stomach and the breathless sensation as he spoke, physical manifestations of fear which were unfamiliar to him, for he had never been trapped like this, never been where he could not run or duck or hide.

He looked at the faces of the others: Blades's frowning, perspiring; Mrs. Graeff's, pale and drawn; Latham's, hard to fathom, because of the glazed myopic gaze . . . then hers. A young face which was mobile and vulnerable, as she was, alert but not perceptive; sensuous but not sensitive. The way she had defended him against the others had touched him. He wondered what it was she had written on the piece of paper when she had borrowed his pen. What? A shopping list? A dramatic letter of farewell to her boyfriend, just in case? Notes on a night in a stalled elevator?

But there was something about her which made him reject the idea that she had a boyfriend. He could not see her in the fickle and giddy boy-girl relationships he had seen his daughter involved in. She was far different from Kathy. Though they must be close to the same age, she was more knowing, despite her unpolished ways; she was more confident. It was not the sort of confidence that would see her through an End of the World Party, where she was apparently outclassed—Kathy would have breezed through that—it was the sort that let her look so fully with her green eyes into his eyes as she asked, "You okay?" It was the sort that let her touch his knees lightly with her fingers, in an attempt to return his pen.

The trouble was, he knew so little about women; he had really only known Mariam.

"We're not going to fall again," Charlie Latham was saying. "We're going to stay loose and keep our cool."

Pray God, Whistler thought; *pray God*.

Mrs. Graeff gave a giggle, "You certainly are the epitome of the modern minister, Reverend Smoke, with all that slang," but there would be no way for him to divine that it was a reproach. She couldn't help her feelings. His background was shoddy enough, without that tawdry street vernacular. Now, of all times, he should behave with dignity; he was a man of God; ". . . hide not thy face, for I am in trouble. . . ." Mrs. Graeff thought of her lovely chocolate fudge cake with the

124

white icing, sitting in its box on some shelf in the Algonquin, the candy-red script hardened on its face:

> Let flags unfurl
> For it's our pearl.

She felt the tears coming, felt the pain in her swelling ankle.

Charlie Latham said, "Do you think I'm groovy, Mrs. Graeff; think I'm a gas?"

"Oh, wow!" Josie Swift laughed. "Where'd you get that?"

"Man, I got it from the flower people; like, it's my hang-up."

Josie Swift clapped her hand to her mouth and laughed harder.

But if Charlie Latham was too nearsighted to see the tears in Mrs. Graeff's eyes, T. T. Blades was not. He was standing there, thinking that he would catch a plane to the West Indies next Wednesday, in time to meet the *Franconia*. He said, "Is it your ankle?"

"Oh, don't bother with me; I have the weepies for some mysterious reason."

"Are you in pain?"

"No, no, let's not talk about me. What were we talking about before? How fine it was for Reverend Smoke to try and keep his marriage intact."

Blades said, "Yes, Reverend. I didn't get a chance to say anything, but I agree; you could have just checked out on the whole deal once she started drinking. Nobody would have blamed you."

"I didn't realize how futile it was," said Charlie Latham. "It was futile." He had said something very similar the night that Gwen had announced she was going to leave him, take Frank with her. It's for the best, he had said; the way things are, you're sacrificing yourself and Frank. It's futile.

She had said, "Charlie? You know I don't want to go. I don't want to leave you here alone."

Greta Garbo had answered her: "I want to be alone."

Charlie said, "Self-sacrifice is always a mistake. Always. You can't give up your life for someone."

"But Christ gave up his life for us, Reverend Smoke."

"Precisely, Mrs. Graeff."

"Was *that* a mistake?"

"We shouldn't confuse ourselves with Christ."

"Ah!"

125

Charlie wondered if the thing to do was just excuse himself, step to the back of the elevator, and go. He wondered
how to put it, say it right out like that.

"You're very deep, dear Reverend Smoke. Just when I
think you're not too complicated, then you turn out to be
very complicated."

Josie Swift smiled. "I'll buy that"—and touched his arm.

The gesture of familiarity irked Mrs. Graeff; oh, 'fess up,
Faith, *she* irked Mrs. Graeff, who said, "Now, Mr. Cougar,
you take your turn. I want to know all about my boys," and
shot a haughty glance at Miss Red Tramp.

At that moment, six policemen and Louis Gillespie were
pounding on the door of a garage on East 38th Street. The
studio of the sculptor Zolto.

The idea was to transport the lumber back to the Gart
Building on foot; by now the streets of New York City were
frozen and impassable.

## 27

There was a favorite record of Joe Swan's; he used to play it
at training camp every year, Joe being the Cougars' swinger.
This voice—you didn't know if it was a man's or a woman's
—would come on real husky and slow, singing, "*You don't
know what love is, you don't even know the meaning of the
word.*"

Before it could get much further, T. T. would hie himself
down to the whirlpool baths to soak his aching bones. Balls
to that mush.

Well, you don't know what grim is until you try to explain
what love is, and the person you're trying to explain this to
happens to be Shirley Fitzgerald Blades, your wife.

"I can understand if you met this girl and got some kind of
thing for her, T. We all make mistakes."

"I didn't make a mistake. I didn't see that I had two
choices and that I chose the wrong one."

126

"You did have two choices, though."

"I didn't have two choices."

"You did, T."

"No."

"One was to never see her again, because you're a married man. One was to see her again. So. You saw her again."

"Yeah."

"So you did have two choices."

"Okay."

"And you did choose the wrong one."

"What am I going to tell you, Shirley? I still want to see her. I have to see her. What am I going to tell you?"

"I'm going to put water on to boil for coffee, T."

"Yeah. We ought to get off this. It's depressing."

"I don't want to get off it. I think we should thrash this out."

"Thrash it out? What is it? Poison ivy at the back of the house or something, crabgrass or something?"

"You tell me what it is, T."

"I said what it is. I'm in love with her."

"Are you really *in* love with her, or do you just love her?"

"Huh?"

"I said are you really *in* love with her, or do you just love her?"

"What's the difference?"

"If you're *in* love, it's deeper."

"Oh. Well, I'm *in deep.*"

"It'll go away, then, T. It's like an infatuation."

"It's not going to go away."

"Let me put water on to boil. . . . It'll go away."

"Now, look, Shirley! Don't get that musical tone to your voice! I know what's going to stay and what's going to go away. Now, this girl comes and goes, but she might as well be here all the time, because she's like mildew. You're never rid of it! You know how mildew is when it gets on a suitcase or something? You never get rid of it!"

"Wait until I put the water on to boil, T. Then you can tell me all about it."

"I don't want to tell anybody about it; I just want to be left alone about it!"

"I want to thrash it out, T."

"Shirley, wait a minute. Stop. Now. Listen. You see, I love this girl. She gets all dressed up——"

"Like some whore in all her finery."

"Not like some whore. You should see her!"

"If I ever see her, she'll be one sorry little prostitute."

"She's not a prostitute. She's a very fine woman."

"Oh, my eye fine! T., what kind of woman goes around with another woman's husband? Answer that!"

"She hates it; do you think she doesn't?"

"She goes ahead and does it. She likes to be seen around town with a big football star. She'll ditch you when you're not a star, T."

"I haven't taken her around town. I wouldn't do that to you."

"You wouldn't do that to *you*. To your fans."

"I wouldn't do it to *you*, Shirl!"

"Ashamed of her?"

"I'm proud of her! We look good together, too. Sometimes when I'm with her, sitting across from her in some little restaurant, I think I wouldn't feel anything about doing it right in front of everybody, in the aisle with her. It couldn't look dirty, because there just isn't anything bad about us together that way. She loves me! I love her! People take one look at us and they know it!"

"She must be something. You want to screw her in the aisle of a restaurant."

"You twist things, and how come you use the word 'screw' now? You always tell me you hate that word, and now *you* use it all of a sudden!"

"In honor of her, T. That's all."

"You can tell me to screw her and I-don't-care-what-word her, but it won't make anything we do together, her and me, anything but great! Great! ... *Decent!*"

"Maybe the Pope will canonize the two of you doing it in the aisle of a restaurant. I'm putting the water on to boil, Sir Lancelot. I'll return to Camelot in a minute. You want some orange juice?"

They had been up all night; he had been out with Lois; Shirley had been waiting for him when he got in at four that morning.

They were both punchy now; was it also true that they were even beginning to enjoy sparring with each other, aware of the humor of their thrusts and parries?

How little people knew of themselves; how sure they sometimes were that for them this sort of thing would not be hard; they'd handle it. T. thought so, went along with her mood, became more and more entangled in the web of words they got off so easily, refreshed himself with coffee, took a swim; they took a walk and then made love and had a nap.

128

When T. woke up she was lying beside him, outside the sheet, smoking a cigarette. He was lying under the sheet. He stretched, made a noisy yawn, murmured, "Hi, hon, what time is it?"

And heard her answer, "Is she better than I am in bed?"

"Not that again. Not now."

"I want to know."

"Why?"

"You can tell me honestly. I want you to."

"She's—different."

"How?"

"She's—she does different things."

"Oh! *That.*"

"No, she doesn't do *that.* But what if she did do *that?* It's not a crime."

"It is so, T."

"Okay, it's a crime. Go arrest half the people around."

"What things does she do? Does she talk?"

"Sure, she talks."

"Says dirty things?"

"Shirley, she's not some floozy. She's not some breast-pin saleslady from the five and ten. She's not a hooker, either. Why can't you just believe she's nice? Decent."

"Decent! Takes another woman's husband? Sleeps around with him?"

"We're in love."

"What's the sexiest thing she ever said to you?"

"I don't know. I'm supposed to remember that?"

"You always remembered the sexiest thing I ever said to you."

"Yeah," he said. "That's different." He had no memory of it.

"Tell me something sexy she said."

"Aw, no."

"Yes. Yes, I want to hear it. Something sexy she said."

T. thought a minute. "It doesn't sound like much."

"Tell me."

"Well, once she said, 'I want you to get me very pregnant. I want to walk down Fifth Avenue with you, big as a house, showing everybody.' "

Shirley looked at him and smiled and put her cigarette in the ashtray. Then she hauled off and walloped him so hard his teeth hurt after. She called him a name he had never been called by anyone, not even by the most foul-mouthed tackle, a name he had never called anyone either, though he had

129

heard it was one of the three most obscene words in the English language.

That was the moment T. T. appreciated that nothing about it was going to be anything but grim, and like the voice on Joe Swan's record said, he didn't even know the meaning of the word.

Hands down, telling Shirley about Lois was his worst mistake.

# 28

The heavyset fellow in Quinn's Bar on 44th Street ordered another whiskey. He said aloud, to no one in particular, "When anything goes wrong, people don't want to listen to you, they want to blame you."

A plump woman with sun-and-fun-shaded hair sat on the bar stool next to him, sipping Seven and Seven. She said, "That's the way the ball bounces sometimes."

"Sometimes? All the time."

"Really?"

"You work for a bunch of lickpennies, the ball bounces that way all the time. One thing I hate is cheapskates."

"Do you work in the Gart Building?"

"That's a good question, isn't it, Stevie?"

The bartender was rinsing out glasses; he answered, "He's the superintendent."

"Was ... You'll see. My head'll roll first."

She said, "I've got a personal friend in that elevator."

"Yeah? You a celebrity?"

"Holy cow, *me?*"

"I just asked because you stick around over there very long you get the idea everybody in that elevator's got friends that are big deals!"

"I'm no big deal. Pssss!"

The bartender said, "I heard Senator Anderson's been over there raising all kinds of hell."

"Sure, that's what I mean. Listen, there's nobody over there just ordinary but Ryan and me, and Ryan's a cretin. I

130

got a bellyful. Big deals! Architects, lawyers, senators—" He turned to the blond. "That's why I wondered if you was a celebrity."

"Are those people going to get out of that elevator all right?"

"I pray to God, lady. What can I tell you?"

He downed the whiskey in a single gulp; he signaled for another.

The bartender said, "You better not get a load on, Fred."

"*Tell* me . . . Know who's hightailing it in from Bronxville? Hillman Skidmore, the elevator King in person. At the personal request of His Honor Senator Robert Big Mouth Anderson."

"He won't make it in this weather," said the bartender.

"He'll break his neck trying. He's got his own jeep, I heard, rigged up with a snowplow—whole bit. He's a one-man Sanitation Department."

The bartender held the bottle of whisky over a supersized jigger. He said, "Say when."

"When my hands stop shaking," said the super.

"Fred, you got nothing to worry about."

"I was warned when I took the job. The owners don't like to shell out for repairs; they're tightwads. They're misers."

"They have that reputation," said the bartender.

"I never seen them, but they must wear rags. . . . You said, yourself, they have that reputation. I was warned they don't like to shell out for repairs. What can I tell you? I didn't beat a path to their doors reporting repairs. I'm not getting any younger, and I got to eat same as the next fellow."

"Was the elevator broken and you didn't report it?" the blond asked.

"The elevator wasn't broken that I know of, lady."

"Hear no evil, see no evil, speak no evil," said the bartender.

"It's a great little motto," the super said, "for monkeys."

## 29

When T. T. finished, he shoved his hands into his pockets and shrugged. "That's it. In our house, cancer's a better word than Lois."

"I'd say you were still in love with Lois," Whistler said.

"I told her it was all over, last week."

"Bully for you, Mr. Cougar! Bully for you!"

"You sure make her sound groovy."

"There's nothing wrong with my wife, either."

Whistler said, "You don't spend the rest of your life with a woman because there's nothing wrong with her. . . . I'll butt out, Blades, if you want me to, but that's my opinion."

"You have a right to it. . . . You just don't understand what pro ball is like. Most of us are married men. It's a very closed fraternity. I know all their wives, they know Shirley. This thing spoiled an awful lot for me. Everybody knew. I'd come into the locker room and you could hear a pin drop. They let me know what they thought of me. . . . And I wasn't playing my best, either."

"You were too busy worrying about what they thought of you."

"Even the fans. They were booing me no matter what I did. They had me so rattled that at the end of last season I wasn't even mixing up my plays. Anyone could have figured it out. I was calling a running play on every first down."

"The tyranny of the mediocre. The fans."

"Is that the way you feel about your customers, Mr. Whistle?"

"My customers don't boo me, Mrs. Graeff."

"It's a pity, Mr. Whistle."

"What bothers you about me, Mrs. Graeff? Because something does! Don't be afraid to just say it right out, whatever it is. I've never struck a woman yet."

"I wouldn't like to be first."

Blades said, "Well, look, Mrs. Graeff, he has a right to say how he feels. There's no point in our game if we don't get involved."

"A comment is one thing, I feel; discouraging a man from reconciling with his wife is quite another."

"If he's that easily discouraged, it isn't that easily reconciled. I'll butt out anytime he wants me to, but I'm not going to lie about my feelings.... Look, I'm on Blades's side in this thing. I wouldn't like my wife to remind me I'm not going to be in top form much longer, I'm not going to be able to do my job well much longer."

"My wife can't help it, Whistler. All pro wives are as aware as the dickens what a limited career football is. Shirley's twice as aware, being Gib's daughter. There's a story that when Gib was with the Bears, he hit up the manager for a raise. He said to him, 'I played my tail off for you, and now I'm old.' The manager said, 'How old are you now, Gib?' Gib said, 'I'm twenty-three.' "

"That's a good story, but these days a pro ball player hasn't got any reason for that kind of insecurity, has he? He's paid a fortune."

Blades sighed. "I know. But it still affects a fellow in strange ways. There's a Cougar tackle making eighteen thousand dollars a year. As soon as the last game of the year is over, he hurries back to the little town he's from in Vermont to apply for unemployment insurance.... Then there's all the stealing from the team: T-shirts, sweat socks, shoes, jackets, even footballs."

Whistler chuckled softly. "Who doesn't put his hand in the till now and then? In my office the inventory goes down with the secretaries every night; they help themselves to everything from paper clips to a year's supply of the company's best stationery. It wouldn't surprise me if these cartons were going home with some office girl." Whistler smiled and shook his head. "I'll tell you something, though. I'd a hundred times rather have that problem than have an employee who has something wrong up here." He tapped his temple. "I'm going to have to let my partner go, because he's got himself all twisted up in psychoanalysis. *You* know the old joke about the psychiatrist's patient: you ask him how he is, he wonders what the hell you meant by *that* question."

Charlie Latham said, "But some people really need that kind of help." Now he didn't think he could go if he had the chance; he was damn near crippled by the pressure.

Mrs. Graeff said, "Psychoanalysis makes everything seem

sinister. My son had a boa constrictor at one time. They're devastating creatures. My son named him Killer. Then this doctor who was connected with my son's school, this psychoanalyst, suggested it was a play on words, and Douglas really meant *kill her*. Meaning me, of course."

Charlie Latham said, "How's your ankle?"

"There's pain, but I realize there's nothing that can be done about it. I'm just sitting here pretending that everyone was hurt much worse than I. It seems to help."

Whistler had more to say to Blades. "You fellows aren't the only ones with peak years. Any man in business has a few peak years. He doesn't maintain his thrust much after them. He rides on what he's done, on how much reserve he's built up."

"I suppose so," said T.

Mrs. Graeff said, "It *was* a mistake to tell your wife about that girl. A woman never forgives something like that. Long after you've forgotten it, she'll remember it."

Whistler continued, "These are my peak years right now. It's now or never. That's why I have to forget the rule book occasionally, like the night of the blackout with my Vesey Street lot. Blades, you of all people should have understood why I did that."

"But that was a big chance to take."

"The only chance I took was the chance of being found out. The food was safe. . . . And I *was* found out; it cost me ten thousand dollars, the whole Vesey Street lot, and four incoming truckloads." Whistler smiled at T. T. "I got fined just the same as you boys do when you step out of line."

"I think it's different."

"Because you're not in business. It's hard for you to appreciate the circumstances."

T. T. said nothing; everyone was remarkably quiet.

Whistler looked from one to the other. "All right, it was a mistake. Isn't that what you're talking about?"

"You were deliberately setting out to put something over on the public," said Blades. "I don't know if you can call that a mistake."

"I paid a ten-thousand-dollar fine for it. I'd say it was a whopping mistake."

"Which is exactly the terminology used earlier when we wondered how our lives had come to be endangered, and by what sort of person," said Mrs. Graeff.

"What do you mean by that, Mrs. Graeff?"

"Simply this, Mr. Whistle: I would have considerable misgivings about purchasing anything manufactured by Whistle Foods. Someone who thinks as dangerously as you do was responsible for our being here. Forgive me, Mr. Whistle, but I do not think premeditated negligence is the same thing as a mistake."

Whistler's fists were clenched at his sides, but he kept his control, speaking to her in a soft, reasonable tone. "I haven't been in the business twenty-one years without learning very well by now what is safe and what isn't. Do you think your local A & P tosses out all the frozen packages nights when the power fails? And you can bet your life the power fails, many a night the power fails, and they come in seven, eight, the next morning with the stuff swimming, and they repair the power and refreeze! I was going to do something that's done every day at some A & P in this city, or some Bohack's or Gristede's or Sloan's—and don't forget to count all the little delis where the electrician comes when he gets around to it, and goods sit sometimes a couple of days, then get popped back into the freezer. What I did was careless, but it wasn't dangerous. I didn't get where I am to chance ruining it all for a few carloads of frozen dinners."

There was a silence in which Whistler's heavy breathing was the only sound. Then Josie Swift said, "*I* believe you, Mr. Whistler."

"I think we should get on with the game," Latham said.

"Which means you do or don't believe what I just said, Reverend?"

"It means I do."

"I'll go along with you," said Blades.

Mrs. Graeff was playing with her fur cloche, which she held in her lap. Without looking up at Whistler, she said, "Nevertheless, Mr. Whistle, there's an old saying: the pitcher that goes too often to the well is broken at last."

There was an audible emission of breath from Whistler. When he spoke, his voice had hardened. "My name is Whistler. Not Whistle."

"Mr. *Whistler*. . . . You do just the opposite from what my son used to do. He was always maximizing danger; you seem to always minimize it."

"I don't understand all this talk of danger in connection with me."

"No, I know you don't."

Josie Swift sighed. "I don't either."

"That hardly comes as a surprise to me, Miss Swift." There was a sudden, silly tilt to her lips as she persisted. " 'Oh, we can't get stuck here,' he said; remember? It was one of the first things out of his mouth. We can't get stuck here. Then he just took over from Mr. Cougar. Mr. Gillespie had made Mr. Cougar our captain and he just took over. Yes, and this car is locked in position," she continued, imitating a gruff male voice, "this car is being held by brakes."

"What are you getting at, Mrs. Graeff?"

"Mr. Whistle, remember those poor children in Tijuana, Mexico? It was a year or so ago; there were reports in all the newspapers. Someone had been careless; somehow or other some pesticide had gotten into the bread."

"Parathion, yes."

"Was that its name? Well, you see, then, don't you?"

"What do I see?"

"That your kind of thinking can be very dangerous."

He stood there looking down at her, his face now flushed with rage.

Latham started to intercede, but before he could, Mrs. Graeff added a few words to what she had said. "You see, I do think you're dangerous. I wouldn't be surprised at what you'd do."

What he did was whirl around and hit the wall of the elevator to keep from hitting her. He hit it as hard as he had ever hit anything in his life.

The elevator lights blinked once, twice; then total darkness.

In which Mrs. Graeff said, "Get ready to fall."

# 30

Faith Graeff's behavior would not have come as any surprise to Roger Tyson. He was well aware that as a provocateur she had few peers.

A short while before the incident occurred, he had been saying some things very much along those lines about his client as he and Senator Anderson were waiting for Hillman Skidmore's arrival.

Louis Gillespie had made available to them one of the sixth-floor suites of Gillespie, Goddard & Ross. Roger and Bob had used the stairway; elevators were available only to members of the rescue team.

What everyone was waiting for now was not Hillman Skidmore's arrival, but the arrival of the lumber necessary to the rescue operation.

The Senator was the exception. If he had any faith in underlings, it was because he had first checked them out with their superiors. When anything went wrong and the buck began being passed, the Senator never waited for it to go its rounds; he arrived where it was bound to stop, ahead of time, usually, demanding answers even before the questions had been put and pondered over.

To read nervousness in Bob's face was not easy. On the surface he wore trouble like the Rock of Gilbraltar weathering the assault of a feather duster. But Tyson knew him well enough to guess he was very damn nervous; the usually piercing light-blue eyes were making no effort to look back at Roger's while they sat there talking on one of the large yellow leather couches, and periodically the Senator would pass one of his hard small hands through his thick white hair, and then grasp both hands together, making his knuckles crack, and glance again at his watch. Those small gestures in a hardnose like Anderson were equivalent to another man's pacing the floor or chain-smoking or tossing down a few dozen in a row. They were sufficient reason to postpone any further lectures from Tyson to Anderson on the subject of marriage and the prospective bride. (Tyson winced inwardly every time he linked the word "bride" with the redheaded number from the firm's bullpen.)

So, staying off that subject, he had somehow rambled into a description of Raymond and Faith Graeff, bearing down hard on Faith's incredible self-absorption, perhaps for no more important reason than the fact it was because of her that Tyson was stuck in this place at this hour.

He said, "My wife says it isn't self-absorption, it's innocence. You know Phyllis: she can make a hailstorm of a typhoon. She says that Faith isn't malicious, she's simply uncomprehending, like a child. She doesn't know she's hurt anyone's feelings or been the catalyst to a quarrel, or any of it."

The Senator was removing coffee containers from a brown-paper sack. They had originally intended to have this coffee break across the street at the luncheonette next to

137

Quinn's Bar. But the Senator was too well known. He had been seen too many times on television presiding over the congressional investigations into racketeering, and his outspoken dove calls against the war in Vietnam had made him newsworthy; his caricature was a favorite with Herblock, Batchelor, and Feiffer. His presence on 44th Street had caused too big a stir among those who were beginning to gather—the trouble watchers, who showed up faithfully, any time/any hour for everything from fires to street fights in Fun City, dispersing only by order of the police, who knew it was less trouble to contain them behind a sawhorse barricade.

"Here's a regular," said the Senator, passing one of the coffee containers to Roger. "Well, maybe your Mrs. Graeff *is* an innocent. Phyllis was always a pretty good judge of character."

Tyson felt like saying: not of yours, Senator; she was so positive Maggie Van Pelten would be the next Mrs. Anderson. "Bob," she always said, "likes a character, and Maggie's a character—give her that." Tyson gave her that, all right, but the Senator was a bit more complicated. Or maybe, in his advanced years, more simple.

The Senator continued, "Someone once said that innocence is like a dumb leper who has lost his bell."

"That's Faith."

"You know, I think I've met Ray Graeff."

"You haven't met *Ray* Graeff. No one would ever call him Ray. He's very Raymond—withdrawn, distant, incapable of small talk. You know the type; if one is going to break the ice with trivia about the weather or the headlines, he'll just stay silent."

"He won the Nobel, didn't he?"

"No. That was something of a mystery to me, too. Raymond's a hard man to know; I don't think anyone's ever been very close to him. He's the sort you can never imagine having ever been a boy, having ever been young, or reckless, or gay. But he used to like to talk to me about his work years ago, when we still lunched together on occasion. He was all caught up in something to do with gravitation; it was his only real enthusiasm."

"I do remember him, now. I met him very briefly during the Second World War. He was part of a radar research team at M.I.T."

"That's Raymond, yes."

"He was the talk of M.I.T. Everyone thought he was the new Einstein."

138

"Except, of course, Raymond disagrees with Einstein." Roger Tyson took a sip of coffee and smiled. "Oh, he doesn't argue that the *general* principles of relativity don't apply to gravity; he simply thinks that Einstein's theories, as formulated in his field equations, are incorrect."

"But I was sure he received the Nobel."

"He didn't. He was working with this Indian physicist. They were both on the same track, and they'd teamed up. Raymond was at his apogee in those days. I remember that he even seemed hail-fellow-well-met, which was wholly unlike him. His excitement about his work was very contagious, too; let's face it, Bob, how many of us ever have the chance to discover something that actually alters our knowledge of the world? It *is* exciting. I looked forward to those lunches with him. . . . Then suddenly Raymond just dropped out of the picture."

"What do you mean?"

"He wasn't available for lunch anymore. If he came into the city at all, *I* didn't know about it. I called him once to find out how things were going; he was so abrupt I imagined that he was just too busy for anything but his project. I met Faith in New York one day; when I asked her about it, she said Raymond's associate had gone back to India. She said Raymond was involved in something else. I remember I laughed and said, 'Good Lord, that's like saying I've left law, isn't it?' 'Is it?' she said. 'Have you, Roger?' I never knew how to take that remark. I never knew how to take any of her remarks, whether they were intended to be amusing or snide. At any rate, a few years later the Indian got the Nobel for his work on gravitation; he and a German physicist."

"Waraich and Plangman. I attended a reception for them in Oslo. Of course."

"Yes. But it should have been Waraich and Graeff. Everyone said so."

"I wonder what happened?"

"It was always my guess that it was Raymond's personality. He's one of the most decent men you'd ever come across, but he's uncommonly rigid. He's probably a very difficult and exacting worker, the perfectionist who just can't give an inch in either direction. It's my hunch he'd be impossible to work with. They probably had a falling out."

"Most likely." The Senator's gaze had drifted toward the window, the snow raging against it. His mind was starting to worry the emergency again, fingers began drumming the formica tabletop in front of him.

Tyson was not up to another of the Senator's blustery patrols downstairs through the various huddles of major and minor officials. Neither were the police sergeant and the deputy fire chief, who were controlling traffic in the lobby of the Gart Building. Together they had taken Roger aside and demonstrated the New York City protector's particular on-duty indifference to overloads. "You keep windbag out of our hair, or we'll restrict both of you from the building."

Desperately Tyson sought to continue distracting Anderson with the discussion of Raymond Graeff. He said, "Still, it doesn't seem like Raymond to just abandon a major project because he isn't getting along with his associates. Why would he just step out of the picture that way?"

But now the Senator was rising and walking across to the window, staring out at the raging snowstorm. "How are they going to get that lumber here in this? There's nothing moving down there; streets are snowdrifts."

"Gil Holland will figure something out, Bob. He's a good man."

"Is he? Then why hasn't he figured something out before this? And where's Hillman Skidmore?"

Ten minutes later Skidmore walked into the sixth-floor suite, shaking snow from his parka, rubbing it away from his eyebrows, striding across to the Senator with his right hand extended. "Senator, it's a pleasure to——"

Bob Anderson cut him short, ignored his hand. "Mr. Skidmore, what's going on in that elevator?"

"Right now it's pitch black in that elevator, Senator." He unzipped the parka and tossed it on the couch. "Mike Farley just threw the power switch. The lumber is here. Holland and Lieutenant Scholz's Emergency Division are ready to go to work now."

# 31

"Did we fall?"

"No."

"I felt us fall."

"We didn't."

"He *is* dangerous."

"Hush. . . . Let me say a prayer."

"Reverend, before you do, stand back here against these cartons with Whistler and me. We can brace them with our backs if it's necessary; where's the carton with the thinner in it?"

"Here by me."

"Okay, Miss Swift. See that the top's screwed on good this time. Is Whistler's undershirt in there with it?"

"Yes."

"Slide that box over in front of us and sit on it."

"Are we going to fall again?"

"No, Mrs. Graeff, but we're going to take precautions. Is everything clear of you? Feel around you."

"Yes. But I won't be able to stand or walk if——"

"I know that. Don't worry. If it comes to that, I'll carry you."

"We're going to fall, I'm afraid; dear God, we *are*, I——"

"We're not, and we didn't; all he did was knock out the lights."

Whistler's voice trembled. "I'm sorry. I don't know what else to say."

"And it's a little late for that," Mrs. Graeff answered.

"It wasn't his fault, it was your fault, Mrs. Graeff, telling him he was dangerous, and talking about pesticides in the bread, and this, that, and the other thing!"

"*Be still*, you little tramp!"

"Oh, har-de-har, har, har! *You* be still."

"Common little——"

"Cut it out, ladies! Reverend Smoke? Say a prayer."

"Be our strength in hours of weakness . . . in our wanderings, be our guide. Through endeavor, failure, danger . . . Father, be thou at our side."

In the darkness, Josie Swift brushed tears from the corners of her eyes; she was not going to give in and cry.

Why did T. T. Blades want the men to stand back by the boxes, if they weren't going to fall?

She tried to think of something to keep herself from crying: the Senator.

Shoot, he'd never marry her, even if she did get out of here alive; Irene was right. She'd always been Losersville; Harlan Francher was right. Remember how Harlan had said it that night, with such a tone of amazement: "Why, don't you know what you are? Don't you *know?*"

"Amen," Mrs. Graeff and T. T. Blades murmured.

Mrs. Graeff said, "Could we sing a hymn, if we sang very softly?"

"What hymn would you like to sing?"

"You decide, Reverend."

"It should be one we all know," he said.

Josie Swift said, "How about number eighteen or number four-forty-one? Everybody knows them."

He didn't answer; she realized what was bothering him. She said, "Eighteen is *Abide with Me,* remember? And four-forty-one is *Faith of Our Fathers.*"

"I know the first one," said T. T. Blades.

Mrs. Graeff said, "I do, too."

Charlie Latham began it: *"Abide with me: fast falls the eventide,"* and the others, save for Whistler, joined in: *The darkness deepens; Lord, with me abide: When other helpers fail, and comforts flee, Help of the helpless, O abide with me."*

While T. T. Blades sang, he held in his hand the gold pen Lois Cadwallader had given him. 7 Sol. 10. He rubbed the engraving with the tip of his thumb. *I am my beloved's* and *his desire is toward me.* He had never received a gift like that before, but the year he really made it big for the first time, he bought this gift for Shirley.

He walked in the door and tossed the box across to her. "Catch."

She didn't catch it; she had to bend over and pick it up. She was wearing a skirt and sweater and a pair of loafers. She had been smoking a cigarette and sipping Tab from the bottle and watching Art Linkletter's *House Party* on television. Through the windows of the apartment at the Dunes, T. T. could see Gib stretched out in his Rock'R Recline chair, on the enclosed porch, watching a Western on his small Sony.

"What's this?" Shirley said, turning the package over in her hands.

"Nothing much." He played it down; he pretended to be very tired and flopped into the armchair, rubbing his eyes with his knuckles, peeking at her through his fingers.

"What is it, a present or something?"

"Just something to celebrate my bonus."

"Well, gee, T. Thanks."

He watched while she tore off the paper.

"Cartier! Thomas T. Blades! *Cartier!*"

"Open it," he said, as though he were not at all excited; what it was was this football T. had had made of sapphires and diamonds and turquoise; it was just a little football, a brooch. It had cost fifteen hundred dollars.

"Oh, T. It's very cute! I hope you didn't spend a lot."

"Not much. I knew you never had anything from a place like that."

"It's a very cute little pin. Was it expensive?"

"Naw. Read the card."

It said: "Something special for someone special, with all my love. T."

"Hey!" she said. "Say!" And then: "How much was it?"

"I don't like that, telling the price of things."

"Then it was expensive."

"It's a good pin."

"How much, T.?"

"No. Just take it; don't ask that."

"Fifty?"

"No. It's a good pin."

"Is it over fifty?"

"I said it's a good pin. It's a pin that's a lot over fifty and a lot over a hundred."

"T.? How much did this pin cost?"

"Enjoy it, Shirley."

"How—much—did—this—pin—cost?"

"Okay! Okay! It cost fifteen hundred."

She just stared at him; she was not able to talk.

T. grinned. He said, "Well, you're my best girl, aren't you?"

She was putting it back in the box.

T. said, "I want you to have nice things. We don't have kids to worry about. I'm making good money. I want you to have, you know, a fur coat—a mink, you know? That's what I want—to give you things." He went across and knelt by her

143

chair and put his fingers out and chucked her under the chin. "You know? Honey?"

She closed the box over the pin.

He said, "I designed it. I told them what I wanted."

"I'm taking it back, T."

"You're *what?*"

"I couldn't wear it. It's too expensive. I'd always be afraid I'd lose it."

"Shirley, it's got a safety catch on it, and honey, did you know it's insured? It's insured."

"It's not something I'd wear. Sure, T., you're doing all right now. You're making good money. But what happens when you're thirty, thirty-one, thirty-two? How are you going to earn a living, T.?"

"I'll take care of us, don't worry. I'm making good money."

"Look out there at Gib. He made good money, too."

"Not the kind I'm making. He didn't even come close."

"For his day, he did all right; now look at him."

"I felt so good on my way home," said T. "I had that package on the front seat next to me, and I really felt it was going to make me very happy to give this to you, honey, because it would make you happy."

"It's all right to throw your money around if you're Bo Belinski or Joe Namath."

"I said, 'T., it's something you designed yourself, especially for Shirley. You never gave her anything like this before. She's going to flip when she sees it.' I thought you would."

"They're kids. They've got years to go. How many more years do you think you'll be making good money?"

He said, "I'm going out for a drive."

"We're eating at six, T."

"I'm not eating at six."

"I'll keep something hot for you, then."

T. never mentioned it to her again; she didn't either, to him. A week later their joint savings account showed a deposit of fifteen hundred dollars.

Eventually T. told it as a joke to other guys at training camp, traveling, he'd imitate Shirley saying, "It's all right to throw your money around if you're Bo Belinski or Joe Namath, they're *kids!*", and the fellows would howl, cracked up by T.'s limp-wrist gestures and the high, falsetto voice and the whole idea of a guy who couldn't unload a brooch that cost fifteen hundred clams on his own wife.

T. T. Blades had fumbled through some of the words in

144

the second verse, then dropped out, leaving only Josie, Reverend Smoke, and Mrs. Graeff to finish the hymn.

Josie, while she sang, could not fight back the tears any longer. Her face was wet. She was glad of the darkness. When she had come to the line "I need thy presence every passing hour," she choked back a sob, for now she felt entirely alone: the Senator seemed as far away and unreal as China.

The only person who had ever been familiar, dependable, was Irene; all right, she was what she was, but she was real; these people were not, this city wasn't. Josie could order her Tanqueray Tom Collinses and wear her Gucci shoes and her Galanos coat, but she wasn't fooling anyone.

She was a Lahaska Swift. They had known it at St. James's in Doylestown, at the Franchers' in New Hope; Maggie Van Pelten had known it in Washington; in New York Mr. Tyson knew it, and here and now in this elevator, they all knew it.

Never mind that her whole life she had tried not to be like Irene; she wasn't any better; she didn't want to be any better. It was too hard being better; learning good grammar and that artichokes had hearts and perfume was fragrance and Senator Dirksen was some minority something in the Congress was too hard. *Go melt back into the night, babe; everything is made of stone;* say that again; and sitting there in the pitch black on that box singing "Ills have no weight and tears no bitterness," Josie Swift weighed a thouand pounds and didn't care anymore if they did fall the rest of the way, for the shaft was like home to her; all her life she had gotten the shaft.

So when his fingers touched her back, then hesitated, she made no sound of alarm, for she was tired of running from herself, from what she thought she was and what she thought she wasn't: what followed seemed to her as inevitable as her confrontation with Harlan and the truth about Irene. She felt the same numb acquiescence as he very lightly caressed her side, shifted in near her heart, hesitated, and as she sang on, moved and cupped her breast.

He had gotten to her after all.

She was more surprised by the raucous noise of the bullhorn, and his hand withdrawing.

# 32

ATTENTION, EVERYONE IN THE ELEVATOR. THIS IS LIEUTENANT SCHOLZ OF THE POLICE EMERGENCY DIVISION.

WE'VE TURNED OFF THE POWER; THAT'S WHY YOU HAVE NO LIGHTS.

YOU'RE IN A PRECARIOUS SITUATION, BUT WE CAN EVACUATE YOU SAFELY WITH YOUR COOPERATION.

THE ELEVATOR CABLE BROKE IN SUCH A WAY THAT IT HAS HAMPERED THE SAFETY BRAKES. THEY'RE HOLDING, BUT THEY ARE NOT LOCKED SECURELY. THAT'S THE REASON THE CAR SLIPPED DOWN BETWEEN SIXTEEN AND FIFTEEN.

WE HAVE LOCATED LUMBER, AND WE ARE GOING TO MAKE A WEDGE BETWEEN THE BOTTOM OF THE CAR AND THE FIFTEENTH FLOOR. THAT WILL FIX THE CAR IN A STATIONARY POSITION SO WE CAN LOWER A LADDER TO YOU FROM SIXTEEN.

THEN WE'LL BE OUT OF THE WOODS.

STAY STILL, SECURE YOUR CARGO AS BEST YOU CAN. DON'T SMOKE.

WE ARE DOING EVERYTHING IN OUR POWER TO HURRY.

There was a moment's pause.

Senator Robert Anderson said, "EVERYTHING'S GOING TO BE ALL RIGHT, JO. I'M RIGHT HERE. DON'T WORRY."

Then there was another, more arresting noise: that of a man urinating on the floor of the elevator.

# 33

The lobby of the Gart Building was a beehive of activity, hornets predominating.

Head hornet Gil Holland was angrily directing the loading of the lumber into a first-bank elevator. It had been a long time getting there. It had had to be cut to size, ten feet, then carried by six policemen the distance from Second Avenue and 38th to Sixth Avenue and 44th.

Frederick Fitzgerald, the building superintendent, was ensconced in the phone booth in the lobby, spitting out drunken anathemas to whoever would still answer his call at this hour of the night, his wife being the most dependable. Somewhere in Brooklyn, the elevator inspector for the Gart Building, his phone off the hook on the advice of a lawyer, was rapidly polishing off a bottle of Johnny Walker red, given him by Fitzgerald, some thirty like it since he was assigned that West Side tour, all gone; he was beginning now to truly appreciate how costly free things were and what a cheap bastard Fitzgerald was: *this* sort of trouble, he should have seen some money; he should have seen a lot of money for okaying those elevators without inspecting them!

The corporation which owned the building had sent a lawyer there. He was standing with Roger Tyson by the directory. Their conversation was no longer about the matter at hand; they had made prefatory comments concerning the crisis, the rest would come in long briefs, their contents still in the balance. They were now discussing the deterioration of the kitchen of a downtown restaurant both had fancied before a change in ownership. It was hours past Tyson's bedtime; he now felt extremely put upon by Faith Graeff. The Gart corporation lawyer had been awakened from a sound sleep for this assignment; his mouth was dry from Doridens; he was still doped by them. There was nothing, really, he could do but observe, which he did, standing there glumly, yawning, keeping up his half of a conversation about lobster.

147

Perversely, Louis Gillespie's mood was improving as the hour grew later and the situation seemed to be improving for the people in the elevator, while growing steadily worse for all connected with the Gart Building. For six years Gillespie had tried to convince his partners, Goddard and Ross, to move to the East Side of New York. He had always nurtured a special hatred for the Gart Building; it had been designed by a colleague who was marvelously successful, whose work was consistently mediocre.

Then, too, Gillespie's spirits were uplifted by the cheerful, enthusiastic cooperation of Zolto, the sculptor, who even now was remaining there to see if there were any way that he could be of more help. His pleasant, warm countenance was a blessed sight in the midst of scowling eyebrows, turned-down mouths, narrowed eyes, and wrinkled foreheads.

Gillespie said, "I'm going across for something to eat, Zolto. Why don't you join me?"

"I want to call my wife. Then I'll be over."

"You know, you really don't have to stay here. There are enough people to help."

There were more than enough; there were too many. There simply was no weather sufficiently inclement to keep people away. Outside, they were there in force; in the lobby, too, there was a peppering of people who looked suspiciously unconnected with the arrested elevator, or anybody in it.

"I want to stay," said Zolto. "You never know. We may still need more wood. It may not be the proper size. I'll stay."

"I'll see you across the street. And Zolto? Tell your wife thanks for the coffee."

But Zolto was not telephoning his wife. He was telephoning a man named Ernest Townsende.

"Townie?"

"Hi. Zolt?"

"Yes. Did I wake you up?"

"Are you kidding? Listen. Here's what I'm doing, believe it or not." There was a rattle of paper, then Townsende read: "Zolto's sculptured figures, ranging up to eighteen feet, carry out the exhibition theme, 'Man and His World,' and the idea is to depict both the——"

"Cut it, Townie. I'm in a phone booth."

"Where the hell are you?"

"Write this down. It's important. I'm in the Gart Building, at Forty-fourth and Sixth."

"At this hour? Are you drunk? It's after midnight, Zolt."

"There's an elevator stuck here. It's been stuck since six o'clock."

"So?"

"There are five people on it, including T. T. Blades."

"The football hero?"

"Yeah. But listen. There's someone else on it who's got to be important, because Senator Robert Anderson is here throwing *his* weight around. He got Hillman Skidmore to drive in from Bronxville; Skidmore's head of the whole elevator shebang!"

"What's it got to do with you?"

"Listen carefully, Townie! It's beautiful! They're using some of my lumber as a wedge to hold the car secure while they carry out the rescue!"

"*Huh?*"

"They came to my studio. The police and the architect who did my place, remember Louis Gillespie? The neighbors were all peeking through their shutters, wondering what Margie and I'd done this time, if we were taking LSD over in our pad or what, police pouring out of my studio—you should have seen it!"

"Sounds exciting."

"It's a lot more exciting than any crap you can hack out about the Ruters Exhibition, Townie."

"You want me to wrte it up? Want me to come over?"

"Townie, sometimes as a press agent you're a good shoe salesman. Sure, I want you to come over. I want you to bring a few people with you, too."

"Like who?"

"Like Gabe Pressman, like Bob Teague, like Jim Hartz, like Jim Jensen. Anyone you can scare up at CBS-TV, or NBC-TV, or ABC-TV. Townie, this is a hell of a good story, and they're not far away; they can come here on foot with their cameras."

"Zolt, you're good, but good enough to get guys like that out of bed?"

"Senator Anderson's that good; so's T. T. Blades. I don't know what I'm paying you for, Townie."

"Okay. I'll try it. I'll try anything, I guess."

"It's not just anything. We've got a couple of celebrities, and we've got Zolto to the rescue. This could be a big break for me, Townie. You *work on it*, hear me?"

"How much longer will it last, though?"

"We'll be here at least two more hours, maybe more. But hurry! Get the networks alerted as soon as you hang up."

"All right, Zolt."

"Townie? Don't tell anyone I told you about it. They're doing everything possible to play this down to the press; they're pretending it's a very insignificant incident."

"Your timber helps the rescue; your hunger for publicity hinders it."

"And keeps *you* eating. No, it won't hinder anything, Townie. They just don't want publicity because they're going to be slapped with a lawsuit before they can say tomorrow morning. It's a hell of a treacherous situation, by the by, Townie; I sound flip about it, I know, but it's a hairy thing."

"Let me hang up and start things generating."

"Townie?"

"What?"

"On your way, pick up some Number-two Max Factor Foundation, hmmm? I'm awfully pale to be on telly."

"Yeah, I'll be sure to do that."

"Beautiful, isn't it?" Zolto Calas laughed. "It's a Happening, man."

# 34

At first the sound of a man weeping sometimes begins like laughter, so Mrs. Graeff said, "I, for one, find *nothing* amusing about it."

"No one does, Mrs. Graeff," T. T. Blades answered.

"Obviously someone does."

"No. No one does."

Then she heard the sniffling, choking noise, heard him let his breath out in a muffled wail.

Blades said, "It's all right, Reverend."

"Oh, no! It wasn't—" Mrs. Graeff left her question unfinished; no one answered it for her.

She could not believe it: that the Reverend would do such a thing, would do it without saying something, *something*; pardon me, I have an emergency; I'm terribly sorry but I can no longer control myself; that the Reverend would simply relieve himself without a *prenez garde*.

Blades said, "Sit down."

"No," whispered.

"Are you all right?"

"Yes." It was another stifled outcry.

Mrs. Graeff exclaimed, "Tch!"

Josie Swift stood up. She found her way back to him through the darkness. She put her hand on his arm. "Come on. Sit on this box where I was."

She was not afraid of him anymore.

What had taken place between them in the darkness was as sordid and as sad as what had followed.

He had surrendered to losing, whatever it was he had to lose and whoever he was. Before she had heard Bob's voice, she had almost given up herself; she had taken that first minute step by feeling no reaction to his fingers but dumb, impassioned submission—something Irene must once have felt a long time ago.

She did not feel pity for him, either; it was something more—the protective concern a near victim feels for the victimized, or the recovered for the sick.

He sat down.

Mr. Whistler pushed a box across to her. "Here's one for you."

"Thanks." But she stood beside him, watching over him. She said, "Mr. Whistler? I guess you're not such a hotshot after all; *you* didn't make the lights go out."

"I guess not," he answered.

Then she said, "I just put myself into the game; here goes my worst mistake. I wish I could say here goes nothing."

# 35

November 19, 1965, early in the morning, still in her pajamas, Josie Swift went into the living room, shut the door behind her, and dialed a number on the phone.

"This is Josie, Mrs. Larsen."

"*Josie?* I don't even think the chickens are up yet, are they?"

"This one is."

"What are you calling about, dear?"

"I'm not sitting with Lizzie anymore, Mrs. Larsen."

"Do you have a Tuesday job, dear? Because we can change the day."

"Nope. I don't have no Tuesday job, Mrs. Larsen. I just don't feel obligated no more to sit for a parrot."

"Aren't I paying you enough, Josie?"

"Mrs. Larsen, I *said* that I just don't feel obligated no more."

"All right, then, Josie. I hope you change your mind, though."

Then she sat there smoking cigarettes and having coffee, so when Irene got up and came in from the bedroom, Irene said, "What's with you? You got this place smoky as a barroom."

"I'm going to get me a job, Irene."

"Huh?"

"I'm quitting High and getting me a job."

"Honey, I always wished *I* had a high-school diploma."

"What for, Irene?"

"Well, they're nice to have. You hang them up and they look very chick."

"I don't care to look chick or put airs on or this, that, and the other thing!"

"You get a better job with an H.S. diploma," said Irene.

"I don't want to be no big-deal anything, Irene. I just want to be me myself and I. Period."

But she was not herself all that winter, far from it.

She would see Harlan Francher zip by in his Sting Ray, and there'd be some of that New Hope clique with him, Fred Wolfe and Billy Inman and Ted Plant and the fancy numbers they took out, and it would be a big production, top-down-in-January sort of thing, somebody half hanging out of the back and the radio turned up real loud, the girls' hair flying in the wind, and just everybody on the street watching, and Harlan sometimes would and sometimes wouldn't call out: "Hey, Josie!"

She would be walking with Howie Waterhouse or something tacky like that, carrying shoes over to Lambertville to be repaired, or getting into Irene's crummy old Buick, and that whole load of them would whip by and look at her, and you could tell how burshwa they thought she was.

152

Couple of times Harlan tried striking up a conversation when they ran into one another downtown in New Hope.

It would go like this.

"Hi, Josie!"

"Oh. Hello, Harlan."

"Well, that's not much of a hello."

"I'm in a hurry."

"Don't you have time to twitter?"

Walk right around the next corner, don't even answer him.

Regretted the only time she ever had.

"Hi, Josie!"

" 'Lo."

"Don't you have a smile for old Uncle Harlan?"

" 'Fraid not, thank you."

"Hey, Jo? How come you quit school?"

"None of your business, Harlan Francher. I don't sit for Lizzie no more, either."

"Who's Lizzie?"

"Lizzie Larsen. The parrot. I don't sit for her no more."

That reached him, all right, because he bent double laughing at that one; he hadn't even been able to straighten himself up and stop by the time Josie got to the corner and away from him. She looked back and saw him there convulsed.

Began to really grate on her nerves; she'd get to thinking about it a lot, what he had said to her that night and all, and then him streaking by in that red job, King of the Road or something.

So what she used to think, boy, would he be sorry if she ever did, she finally did.

She spread it all over town, by writing it in only four places.

She wrote it on the large sign outside the Bucks County Playhouse, in lipstick.

She wrote it with a ball-point pen on the front of the white cover on the new Random House dictionary in the New Hope Library.

She wrote it in the rest room at the Delaware, in pencil, near the mirror.

She wrote it in white chalk on the sidewalk in front of the high school.

She got Howie Waterhouse to help her.

She wrote: HARLAN FRANCHER IS A FAIRY.

It caught on.

It wasn't a week before there were similar epigrams all over town.

There was a war memorial on the main street—a large

153

black cannon with cannonballs beside it; someone, in white paint, wrote across the cannonballs: "These are the balls Harlan Francher used to have."

A gang of boys put up a large sign late one night on the Francher lawn: FRANCHER AIRPORT. *Fly with Harlan!*

Never mind all the filthy, dirty, predictable ones; it wasn't a week before they were everywhere.

It was ten days to the day that Josie took her little walk through the city with Howie, that some other boys took Harlan for a walk. They took him down the river road, in the direction of Point Pleasant, late one night, at a time when it is usually foggy and trafficless and dark. They stopped near the canal. He was found on the bank in the mud, next day, beaten to a pulp, but still alive, his clothes ripped off him, women's underwear in their place.

There was an article in the New Hope weekly about how the incident would always leave a mark on Harlan Francher, but how it would always leave a mark on the city, too.

A much worse mark.

Wanna bet?

# 36

Charlie Latham, a memorizer of everything from hymnic responses to the state papers of Theodore Roosevelt, to Milton, Stalin, Huxley, and Caedmon, remembered, while she spoke of Harlan Francher, some lines from Francis Thompson: *"My mangled youth lies dead beneath the heap/My days have crackled and gone up in smoke."*

He was the only kid in Luda Grove, Iowa, who wore a Prince Charlie haircut when he was two, three, four, and those little extra-short shorts with the high knee socks, and the navy cap and short navy coat with the gold buttons.

In kindergarten he already had that confident tone, flawed slightly by the tiniest baby's lisp; he made sure, "Spell my name Charlie. Not Charles."

There were plenty of Luda Grovers to say, "If they're

154

going to strut Miss Fancy over there to the Latham farm, why do they call their only son Charlie? No middle name, either, I hear."

"Poor does what rich pleases. Rich does what it pleases."

"All three speak French at supper, I hear."

"Heard he's got a key, a vest key, kind they give for having more brains than the rest of us."

"He couldn't have had so many more than us; he'd of never come to Luda Grove to live."

The Lathams were not rich, except in knowing ways of enjoying life without much money. Charlie's clothes were made for him by his mother; his parents had always spoken French to him; the three could also converse in German and in Latin.

The property in Luda Grove was inherited from Charlie's uncle; Charlie's father, a scholar who specialized in dead languages, had taught college for fifteen years before moving to Iowa; it was time to write a book. The idea of his son growing up on a farm intrigued the father, too. Charlie's mother was the old-fashioned, well-bred sort who did what her husband wanted and went him one better doing it. A city girl, she took to the country with amused enthusiasm, finding time to do the usual housework, then bake bread, feed the chickens and cats, sew, put up preserves or perform whatever seasonal task was fitting, and cook the kind of meal each evening you could not buy within a hundred-mile radius of Luda Grove, if then.

They had élan, and if Luda Grovers did not know what élan was, they did know that the Lathams had something which made it possible for them to do what everybody else did, plus a dozen things nobody else did, with a certain grace and style never before managed in that county.

Then, of course, when the airplane from Des Moines to Chicago crashed, killing all eight passengers, pilot, and crew, all aboard but little Charlie, people said, "It just goes to show you; you can have everything one day, be the biggest things around, the next day somebody's giving your name to a funeral director."

People said, "Well, the poor little tyke. Who'll raise him?"

"Heard an aunt was coming to raise him."

"You think a little kid like that knows?"

"He knows; he's six."

"They been here eight years? Seem strangers still."

He knew.

His Aunt Kate said, "You better be awful good from now on in your life, Charlie, because God spared you."

"Yes, ma'm."

"He must have had a reason for sparing you, son."

"Yes, ma'm."

"So you be good for Him, and never forget you were spared out of all the rest."

He was good. Luda Grovers, far from feeling the name Latham was a stranger's anymore, claimed Charlie as their own, proudly, everyone of them with maternal and paternal feelings for the boy, who seemed incapable of doing anything without skill. Superior, excellent, cum laude—these became familiar words in any sentence containing Charlie Latham's name, in any reference to the boy who grew up stunning, amusing, brilliant, popular, and dashing.

Very dashing; some said all too dashing, as though the crash had made him feel that Fate could not fell him; he took chances. It was the worst anyone in Luda Grove could say about him, but it was a fact, it was his only flaw. He was a daredevil, whether he was going down Fine Daughter Hill on a sled, heading into traffic, or swimming summers out beyond a point he could be seen on Swan Rest Lake. He liked to gamble, too; he followed after fairs and carnivals to do it, Aunt Kate a step behind him, after him to stop. But Charlie could charm the birds out of the trees, and Aunt Kate, after a heated confrontation with him over the gambling, or going without his coat in freezing weather, one or another fool thing old maids worry about, always had to turn her back on Charlie, so he would never see he'd broken her resistance, she was smiling. *Darn fool!* Always got her to smiling that way, right when she least wanted to.

He was valedictorian hands down; Luda Grove High would never see the likes of him again. He won a scholarship to Princeton. Nearly every pretty girl in the county, at one time or another, had had Charlie Latham's attention, but that summer before he went east, he spent an idyllic three months, lolly-gagging around the Armstrong place, courting Gloria Armstrong, who was going east herself in the fall, to Smith.

Mr. Armstrong, a banker, a cattleman, everybody said one of the wealthiest men there was in Iowa, thought so highly of Charlie that he invited him along for a huge family reunion in St. Louis. There they all were, all the Armstrongs and all the Kieselhorsts (Mrs. Armstrong's branch of the family), a few Paddlefords, and a Benoist, all gathered grandly at 31 Pershing Avenue.

Nobody back in Luda Grove believed Ida Kieselhorst Armstrong; everybody said Charlie was probably doing no more than going to the bathroom in the bushes. Charlie wasn't *crazy*, after all; then why would Charlie do a crazy thing like expose himself to the little Kieselhorst girls, whose parents were twelve feet away on the veranda?

Nobody liked Ida Kieselhorst any the better for passing on the story; everybody put it from their minds, until a Luda Grover since moved east sent back a clipping about Charlie, years later. He had been picked up on a charge of indecent exposure. He was a professor at a college, married, and he had a son named Frank.

What did it all mean, a man who had everything, and with one sudden foolish impulse, cast a shadow on his own good name, irrevocable as a brand across his flesh to mark him from the rest?

Why did he make it seem he should have died in that bad crash with all the rest, and not been privileged to survive?

There are always people who will not wait for, aren't concerned with, answers, who set out, be it in New Hope, Pennsylvania, or Yansetti, Virginia, to make things right; that time in Yansetti so badly Charlie could not open his mouth to talk; his jaw was broken. But he did not have to open his mouth for much; his classes were abruptly canceled, his career at yet another place of learning terminated.

Charlie Latham, while he listened to Josie Swift tell her worst mistake, thought of the irony of his being too embarrassed to say what it was he had to do; for no one but Charlie Latham would have felt the intense shame of that emergency and be just as unable to apologize as he had been to excuse himself beforehand.

He had thought that it was laughter which would emerge from deep inside him, but he knew nothing about himself; he understood nothing about others, either, for why was the redhead suddenly so solicitous, when he had entirely forgotten her?

# 37

The summer of 1951, Whistle Foods' executive office was a trailer on a lot in northern New Jersey. The lot had been a dump before Will and Ben had put down five hundred dollars apiece, against five thousand dollars for its purchase.

Ben and Will were living in the trailer, too. Mariam, in the last month of her pregnancy, was in Florida, at her parents'; Fran Hyde was staying with her mother until Ben could afford a place for them.

On the lot there were singed tin cans; rats hiding in the decaying skeletons of discarded automobiles; wanderers living on its fringes, cooking meals nightly over tiny bonfires; and the noise from roadhouses nearby, coupled with the stench indigenous to that part of the state.

"What you do nights is your own business," Will told Ben after a month of living there. "But I don't like having her in the trailer."

At first he did not mind coming home to find her there. He would have been out since early morning, as Ben would be, calling on everyone from small grocers to major distributors, from restaurant chefs to buyers, and checking operations at the plant Whistler leased outside Newark. He would be later than Ben getting back to the trailer, for Will was also involved in efforts to finance a small building for the lot, a new plant site which Whistle Foods would own. The builder wanted five thousand dollars down on twenty-five thousand or clear title to the land. No bank would lend Will the money, so he would have to squeeze into his schedule appointments with prospective moneylenders, none of whom were enthusiastic about the future of frozen foods, much less Whistler's puny force.

She was a short, thin girl with a tiny waist and long, slender legs. She had very large breasts for such a short individual; they pressed themselves forward from her supple body like an insult or a demand. Her yellow hair was pale and soft,

158

spilling past her shoulders, and she favored the color blue, sky-shaded. To Will's horror, she wore around her neck on a gold chain a rabbit's foot which had been dyed that shade.

She was an eight-to-four waitress in the Dutch Shoe, half a mile down the road. She was a strange, quiet girl, undemanding but not servile, polite with Will but not beholden. Tired from a hard, long day, Will would like it that she offered to heat up some dinner for him when he arrived; she would serve it to him, smiling with her dark, bright eyes; she was solicitous: "Did you have any luck? . . . You will, though. . . . Is the coffee hot enough; here, let me heat it up. . . . You're awfully tired, aren't you?" Pittances. But Will would receive them, glad for someone feminine to be concerned and there to do things men were clumsy doing.

"Why the change of heart?" Ben wanted to know when Will asked him to have her stay away. "I thought you liked Nadine."

"I do. But she's been around here too much, Ben."

"What does she do that's wrong?"

"It's wrong for her to be around. You're married. I'm married. What does she want here?"

"Nadine is just Nadine. She doesn't *want* anything." He laughed in his cocky way. "Just to watch me." Then, petulant, "My God, we don't bother *you*."

Will usually went into the bedroom of the trailer before she left. There he would write his nightly letter to Mariam, missing her at that time of day with the particular urgency of a man who had come home to the same woman for eight years straight, with all the excitement in him that had been there when he had first set eyes on her and felt stabs of wonder and desire leap up through his throat.

If anything went on there in the trailer, Will didn't know about it. He doubted it. After writing his letter to Mariam he would strip to his undershorts, fall on the bed, and pass into a deep sleep which lasted until the sun sifted through the slats in the Venetian blind. Nadine lived a mile away in some boardinghouse. Ben would drive her there at the end of the evening. He supposed a lot went on inside Ben's car; he often felt a streak of pity for that kind of girl. If Fate had moved a little this way, and a little that way, she could very easily be the pretty, poised, intelligent co-ed of some bright green campus with its sturdy and ancient shade trees, strolling with the would-be lawyer or the med student, some winning potential breadwinner who would bed her down eventually in some suburban town, where she would give him kids and do good works at local hospitals and hostess all his important dinner parties.

As it was, the Bens of this world would have their way with her, and leave her to be years hence one of those aging, swell-guy waitresses with faded traces of former beauty and that kind of undaunted good-nature one always came across among their kind in diners by the roadside. Ben said she waited tables down in Florida winters; he said, "She's got it soft; she simply follows the sun!" For Ben, there was no more to it than that.

"I wish you'd keep her out of here," Will insisted as they discussed it that night.

"My money's in here, too, Will."

"Yes, it is." Will refrained from reminding him it was the only money he had ever invested in Whistle Foods.

Ben said, "I won't have her here as often. Okay?"

"Okay."

He didn't, and Will didn't make an issue of it those nights he came home and found her there. But Will could sense that Ben had told her of the conversation. She no longer offered to do anything for him; her attitude was cool but pleasant; she refrained from asking him about his day, and Will would set about fixing himself a sandwich or a bowl of soup in the tiny trailer kitchen. Soon after Will would come in the door, she would mention getting home early, make motions to go. Another thing, her eyes would never meet his now. She seemed newly timid or ashamed or hurt, and Will supposed that he was responsible, that Ben had put it in some thoughtless Ben Hyde way which made her feel common and inferior.

Will said to her one night, "I guess I talked myself out of a home-cooked meal for good," hoping to lift the cloud of unhappiness that had seemed to settle over her.

Ben laughed and slapped his knee, but Nadine just shrugged and answered, "Anytime. Just say so," looking down the way she did, as though she had done something, was something, wrong.

Will never got around to pursuing it beyond that point.

The same day that Will finally swung the deal, Ben went to personally answer a New England wholesaler's complaint about a damaged Whistle shipment. There were better deals than the one Will had made. He had signed a five-thousand-dollar note to get four thousand cash; he would pay six-percent interest on the five thousand for twelve months. It figured out to be an interest rate of thirty-two percent. Without it, though, Whistle would have gone down the drain;

if it wasn't much, it was all there was, and at last there *was* a beginning. It took Will from four that afternoon until eight-thirty that evening to work out the arrangements, with intervals in between when it would look as though even *that* would fall through.

When he was finished, everything signed, it sank in that he now had his start, and an elation far out of proportion to the facts spread through him, so that on his way back to the trailer he was actually singing aloud along with the radio. He sprang out when he arrived and ran in, realizing only then that Ben was away; the trailer was empty. He leaped to the phone and placed a call to Mariam in Florida. There was no answer, and he felt a disappointment almost as sharp as the one he had experienced after the click of her suitcase closing, during their last embrace.

He was in the kitchen opening up a can of Campbell's chicken noodle when Nadine appeared.

Her yellow hair was piled on top of her head, held by a light-blue velvet ribbon which matched the sleeveless, full-skirted silken dress that clung to her. She wore white shoes with spike heels, and under her arm was a white beaded bag. For the first time he saw that her eyes were that color blue, their lashes long and dark. She was very tan, her face and arms, her slender legs, bare, with thin, delicate ankles. Nervously she fingered the blue rabbit's foot around her neck which so repelled Whistler.

"Ben's gone away," he said, realizing how gruff his tone sounded; he attempted to soften it as he added, "He went on a business trip. He'll be back in five days."

"I didn't see his car. I wondered."

"Well, he's gone."

"I won't see him," she said rapidly, sensing his discomfort; "I'm going to Florida."

"Do you want to leave an address?"

Beyond her in the doorway, far out across the dump, Whistler could see a tiny bonfire burning in the night, and fireflies. It was a lonely place. He felt a surge of pity for the girl, increased by her answer to his question. "It doesn't matter," she said.

The screen door banged shut.

Whistler had no appetite then for the soup. He reached for his pack of Camels, lighted one, and walked across to the door. He could see her making her way cautiously through the strewn lot down to the bus sign by the highway.

He searched around the trailer to see if Ben had left a

161

bottle there, but there was not even the usual cold beer in the refrigerator.

Stripping to his shorts, he stretched out on the bed, put out the light, and closed his eyes. He was asleep in seconds.

No dart of morning sunlight awakened him. What did was an immense hunger. He remembered that he had not eaten since eleven-thirty that morning. He sat up and put on the light and saw that it was only eleven o'clock. Again he lunged for the phone; he put the phone's arm back in its cradle, afterward feeling a thick depression surrounding him like some sudden, evening, oceanside fog.

Then he shook his head in amazement at himself for giving in to self-pity. He stood up and went across to the sink and doused his head under the faucet, dressed, and dreamed of a huge plate of steak and mashed which he would order for himself in the first place on the road he came to.

"Rare. Blood rare," he told the waitress, and while he waited he downed two double bourbons.

He watched some couples dancing to the jukebox on the small floor in front of the bar; the whiskey tasted good, and for a change the music did not sound like just so much noise. He enjoyed a very healthy, optimistic frame of mind while he ate his dinner, and the dinner, he enjoyed, and even when he looked across at the bar and saw her sitting there talking with some fellow, he enjoyed seeing her. He also felt badly about his treatment of her, and about Ben's treatment of her, too.

"Hello, Nadine."

"Enjoy your dinner? I thought you were having noodle soup." Her lips slid into a playful smile, and she looked him in the eye now, as though she were telling him bygones were by-gones.

He laughed. "Would you like a drink?"

"I have one nearly full."

She excused herself then and danced with the thin, tieless fellow she had been talking with.

Whistler ordered a bourbon and stood with his back to the bar watching her. He supposed that in between the Bens she hung around with the sort she was with now. He was clearly ineffectual, unambitious, uninteresting. Nadine followed him mechanically, performing all the elaborate twists and turns and dips with an expressionless face, and he was chewing gum, not watching her either. About to be a father, Whistler felt a fatherly concern for her; when she returned to the bar, as her dancing partner wandered over to the jukebox to feed it money, Will said, "What kind of a life is this for you?"

"Nothing to talk about," she said, "so let's don't."

She sucked at her drink for a few seconds and then she said, "I'll sure miss Ben."

"Why?"

*"Why?* I liked him. We had a lot of laughs."

"Is that what it's all about, Nadine?"

She sailed off for another dance with another fellow, this one also tieless, wearing a short-sleeved sports shirt outside his pants. She did not watch this fellow's face any more than she had the other one's, but she did watch Whistler watching her, and in those moments, moving with the music, eyes meeting his, she seemed so knowing, and so caring, too, as she had sometimes seemed when she was setting Whistler's dinner down in front of him and saying, "You're awfully tired, aren't you? . . . Did you have any luck? . . . You will, though."

Whistler had another double bourbon, but although she watched him right through every dance, watched him and only him, she did not come back to him there at the bar. At one point when there was a lull in the music, she joined a booth filled with a motley bunch, and sat so she could look at Whistler, and once she tipped her glass to him in a sort of salute. Whistler beckoned to her with his finger; his lips formed the words: "Come here."

She didn't.

When the music played again, she was back on the floor again with the first thin, tieless fellow.

After that, she didn't look his way at all; she ignored him.

Whistler polished off his bourbon, swung down off the bar stool, went out to the parking lot, and got into his car. Silly nonsense, he said aloud, and he laughed at himself while he whipped the shift in gear and took off with his wheels squealing.

Halfway to the trailer, he turned the car around.

The fellow she was dancing with looked surprised, but Nadine didn't. The fellow seemed on the verge of protesting, but Nadine shushed him with a silent gesture, a finger to her lips. She followed Whistler, stopping by the bar stool to pick up her white beaded purse.

"What do you want to talk about?" she said when they got in the car.

Whistler did not answer her. He kept driving.

She pushed in the cigarette lighter, waited for it to be hot, then lighted a cigarette, blowing out a cloud of smoke. She puffed at it all the way to the trailer, in silence.

Inside, he wanted to take her quickly, in a sudden rush of

163

violent feeling, but as he grabbed her, she said softly, "Careful of my dress. It's new."

She laid her beaded purse on the table by the bed; then she sat down on the bed and leaned back so that her whole body gave an impression of slight mockery as she patted the wrinkled sheet where Whistler had lain earlier that evening.

He heard a groan escape from deep inside himself as he pushed her back and put himself on top of her. "My dress——" he drowned out with his mouth pressed hard on hers; he felt the shape of her body outlined against his chest; his hands moved to her breasts, and with a twist of her body she took her face from his. "I want to take off my dress."

His hands were clumsy with the buttons. "I will." And he tore one, heard it roll along the floor under the bed.

"I knew," she said.

"What did you know?"

"I knew all along you'd be this way."

"You like it, don't you?" and she did not answer as he forced her breasts up from her bra and bent his head down in their round softness.

She said, "You didn't want me around. I wasn't good enough." She gave a cynical laugh.

She was not wearing panties.

When he woke up there was no sun, and he could hear the rain beating down hard on the roof of the trailer. He could hear the telephone ringing, too. He answered it, not even remembering about Nadine until he was midway in the conversation with his father-in-law.

". . . in labor for ten hours, but it's a healthy little seven-pound girl. And Mariam is fine, just fine."

"I tried to call last night."

"We were at the hospital."

"Well, that's just wonderful news!" he said, wondering if Nadine was in the other room, in the bathroom, where she was.

But Nadine, he discovered, had gone, and he was very glad of that.

For about fifteen minutes.

It took him that long to think to look in the book in his desk, for the envelope containing the four thousand dollars.

That was gone too.

The New Jersey police had Nadine traced while she was en route to Florida. She had twenty-two dollars with her; there simply was not any way that they could pin it on the girl;

there were, after all, tramps who camped near the dump; any one of them could have entered the trailer while Will was sleeping.

But Ben Hyde knew as well as Will that only Nadine would have thought to look for the money in *The Eastern Retail Grocers Directory;* they had kept money there before; it was no secret to her. And Will had had to admit to the police that she was in the trailer that evening; he had described how she had come there looking for Ben.

"I don't blame you if you fire me, Will; you warned me about having her around."

"Forget it! Just forget it!"

Whistler paid off his loan and built his plant with money borrowed from Mariam's father.

As Josie Swift described *her* way of making someone pay for looking down on her, Whistler was not surprised when she said, "I wasn't good enough," in the same tone as Nadine. Different as they were, their similarity had compelled him to reach out for her, but not in the rough way that he had for Nadine. For as they were all singing hymns which were unfamiliar to him, there in the darkness, with unreceptive strangers, he had thought only of pressing her hand, a gesture of thanks for her defense of him. But when he touched her, it seemed suddenly as though she were waiting for him to do it; she stayed so very still, though he could feel her heart beat wildly.

After the bullhorn forced him to stop, he was amazed at the lingering excitement.

# 38

In six-nineteen the Senator was munching a hamburger; his tie, coat, and shoes were off; he was stretched out on the couch.

"How's it going out there, Roger? I've been confined to quarters again."

Roger Tyson's bald head was wet from the snow; he was out of breath, having raced up the six flights.

"It's going all right. I've come to get you out of here, Bob."

"Why?"

"I was across the street at Quinn's just now. I looked across and saw them marching toward here with television cameras. Bob, all three networks are outside setting up."

"It'll be a live and very wet show, won't it? Is the wedge in place yet?"

"They're working at it. . . . Bob, across the street all the reporters are trying to figure out who it is in the elevator you're so concerned about."

"Do you think I care about the reporters? If you're so privileged with access to these surroundings, go find out what's taking them so long to put that lumber in."

"Bob, I wish you'd think for a moment. I wish you would. Phyllis is right, you know, you're an old fool."

"She's had a lot of practice in spotting one."

"If you were some decrepit duck in his seventies, I'd say go ahead, and more power to you, but you have years of useful life left, Bob. You have a lot more to contribute."

"What's the matter; do you think she's going to wear me out?"

"Oh, Bob. We're never so unsure as when we can't do anything but joke about it."

"You're right, Roger."

"Am I finally getting through?"

"You are."

"What are you going to do about it?"

"What do you suggest, Roger?"

"Do you mean it?"

"Yes."

"I suggest you get out of here as fast as you can, right now. Then, when this is over, I suggest you give the girl a thousand dollars. Tell her you have every confidence she'll find someone more suitable to marry."

The Senator finished his hamburger, wiped his mouth with a paper napkin. "Yes, all I can do is make jokes right now. I am unsure. About getting her down safely, so I can marry her this August. Roger, you tell Phyllis that it's going to be the social event of the season, and if she doesn't stop calling me an old fool, I'll put her way back in the church behind a pole with her sister. . . . What I hate most about the waiting is not being able to see what's going on; how the hell is it *you're* free to come and go?"

166

"I'm not. I got permission to speak to you, that's all."

"Well, you've said your piece."

"Robert?"

"I haven't heard you call me that since we roomed together, Roger."

"I haven't felt you were as immature as when I called you that, until this evening."

"Roger, men of our age can't be called immature anymore. Senile is the appellation, I believe."

"My God, I'd any day of the week rather see you marry Maggie. I'd see that any day of the week before I'd see this."

Anderson laughed and tossed the hamburger wrappings into the wastebasket. He said, "You wouldn't if you were the groom."

"May I ask you one question, Bob? Seriously?"

"Fire away."

"This girl's occasionally taken dictation from me. I've heard the way she speaks. 'No more' for 'anymore.' I don't have to tell you, I suppose."

"She's gotten a lot better about 'no more.' I hardly ever hear her say it no more."

"What will you talk about with this girl, Bob, night after night?"

"Well, maybe you and Phyl will send us over one of your games for a wedding gift—Monopoly, Scrabble, Chinese Checkers, Careers—whatever it is you two are playing evenings nowadays. We'd be most grateful, Roger."

But after Roger Tyson finally gave up and left six-nineteen, the Senator regretted the remark; it was unnecessary, petty. He should not expect Roger to react any other way. Few people would accept it without ridiculing it or attempting to dissuade him, some such thing.

He had had his first taste of it at Maggie Van Pelten's.

He had gone there to inform Maggie of his marriage plans. It had been a long time since he had owed her any explanation, if he ever did, but there he was late one Friday afternoon, standing on her doorstep, hat in hand. She had just come from a reception at Dumbarton Oaks, which was practically across the street. She was feeling no pain, admitted it as she opened the door and saw him, then proved it by bumping into her Tambour desk as she hurried to the buffet to fix him an old-fashioned.

"I wouldn't mind taking these right into the bedroom," she said. "Do you have a dinner date?"

"Yes."

"You want to cancel?"

"I can't. . . . And no, I don't."

"Oh, my, my, my, my, my—sounds serious."

"That's why I came by, Maggie."

"Cut it *out!* You're not here to announce something?"

"My marriage. Forthcoming. August."

"Not to that little——"

"Easy, Maggie. Yes. To that little. Her name is Josie Swift."

"Anything to wake up Peter, hmm?"

"Did he ever fall asleep on you?"

"*I* wouldn't let him. . . . Cut it *out*, Bob! You're actually going to marry that little tramp?"

"You don't even know her."

"I've heard pull-lenty, dear heart! I've heard she's a moronic little markdown, for openers."

"Thanks for your blessings, Maggie." He stood up.

"You don't even want the drink?"

"Let's have one another time."

"The bar will be closed to you, lech!"

"As I said, thanks for the blessings. I'll find my way out."

"Thanks for dropping by with the news you're marrying a little markdown who has your dick throbbing away in your long underwear! Oh, you old goats make me laugh! You really do! You'll go to any lengths for a lay! I heard she can't even speak the English language!"

He left her fuming there in her living room, under her crystal chandelier, looking every single one of her fifty-five years. Walking down R Street he thought: at any rate the worst is over, where Maggie's concerned, never knowing he was a mere twenty-four hours away from the now famous artichoke incident.

It *was* an interesting question, the one Roger had just posed: what would he and Jo talk about night after night? What was interesting about it was what had he talked about night after night with people before he met Jo?

It was typical, wasn't it, that the person who made such a remark was so often someone with whom one had never had a memorable conversation, much less a conversation that could even be remembered.

# 39

The movement of the elevator was almost imperceptible. It began just as Josie Swift had finished what she was saying; it was confused with the tunneled shouts of men somewhere beneath them and the hammering of their tools.

But Mrs. Graeff acknowledged it by sucking in her breath, saying, "There. Did you feel it?"

Josie Swift was determined to persevere. "We have to expect it. They're working in the shaft."

T. T. Blades asked, "Was it one of the workmen who spoke to you?"

"Someone I know; yes."

"I hope he's good at what he does."

"He is."

Blades was aware now of a sharp pain near his old shoulder injury. It had begun as a small, nagging ache a while after the boxes fell against him and knocked him over; it was growing more severe, thrusting down near his ribs.

He said, "Mrs. Graeff, how's the ankle?"

"I'm bearing up."

"We all are," he said, hoping it was true and that he could, and he included the Reverend, who had made his way back to stand against the boxes with Whistler and him. He took it as a sign that Smoke had pulled himself together, was functioning again. "Okay now, Reverend?"

"Uh-huh." But Charlie Latham had seized this opportunity to get away from Josie Swift. She had persisted in standing very close to him while he was sitting down. He would move his shoulder and feel her blouse at the back of his head; if he had leaned back, his head would have been cushioned in the smothering softness of her large breasts.

He did not understand why she had stayed so near him. It was the last thing he had wanted. Her proximity gave him an acute sense of suffocation, and then the intense feeling of nausea, which he was trying to contain, standing there be-

169

tween Whistler and Blades, with his back turned on her, facing in while they faced out.

It was as difficult for Faith Graeff to forgive things she did not understand as it was for her to feign a tone of forgiveness, but she managed to sound somewhat like her old self as she said to Reverend Smoke, "I think we might pause here for another hymn. Reverend?"

She was not angry with him; but what he had done had hurt her, for it had been so very rude.

When there was no answer from him, she was more hurt; it was not only her relationship with him which she was thinking about; she wanted the familiar comfort of a devotion. After Douglas's accident, she would often stop in at church on an ordinary afternoon and simply sit there until she felt her spirits restored by the idea of a God whose wisdom showed itself in mysterious ways.

"What do you say, Reverend?" said T. T. Blades.

Charlie could not answer him.

Whistler felt two things—sorry for the poor bastard and pulled by the girl's nearness.

For Smoke to pee on the floor so soon after Whistler had sneaked his fingers along the girl's body in the darkness was lowering to Whistler; he felt allied with him. He sensed Smoke's shame, but Whistler's own shame was diminished by the knowledge that the girl had not even slightly drawn back at his touch. Diminished, too, by his body's refusal to register anything but desire.

It displaced fear and hunger. Incredulous at himself, he ran through practical considerations like his will, insurance policies, his capital, all of that again, as he had been doing from the beginning, but now he felt something the Germans describe as *Fingerspitzengefuhl*: the feeling of excitement at the fingertips.

Beside him, Smoke seemed to be choking back something: rage? sobs? He was coughing softly, clearing his throat, again coughing.

Whistler said, "Why don't we forget the hymn-singing for a while? I'd like to say something, unless anyone wants to comment on what Miss Swift told us."

He was not sure what it was he was going to say, but he felt like getting it across to all of them that he was a man of good intentions; perhaps he wanted nothing more than to tell her that. He was human, he wanted her to know; they both were; if this crisis had created a feeling between them, it was not an ugly one, not one they should fear. *Wie es kommt, wird es gefressen;* there was a place for such fatalism.

170

T. T. Blades said, "I don't have much to say, Miss Swift. We had a rookie once who turned out to be queer. I always thought I'd be disgusted by anyone like that. When I found out about him, it just made me sorry as hell for him. We all felt that way."

"You see, I feel sorry for Harlan now. But then I didn't know about those things. I just thought they were yikky. You know?"

"Sure."

Silence.

"Whistler said, "May I say something?"

"Go ahead, Whistler."

He moved away from the boxes, careful not to move up too close to Josie Swift. In an instinctive motion he straightened his tie and stood as though he were taking the floor in a stockholders' meeting.

"First of all: that business about the warehouse. It wasn't a mistake. Okay?"

Blades said, "Okay."

"I meant that for all of you to hear. . . . I'll tell you something I never thought of until tonight. I went into the frozen-food business at a time when the wholesalers weren't even interested in taking my free samples. Do you know why? It wasn't just that frozen foods were still in the luxury class. It wasn't even that refrigerated transportation was inadequate. It was that during World War Two, some packers had gone in for a fast buck. They were careless, and they delivered inferior goods. Frozen foods had a lousy reputation because of it. So when I did that with my Vesey Street lot, I was doing something that twenty years ago I hated other guys for doing. It wasn't a mistake; you see what I mean?"

T. T. Blades said, "I think you were right earlier, Whistler. Your worst mistake was getting into this elevator. I don't know where I got off, jumping on you."

"I had it coming. . . . Mrs. Graeff, you're right about one thing. I don't think I'm dangerous, but I was trying to run things, take over. And I guess I'm more of a hothead than I ever realized."

Mrs. Graeff did not dignify the comment with an answer.

Whistler continued, "I learned something else about myself. You remember this partner of mine I mentioned?"

"Ben Hyde," Josie Swift said.

He was surprised she remembered the name; he was foolishly pleased that she had listened to him so attentively.

"Yes. Ben Hyde. We were very close once. Then he got

171

himself all involved with this psychoanalysis thing. It was all he could talk about. I think it embarrassed me; maybe I was embarrassed for him—I don't know. I used to feel the same way about drunks when they'd spiel out a lot of things you don't want to hear.

"You see, I always did what I did, and I didn't want to know why. My interest in myself centered on what I'd do if this happened, or that did—not on why something happened in the past.

"But I learned this tonight: the only way we've been able to tolerate each other was to find out more about each other. The only way to do that is to review the past. . . . How long do you think we would have stayed interested if we'd talked about what we were going to do when we got out of here?"

T. T. Blades said, "On the day before a big game, my wife usually makes plans for a celebration party somewhere, so if we win, everything's set up. That's one thing I don't want to hear anything about, not a detail, and Shirley knows that. . . . It's something like what you're saying, Whistler: it's bad luck to talk about what's coming."

"Something like that," Whistler said. "But more."

"I know what you mean, Mr. Whistler," said Josie Swift. "You mean we wouldn't care enough about each other, unless we knew enough about each other to care."

"That's it exactly."

"Like I wouldn't really care that Mr. Blades has missed his boat, except that I know how important it was to him, because of his wanting to get away from Shirley. . . . And I wouldn't really care about you, except I know all about you, what you're like."

Whistler had a sense of elation and lightheadedness. "Yes," he managed.

She was thinking that somehow before this night was over, she was going to tell him what she knew about Ben Hyde.

T. T. Blades said, "It's Lois I'm trying to get away from. Shirley's my wife."

Then Mrs. Graeff said, "I wonder what time it is now?"

"I don't know," said T. T., "but I wish I could smoke. Whistler? If we *were* talking about what we were going to do when we got out of here, that'd top my list: I'd start with a cigarette, that new extra-long-length brand that gets caught in elevator doors." He laughed. "What would you start with? A steak?"

"I said I'd *learned* something tonight, Blades. Look back; don't look ahead."

172

"Then you're 'it'," Josie Swift said. "Let's hear your worst mistake."

He was nearer to her now than he had been when he had started talking; without even being aware of it, he had moved closer to her. But he made himself stop where he was; could he touch her if he reached out?

He didn't try; he tried to act as though he felt nothing unusual.

He said, "Let's get back to Ben for a moment. He's a pain in the neck. You just don't know. This analyzing is a daily thing with him. For example, once I wanted to produce some diet dinners. Ben got the idea we ought to come out with just the opposite, with oversized frozen dinners. We were arguing about it, and finally Ben said, 'You know what your problem is, Will? You're afraid to admit your weaknesses; you won't even admit you have any. That's why you can't see producing the giant-sized dinners. You relate it to gluttony.'

"That's what I put up with. Believe me, we go to get a sandwich, and the next thing I know he's telling me I like soft things like noodles or cream cheese because I need mothering.

"You try working with a screwed-up sales executive like that sometimes."

Blades said, "Why don't you fire him?"

"Right! Exactly! Never mind that he can sell yarmulkes to Arabs, there's a lot he can't do for Whistle Foods, a lot he won't do. Never mind that I hired him to sell and he sells. He should do more. Right! I was telling myself this very evening!

"Never mind that I know Ben like the back of my hand, been working with him for twenty years. The next guy could believe in phrenology. Never mind that

"But you survive by sticking together, don't you? I might have made a lot of mistakes, and one big one, but hiring Ben wasn't my worst mistake; you want to hear my worst mistake?"

Josie Swift said, "Yes. What is it?"

"Before I got on this elevator tonight I wrote a letter to Ben asking him for his resignation. *That* would have been my worst mistake."

Josie bit down hard on her lower lip to keep from saying anything.

Then Gil Holland's voice came over the bullhorn.

# 40

In Italy the number is never used in lotteries; in Paris no house bears it, and persons called *quatorizièmes* are available to prevent having that number at table. Sailors strongly object to leaving port on the day of the month with that number, and on 44th Street and Sixth, in New York City, there is no thirteenth floor in the Gart Building.

Gil Holland, bullhorn in hand, spoke first to the men gathered around him. "We are entering the shaft here on fourteen, although the elevator now rests between sixteen and fifteen.

"We are doing this to anticipate more movement as we open the floor door.

"We will secure the wedge across the shaft and under the car. We take the chance of the car's gaining sufficient momentum between sixteen and fifteen to split the lumber or push it out of position.

"The brake shoes will probably prevent this, although their grip is fickle; the car should inch down slowly to make contact with the wedge.

"We are optimistic—" Gil Holland paused and put his fist to his mouth and made an awkward gesture between a cough and a gulp. "We hope very much," he corrected himself, "that the wedge will hold, that we will be able to begin evacuation at last.

"Everyone in position!"

He showed crossed fingers.

Then he put the bullhorn to his mouth.

"THIS IS GIL HOLLAND. THE CAR MAY MOVE SLIGHTLY, MORE NOTICEABLY THAN IT HAS SO FAR. ANTICIPATE THIS. STAY QUIET. SECURE ANY CARGO SO IT CANNOT FALL ON YOU. WHEN WE HAVE PLACED THE WEDGE IN SECURELY, THE LIGHTS WILL BE RESTORED. WE'LL BEGIN EVACUATION SOON AFTER."

He left it at that.

174

He was a workman, not an emergency-squad lieutenant who was practiced at talking with people whose lives hung in the balance; nor was he a senator who spoke of certitudes with godlike pomp.

He was not a religious man, but he carried a St. Christopher medal on his key ring, and he often crossed his fingers for luck; he supposed what he was was a superstitious man, and one intelligent enough to appreciate the fact that fourteen does not come after twelve.

He had hope, but not high hopes.

# 41

Then let him pout!

Wasn't that what he was doing back there, refusing to say anything, ignoring her attempts to put things back on their old footing?

She was not going to give him the satisfaction of imploring him to pray or sing a hymn; she *was* entitled to a modicum of self-pity, was she not? Her ankle pained her terribly, and if the car were to fall again, as Mr. Holland had implied, who would be worse off; who was the incapacitated one?

Some small word of comfort was certainly due her from him; a minister, he had said, but also a man.

Oh, very much so.

In the long run, they were all little boys; she had learned that much about men in her lifetime; they all were. They could hide behind façades of huff and puff, and stamp around in heavy shoes, and boom about the things they'd do and wanted done, but in a crisis they so often came apart like teddy bears, with all the sawdust spilling out, and at such times Faith Graeff could handle them.

Let him pout, for she would show him she could carry on, as bravely as she would have had he brought some solace to her; it was to him that she meant to direct her words, when stalwarthy, after Mr. Holland had had his say, she said, "And so, we'll carry on like human beings."

There was a respectful silence.

"We'll continue with the game," she said. "There seems to be no choice."

She could not help the tremor in her voice; let it be on his conscience.

She said, "If you'll all be courteous enough to listen" (more courteous, oh! by far, than you have been, dear, weak, man!) "I'll tell you of my worst mistake."

She heard them settle themselves in the darkness.

"I think we'd better just continue on like human beings!" How often she had said that in her lifetime to her menfolk.

Remember that awful night when the policemen brought Douglas home?

Two hulking, uniformed policemen, with poor Douglas between them; he didn't even come up to their waists, that was how young he was at the time. What? About eight years old?"

"We'll pay for the installation of new windowpanes; how many did he break?"

"Every single one, Mrs. Graeff. It's a big, two-story house."

"I know the house! I pass it every day. He broke them all? He couldn't have. He's just a little boy."

"Well, ma'am, he did. He broke them all."

"They're never home. They ought to board it up. Oh, well, we'll pay for all of them, then. I doubt, though, that he broke them all."

"Just ask him, ma'm."

"I *said* we'd pay the damages."

"He smashed the windows with a stick. Last week some windows were broken in the Bartleys' boat-house. The week before, most of the windows in the Keller place were broken."

"Apparently there's some sort of epidemic of window-breaking."

"Or there's a little boy who breaks windows."

"He's always been a copycat. He's probably seen older boys do it and thought it was the thing to do. Children are always trying to act older than they are. I don't know why that is."

"Has he been moody lately, angry?"

"He's just a tot; good heavens! We're going to pay for the Neilson's windows. I don't know what else we can do, except apologize to the Neilsons, when and if they return to the Landing. I often wonder why people have such a pretty
176

summer home and choose to spend the summer elsewhere. The grass is greener, I suppose."

"You'd better keep your eye on him, Mrs. Graeff. We're going to."

"Now, *really*, now! He's not the big bad wolf!"

Oh, that was quite a summer, that was.

Quite a summer!

For one thing, Raymond talked of nothing else but Bhrigu Waraich; he was this physicist from India who was working with Raymond on some project to do with the weakening of gravitation with the passage of time, completely contrary to Isaac Newton, but never mind. They were all caught up in it, and Raymond was always over there in Fogg Valley at the Waraichs' home.

He would come in very late at night and make himself a sandwich in the kitchen, and Mrs. Graeff would come downstairs in her robe and sit with him in the breakfast nook while he ate it.

It was Bhrigu this and Bhrigu that; Bhrigu did this and that, saw this, lived there, had that, wanted this, ad infinitum.

So one night Mrs. Graeff remarked, "What's her first name? You call him by his, but you always call her Mrs. Waraich."

"Her name's Subhadra."

"Bhrigu and Subhadra; aren't they strange names, rather lovely."

"Yes."

"And what's she like?"

"Oh, I don't know; she's young. He's very striking."

"Older than she is?"

"Yes. He has a very clipped British accent; remember Krishna Menon? He sounds like him."

"I hope he doesn't have his temper."

"Oh, Menon wasn't typical. Most Indians are quite serene, philosophical."

"Fatalists."

"You might say so."

"We make our fortunes and we call them Fate."

"Well, that's not exactly how a fatalist views life."

"I know. It was Disraeli's view; perhaps it's mine as well."

"The Indian is more of a mystic than that. More of a romantic."

"When do I meet your great Bhrigu, Mr. Best Friend?"

"I hadn't planned on anything."

"You haven't thought of having him to dinner?"

"Quite frankly, no."

177

"And fixing them a curry? Your Penang shrimp curry?"

"A curry wouldn't be much of a treat for them, I don't think."

"Then something else."

"Perhaps."

"You ought to show him what a cook you are; I bet he doesn't know."

"He's tasted more exotic meals than I could ever find recipes for; he's lived everywhere, you know."

"He has?"

"Oh, yes. Hong Kong, Sumatra, London, Cairo, Berlin. Everywhere."

"He must be quite sophisticated."

"Very."

"I wish you'd share him with me, Mr. Best Friend."

"Yes. Well, one night, then—"

"Promise?"

"I said, one night we'll have them over."

"Don't look so cross; you *didn't* say it until just now."

"All right, I didn't. Now I did."

She saw to it that he kept that promise, one very warm night near the end of July.

Dr. Waraich was very Lincolnish for an Indian, tall and gangling, with a coal-colored head of hair and beard, a formal sort not good at small talk, and she came whisking in in this bright-yellow sari with that red mark they stuck on their faces for whatever reason, seldom speaking much above a whisper. They talked trivia and ate *poularde soufflee rose de mai*, which Raymond fixed ahead of time; then coffee on the veranda looking out across the Hudson.

It was a stunning night of fireflies and katydids and just enough cool breeze, and stars all over in the sky.

"Put on the garden lights," said Mrs. Graeff, "and take Subhadra down to see the roses, dear."

And after Raymond did this, after she and Bhrigu had bored each other unto death for some ten minutes side-by-side in rockers, Mrs. Graeff revealed the fact she wasn't quite the queen of fools he thought she was.

"I am a very deliberate person when necessary," she began, and she continued, caring little that at first he wiggled with embarrassment, born from his first impression of her as ineffectual and fatuous.

Yet finally he did go to collect his wife, if for no other reason than to escape his hostess; he went toward the forcing house swiftly, still with some stealth, too, for he was by nature not a man unused to believing the impossible was possible.

Mrs. Graeff gambled only that her timing might be off, the odds of which were heavily in her favor, for Raymond's tempo was as familiar as her own; he was the only other human being she really knew.

The Waraichs left, of course, soon after Bhrigu Waraich set off down the garden path.

They did not say good night to her; she understood.

Raymond found her in the kitchen, sipping iced coffee in the breakfast nook. For the longest time he didn't speak; he stood there in the doorway watching her. And then he said, "How could you do it that way?"

"You knew our little rule, Mr. Best Friend."

"And how did you know?"

"I knew because you didn't mention her. Oh, you came so close, like being warm in hide and seek, the way you talked so much of *him*."

He sighed. He murmured, "So careful to avoid her name."

"Too careful. That was how I knew. Since when do *you* care what a Bhrigu looks like, talks like, where he's lived, or what he eats, or what he anything besides the physics end of it? . . . You see, I know you pretty well by now."

"Yes. Don't you just."

He stood there wordlessly while she finished her coffee, took the glass and spoon across to the kitchen sink, and soaped and rinsed and dried them. She turned to him then and said, "Let me give you a witch-hazel rub, all right? I put some in the fridge today so it would be cold in case we wanted rubs."

He stared out at the night, his voice emotionless. "No, thanks. . . . You think of everything. Of *everything*."

"Yes, well, now I hope that after this you will, too. I like to know about your little crushes; that was our little rule, I thought. You wouldn't go behind my back. Remember?"

He didn't answer. His back was to her now.

"*Remember?*"

He said, "Little crushes. You reduce everything to such a level of absurdity."

"I do, or you do? It doesn't matter. You used to like to tell me. You used to brag."

"This wasn't like that."

"*That* wasn't much fun, Mr. Best Friend." She went around to face him.

He said, "None of it's been much fun for either of us, has it, Faith?"

179

She had never seen him cry; the shock of tears glistening in his eyes compelled her to gush self-consciously in a nearly musical tone, "Oh, we make do."

"Why?"

"I beg your pardon?" she said, turning from him, finding something or other to fuss with back at the sink.

"I said, why?"

"For his sake."

He put his hand to the screen door, going for a stroll; he often did when he was upset, but before he pushed at it he said, "You can't even bring yourself to say his name anymore."

And that exasperated her. She crossed the room to call after him, "Oh, don't try to be so deep; you just sound silly. I'm sorry, but you do." She knew that he was standing out there on the gravel path, despite the fact that he did not answer her. She said, "You sound silly and just like him. He's always saying sneaky things, and he gets *that*, Mr. Best Friend, straight from the horse's mouth. Same as he takes those walks all by himself. I'm sorry, but it's true!"

Well, to get back to him and his prank.

"What a thing to do, Douglas," Mrs. Graeff had said after the policemen left. "I can't say that the Neilsons' was my favorite house, either, but I don't think that would inspire me to run down and break their windows."

Raymond said, "Doug, I'm going to stop your allowance until you've paid for them."

"You'll do no such thing, Raymond," said Mrs. Graeff. "I'll pay for those windows. We are not going to make an issue of this episode."

"Just what do you suggest we do, then, Faith?"

"I suggest we do what we've always done here at Sunyata. We continue on like human beings."

And so they did.

But what a summer it had been!

Cutworms had gotten at nearly all the tomato plants Mrs. Graeff had grown out behind the forcing shed, and near the end of August, Douglas had brought home the first of his hissers, that monstrous boa constrictor which he named Killer.

What she told the people in the elevator of that summer was her mistake in letting Douglas have those things for pets.

"You see," she said, "he identified with them. They were

180

so unattractive. If one feels unattractive, one becomes quite capable of doing very unattractive things."

She felt the elevator move.

# 42

"Like what?" said T. T. Blades.

"What do you mean, Mr. Cougar?"

"What unattractive things did Douglas do?"

"He watched them eat. They ate live things."

Their words came slowly, with great effort.

She said, "He spoke to them."

The impact of a barrage of hammering jolted the car; the boxes at the top of the pile swayed. T. T. grabbed them and was tortured by a push of pain across his shoulders and down to his ribs; he could feel his heart socking at his chest, perspiration dripping from his forehead. He could hear Whistler's heavy breathing, feel Smoke beside him, thrusting his body against the pile.

Mrs. Graeff's voice trembled as she continued. "He called them all by name and talked to them sometimes for hours."

"Kids will do that," said T. T. "That's not unusual." The movement stopped. He straightened his shoulders, and the pain came again sharply.

"Snakes don't bother me," said Josie Swift. "I had one once. I used to wear it around my neck. It was a ring snake, no thicker than the end of a penholder. Blue-black, with this ring around its neck the color of a tangerine. Heck. I liked that snake."

" 'Douglas,' I would say, 'you do practically everything but sleep with those hissers. What satisfaction do you get out of them?' He said, 'I trust them.' I said, 'Oh, Lord in Heaven, *that's* a good one. You trust snakes. They were despised even in the Bible, but you trust them.' He said, 'There are other religions which aren't based on the Bible, Mother: the Egyptians, the Greeks, the Romans—' I said, 'Oh, Douglas, talk

181

about things familiar to us here in the United States of America, *please!*' 'All right,' he said, 'even today the symbol of healing in the United States of America is the serpent form of Aesculapius, god of medicine.' Well, I never had an answer for him, not for him; like his father, he always had a mind as quick as lightning when it came to intellectual things. That way he was most superior."

Whistler let go of the boxes, testing their stability. He turned and faced front, bracing his shoulders against the pile. Josie Swift sat a few feet away from him. He had heard her gasp of alarm when the car inched down. He had almost forgotten the cargo and reached out for her. He was relieved when she spoke; her voice was firm and clear.

T. T. Blades pursued the conversation with Mrs. Graeff. "In what way wasn't he superior?" It wasn't ten years ago he had received that write-up, nor five, nor three; it was just last year, in Larry Merchant's column: "*T. T. Blades has no superior; football has never seen his equal; he can throw long or short; he can throw in wet or dry weather; he can throw bullets or slow, easy lops. His timing is beautiful! Whatever he throws arches down toward the hands and arms and chest of his receiver.*"

"He was weak," said Mrs. Graeff. "He was afraid of things, even near the end, no boy should be afraid of anymore. If ever; if at all. . . . Oh, he was afraid his father would have an accident in the car, afraid there'd be another accident with his snakes, afraid at night—he always slept with a light on; afraid our house would burn down, afraid the gas was on, afraid something horrible would happen at Sunyata. I'd tell him what a silly boy he was; I'd say, 'If anyone at school were to know how silly you are, you'd be a laughing-stock.' He would have been, too."

T. T. said, "How old was he when he died?"

"Seventeen. . . . He gave in to himself too often. He was like his father in that way, too. He lacked forbearance. That's such a wonderful, old-fashioned word. Our ancestors understood what it meant; what we suffer isn't important, it's how we bear our suffering. I used to tell Douglas that when he was a little boy; I used to ask him if he thought Abraham Lincoln went around telling everyone he was afraid of the dark, if he thought George Washington wouldn't go to sleep unless there was a light burning in his room. "Ask God for forbearance,' I used to tell him. I memorized a little prayer when I was on my honeymoon in Scotland. Since a certain party is no longer bestirring himself to offer up a supplication, perhaps it would not be out of place if I did."

182

The hammering from down below nearly drowned out T. T.'s, "Yes, go ahead."

"Give us strength and grace to forebear and persevere," she said, in such a ringing, forthright tone that everyone became alert. "Give us courage and gaiety and the quiet mind, spare to us our friends, soften to us our enemies."

"Amen," said T. T. "It's a very moving prayer, Mrs. Graeff." Winston Churchill said, "There is, however, a limit at which forebearance ceases to be a virtue."

Whistler chuckled. "That's pretty good, Reverend. You sound just like him."

"Oh, wow. Richard Burton."

Whistler touched her shoulder gently. "Churchill," he said, "not Burton."

Blades said, "She probably doesn't even remember Churchill."

Mrs. Graeff said, "You've been very naughty, Reverend, pouting back there, but I must say I'm glad to hear you speak up, even if it's only to tease me." A smile slipped to her lips while she stroked her fur cloche on her lap and waited for him to answer. When he didn't, she said in a playful tone, "Shall I call your bluff, hah? *When* does forbearance cease to be a virtue? . . . Ah! Cat got your tongue again?"

Sir Winston answered, "When we beat our children with the bones of our ancestors."

There was a sudden pause.

Then Mrs. Graeff said in a small voice, "That isn't very nice. You didn't mean that."

The hammering continued, and the noise of men shouting under them.

Whistler removed his hand from Josie Swift's shoulder as she put her own hands back to push her hair away from her neck and stretch.

No one seemed about to pick up the conversation; the silence worked against Whistler, made her nervous, he was sure. He said, "It's hard to raise a boy, I think. I wanted a girl, and that's what I got."

T. T. Blades said, "Lois and I used to talk about that— about people who wanted their child to be one or the other. We both agreed we wouldn't care; we'd just love to have a child."

Whistler said, "I probably wouldn't have any patience with a boy; I'd expect too much from him. If a girl's weak, it doesn't matter that much. It doesn't break your heart."

Another pause.

Then Mrs. Graeff said stiffly, "He didn't break my heart, Mr. Whistler. He was my son."

"It's just an expression, Mrs. Graeff. *You* know. He breaks your heart; it's just something you say."

"He breaks my heart. I know. But it wasn't Douglas." She made a belittling noise: "Pssss. A broken heart. That's something that I always thought was far more applicable to teenagers and their crushes. Adults, mature adults, don't walk around with broken hearts. Time mends the vulnerable mind; we learn to steel ourselves against emotion, to deal with emotional ups and downs. . . . My son was a great comfort to me. His father was often busy. My son and I spent a great deal of time together. He became my best friend."

The hammering grew louder; the car shook.

"Grab the boxes, Whistler!" Blades shouted.

But one fell to the floor before Whistler could jump back and secure it.

"Is it closed, Whistler?"

"Yes."

"Can I help?" Josie Swift asked.

"No. We've got them now."

Mrs. Graeff said, "There's someone who could help. Pray for us, Reverend Smoke. I may forgive your dereliction, but God will not."

The Frenchman said, "Dieu me pardonnera; c'est son métier."

"You're being *very* naughty now! Oh, what's got into you?"

Boris Karloff said, "A strange and horrendous power forbids me to continue with my masquerade. I am in the grip of a devastating and terrifying reality."

"And that meany thing you said to me about my treatment of my son."

Jimmy Stewart said, "Well, shucks, I didn't mean any harm, ma'm."

"About bones of ancestors and beating. . . . I cried so after his accident, sometimes I had to get in my car and drive to church in the middle of the day. I'd sit there until I appreciated there is a greater scheme to things than we can perceive; God moves in mysterious ways. He wanted Douglas for a reason I could never be privileged to divine."

Humphrey Bogart said, "That's the breaks."

"Oh, stop it now. Reverend, don't keep teasing me. I loved my son so very much."

Orson Welles said, "Rosebud . . . all I really cared about."

T. T. Blades snapped, "Knock it off, Reverend!"

"*I'll* handle him, Mr. Cougar. He's mad at me. He's trying

184

to punish me. Little boys do that. They do bad things to try and make their mothers feel guilty."

Sidney Greenstreet said, "I find your guilt an unbearable onus on this tedious journey, my dear woman. It blinds you from immediacies. It reduces you to the last resort, your so-called God."

"*Now,* you know, *I'm* good and mad at *you.*"

Greenstreet persisted. "You resort to fragile communication with Him to avoid the substantial but distasteful confrontation with your fellow man, a confrontation I find equally ill-omened."

"Pssss! Do you call yourself a minister?"

Gary Cooper said, "Nope."

"Oh, *no?*"

"Nope."

Whistler spoke up then. "I don't think he feels very much like being a minister right now. Why don't we get off his back?"

"I'm not a minister," Charlie Latham said.

"Oh, don't be silly!"

"I'm not a minister, Mrs. Graeff."

"You are so!"

He didn't answer her.

She said, "Don't be silly! You are! You're an Episcopalian minister!"

"Hunt-uh. I'm just another weak bastard who sleeps with the light on."

Josie Swift said, "It doesn't matter."

She was surprised when Mr. Whistler suddenly took her hand.

"That's right," he said. "It doesn't matter. You sure sounded like one when it counted."

Then Whistler jumped back as the car lurched and the sound of metal rubbing metal rent their ears.

"It's stopped moving," T. T. Blades said after several seconds, but he could not hear his own voice for the sound of hammering, the bullhorn blaring under them, the workmen's shouts. He reached in his back pocket for his handkerchief and mopped his brow. He moved his shoulder, testing for pain; it was there, but not so sharply. It might not be as bad as he had thought; his recuperatory powers were exceptional; word would get around the league the party was over for him because of this bum leg and that bad arm, but he would always make it back. In sixty-six he was bothered by an ankle that required a cortisone shot before each game, yet he still managed to set two league passing records and tie another. He stood there in the darkness testing further, moving his shoulders first one way, then another, bringing his arm up slowly in the motion of throwing.

His confession, the miserable stench, the noise, the soreness of his strained eyes—none of it mattered now to Charlie Latham.

He supposed that Gwen would answer the phone. He would simply say, "I called to talk to Frank."

She'd probably say, "Oh, Charlie, are you pulling *this* again?"

He couldn't blame her.

"Gwen, it's all right," he would say. "I'm absolutely sober, and *I'm* all right. I want to talk to Frank."

When Frank came on he'd say, he'd say . . .

"Frank, this is Dad."

"No *kidding?*"

"Who's it sound like, Batman?"

"Dad! Hi, Dad! Are you coming down to see me?"

"Not if you don't want to go fishing with me!"

No. . . . Wait a minute. Cross that out. Fishing? It was February, even in Virginia. . . . What, then?

"Not if you don't want to—"

Start over.

"Dad? Hi, Dad! Are you coming down to see me?"

"No, mister. You're coming up to see me."

There were a thousand things you could do with a boy in New York City.

"Really? Swell! Can we go to the Hayden Planetarium?"

"Get ready for the Sky Show. From Stonehenge to Palomar!"

"Oh, boy! Hey, Dad? Can we go to the Museum of Natural History?"

"From the Halls of North American Mammals," Charlie sang to the *Marine Hymn,* "to the Halls of Indians of the Plains!"

"*Oh, boy!*"

The noise stopped suddenly.

Just as suddenly, as though she had been waiting for this moment, Faith Graeff, in a voice which was scarcely audible, said, "I won't say for no reason, but it seemed to be for no reason, that one Monday morning after a big breakfast of French toast and sausages, Douglas went upstairs to shave, and then, instead, he took off all his clothes and slashed his body in a tub of water, and just—killed himself."

# 43

"You can't go inside."

"My husband is on that elevator."

"Nobody can go inside."

She was carrying a wicker suitcase; she wore brown, fur-topped boots, a belted polo coat, and a bright orange scarf around her head.

"I have to go in. Please."

"I have orders. What do you want me to do?"

Their breaths puffed up between them in the frigid air. The wind had blown a dust of snow across the policeman's dark uniform.

"The policeman back there said I should talk to you." She looked over her shoulder at the police blockade across the street from the Gart Building. Half a dozen policemen stood guard in front of sawhorses which separated them from a crowd of onlookers. Overalled workmen were clearing the sidewalk in front of the building, shoveling away the snow as rapidly as it came down, pouring salt on the ice. At the curb a fire truck, two ambulances, and an R.E.P. car waited.

"What policeman said that?"

"One of them. I don't know which one."

"You shouldn't have gotten as far as you did, lady. You can't stay here."

"Who's in charge?"

He felt her hand brush his glove. He looked down. There was a twenty-dollar bill crumpled in the palm of his glove. He looked up and into her eyes. That look; he had seen it so often on the faces of women: mothers of lost children, wives of firemen trapped inside burning buildings, victims of robbery, violence; that look, he told himself, still got to him, even after eleven years on the force.

"I don't want this," he said.

"Keep it. There must be someone inside I can talk to."

"I just turned a woman away; how can I make an exception?"

She began fumbling in the pocket of her coat; she withdrew a wallet.

"No!" he said. "Listen. Listen, just inside there's a fellow with white hair. Hillman Skidmore. He's running things, far as I know."

"Thank you."

She started to go by him.

"I can't promise you anything, lady."

"I know. Thank you."

He made another halfhearted gesture to return the money. She brushed past him; he pocketed it.

He stood there for a while watching the television men assemble their equipment to the left of the blockade, CBS, NBC; an ABC reporter wearing a duffle coat and earmuffs was already on camera, standing in the street talking into the microphone.

It dawned on the policeman then to wonder why the woman was carrying that wicker suitcase; a sliver of panic darted at him as the thought occurred that she could be some crackpot; worse, that whatever had gone wrong with the elevator in the first place was connected with her, that the whole thing might be some plot . . . the Senator inside and everything; maybe somebody in the elevator was an international VIP. . . . Christ, after Dallas, anything was possible.

He whirled around and went inside the building.

A helmeted fireman was standing just inside the door, wiping perspiration from his neck, smoking a cigarette.

"Did you see a woman with a suitcase?"

"Naw."

"She just came in, just went past me."

"I didn't see her."

The policeman looked around the lobby. He saw more helmeted firemen, two interns, other policemen, and men in mufti gathered together in small groups. Ladders and hoses were being carried in; stretchers, blankets, oxygen tanks, portable first-aid units.

There was no sign of a woman anywhere.

There was no sign of Hillman Skidmore.

It was two-fifteen A.M.

Wearily, the policeman walked across and leaned down for a drink of water at the lobby fountain.

He was away from his post just long enough for a *Daily News* reporter and a tall brunet to sweep through the door and hurry around behind the newsstand, out of sight.

188

# 44

"It took guts to say that," Whistler said.

But Mrs. Graeff did not answer him; she was finished talking.

Blades stood with his arms folded across the top of the boxes, his head buried in his arms, also silent; Latham, too.

Josie Swift whispered something to Whistler.

He leaned forward to hear.

"I wish he'd pray again."

"He doesn't want to," Whistler whispered back. "I don't blame him."

"I think she'd like him to; I feel so sorry for her."

"Yes. Well—" His voice trailed off.

"I wish that *I* knew how to," she said.

"How to pray?"

"Yes . . . I . . . it's spooky."

Behind her, T. T. Blades added, "Waiting like this. . . . We've said everything, I guess."

"Are you afraid?" Whistler asked her.

"A little. I wasn't."

"But now?"

"I don't know."

"It's so quiet," Blades said.

"Maybe it's the darkness," Josie Swift said; "like, sitting here in the dark and not talking. You know?"

Mrs. Graeff began to cry very softly.

Blades said, "I'll go over. Watch the boxes. Whistler? Smoke?"

"Latham," Charlie said. "Charlie Latham."

Mrs. Graeff's sobs became more audible.

Blades found his way to her; he knelt beside her. "I don't know a prayer," he said, "but I think we're going to come through this all right, Mrs. Graeff. I pray we do. I pray to God we do," he tried awkwardly.

"We all pray we do, Mrs. Graeff," said Josie Swift. "We

189

all hope God watches over us. I don't know how to say it, but—" and she could not finish.

Then Whistler said, "All right . . . I remember something."

And he began: "Hear, O Israel, the Lord is our God, the Lord is One. O Lord, by Your grace You nourish the living, and by Your great pity, You resurrect the dead, and You uphold—"

T. T. closed his eyes, trying to receive some comfort from the prayer.

All he could think of was how ironical, if this was it, that he would go in such a setting; indoors, confined to this small area, having no choice but to remain passive.

What had been best, there was no doubt, was the game of football.

It had lifted him up like some large hand and delivered him from the ordinary world to one of a strange physical beauty; an end faking out and bending in and then taking the ball on a dead run for a forty-yard touchdown, or just the simple movement of a defender angling in, a blocker sprinting down to help, a player jogging around to loosen up.

You were always aware of body movement; you were always studying the films in slow motion, watching the natural elegance of a man leaping for a high ball, or a quarterback with such exact timing that all the receivers had to do was run their patterns.

What had been the best was football; of that there could be no doubt; but when he had been with Lois Cadwallader he had been his best, too; he had excelled at something; some of it was their mutual ability to be graceful with their bodies and free with each other, to enjoy everything, but so much more was the glow it left, much like the glow T. felt after a good game, and then a good season—the feeling that if he stretched just this much, he could reach anything he wanted to, if only he could think of what it was he wanted. For he seemed to have it all, to have won again. It was a glow which made him feel he had used everything there was to use about himself, and what was there was first rate.

Now that he really faced the possibility of dying, T. T. realized that hardest to fathom never doing again was playing ball and being with that woman. Yet he had forfeited both already.

Figure that out!

". . . in the dust. Who is like unto You, O merciful Father, and who could be like unto You?"

Josie Swift said, "Thank you, Mr. Whistler. That's a Jewish prayer, isn't it?"

"Yes."

"Can you say some of it in Jewish?"

"In Hebrew . . . . Shema Yisrael adonoi Elohenu adonoi Echod . . . that's how it sounds."

"It's beautiful."

"Yes."

He stood there wondering how a man could fear for his life, say a prayer, and still want to reach out for the soft flesh of a strange woman.

Not *even* a woman.

He sighed heavily.

T. T. Blades said, "Whistler, why don't you sit down, take a rest? I'm coming back. I'll take over for you."

The answer to his prayer? She said, "Sit here by me."

He did, when Blades had stumbled back in place.

And Latham cursed, "Oh, Christ, it *stinks* in here!" and coughed, and seemed to gag.

He added, "Don't anybody say the obvious. I know all about the skunk's adversity."

"Does it feel good to sit down, Mr. Whistler?"

"Yes." The only thing he could think to say to her anymore: yes.

Behind them, Blades said to Latham, "I'm lucky; my sinuses are always blocked."

"I wish mine were. When you're half blind like me, your other senses overcompensate."

"The same thing happens sometimes if a part of your body goes on the blink; one leg will run harder for the other."

"You'd run like a gimpy, wouldn't you?"

"It's still running, isn't it?" T. T. laughed.

Which was the point when Whistler put his hand out, and in the darkness hit hers as she was raising hers to her head.

She said, "Oops! Don't spill it. It's Miss Blanc. It's my——"

"Trademark," Whistler finished her sentence for her; then he pushed the box he sat on back a distance, but there was no distance he could reach to prevent the assault of the gardenia odor on his nostrils.

Once, twice, three times he sneezed.

"God bless you, Mr. Whistler," she said. "Reverend, is that better?"

And with what Whistler viewed as unparalleled generosity, Charlie Latham told her, "Yes. Smells like a senior prom."

It was not too long after that, though it seemed a very long long time, that Gil Holland's voice came over the bullhorn; simultaneously the lights in the elevator went on.

"DETACH YOUR ROOF HATCH. WE'RE LOWERING A LADDER."

Whistler scrambled up atop the pile of boxes, wheezing, sneezing, going for the clean shaft air, all dreams of falling forgotten as he made his ascent.

Josie Swift stood up, pushed the box she was sitting on behind her; she was grinning. "Hey, we made it!"

The hatch was thrown back; then Whistler jumped down to receive the ladder.

Everyone was stretching, smiling, beginning to feel more like their old selves, T. T. Blades so much so that automatically he did the thing he said he'd do first off, and doing it, careless with euphoria, dropped a burning match.

It fell through the crack in the box containing Whistler's undershirt and the can of rubber-cement thinner.

For a while it was unnoticed.

"Leave the coats!" said Whistler when Josie Swift reached out for hers.

"Are you kidding? A Galanos?"

"Come on!" He laughed. "They'll get everything out for us! Hey, can't you fellows wait to smoke?"

"Do I have to go up the ladder by myself?" Josie Swift said.

"They'll send someone down to help us."

"Mrs. Graeff," said T. T. Blades, "don't worry any more now. You'll be carried out of here like a queen."

She put her handkerchief inside her bag, braving another weak smile. "By you, Mr. Cougar?"

"I did something to my shoulder. I have to be——"

And then Latham shouted, "Look!" for he had noticed the small puff of light a moment ago, disbelieved what he saw; he always saw illusions with his glasses off; then following the puff, a dark hole formed on the cardboard, widening, its edges curling as it grew.

By the time he shouted, the flame leaped out and licked the air.

# 45

The first graying of dawn was appearing in the sky when Stanley Ryan crossed 44th Street and went into the Cookery.

He walked across to a slim young fellow half-asleep over his coffee at the counter, and he said, "They're bringing them down in a few minutes."

"Are we still set up out front, or did we make the lobby?"

"The lobby. The camera doesn't look like much."

"It'll take your picture, Stanley. That's what you're after, right?"

"Sure. I ought to get something. It was my idea saved them."

"So you've said and said and said."

"Then why would you interview Zolto on the TV before me? I should have been interviewed first."

"Well, Stanley, it was his wood, and he asked me to."

"So did I. I asked you to. You said wait. I waited. I've been here eleven hours."

"We'll get to you. You'll be on the six-o'clock report tonight, probably, Stanley, if you want to have the wife see you."

"Probably?"

"Probably . . . . Was anybody hurt?"

"They took up stretchers. That's all I know. Why probably?"

"There's a senator over there, and a few other people who might have priority."

"The Senator left a long time ago."

"Let's get the lead out of our shoes. By the way, did you ever find out who the brunet was?"

"She came with the fellow from the *Daily News*."

"I know that. She's been here as long as I have. Who is she?"

"Nobody knows. She's waiting for someone who was on that elevator, though."

She was waiting for him, and he was the first to come off the elevator, followed by Gil Holland, Hillman Skidmore, Lou Gillespie, and Lieutenant Scholz.

He walked in that easy, sure, long-legged gait of his, smiling broadly at the cameras and the newsmen, not seeing her at first.

The others brushed past the media people, refused their questions, but he knew instinctively that they had waited out the night, the way they waited after games sometimes for hours before the locker room was cleared, the crowd outside thinned down.

"T.?" one of the television reporters said. "We hear you were a hero."

"Was? Past tense?"

The reporters guffawed appreciatively.

He said, "Thanks for waiting around"; he always said the same thing after games. He said, "You fellows must be beat."

"How do you feel, T.?"

"There were moments there when I thought we were going to lose."

They laughed again, and one said, "T. T.? Are you going to bring suit against the owners of the building?"

"I haven't got any plans right now but to get some sleep."

Then he saw her. He did a double take. "Excuse me," he said, and walked across to her.

"Hi."

"I heard about it on the radio, T. So I—"

"Came here. I was hoping . . . "

The reporters tagged after him.

"T. T.? Can you tell us about the people on the elevator with you?"

"There were five of us."

"What did you do while you were waiting to be rescued?"

"Talked. That was about it."

"T. T.? What'd you talk about?"

"Ourselves. You know."

"Where are the rest of them? The other four?"

"Probably hiding out from you guys."

"Did you see Senator Anderson upstairs, T.?"

"T. T., was anybody hurt?"

194

"T.? Someone said there was a fire."

He said, "Hey, hold it. One at a time."

He kept looking down at the brunet, but he was aware of the reporters and the cameras and the small crowd of maintenance men and minor officials beginning to form around him. He signed some autographs; then he stood hand-in-hand with her as he was being interviewed by other reporters who had pushed their way forward with mikes, pads and pencils, and portable tape recorders.

He lingered there with the press, saying he was looking forward to a good season next year, tired as he had to be: T. T. Blades, age thirty-three, one of the survivors, enthusiastically dividing his attention between the woman and more talk of football.

# 46

The snow had stopped. The ambulance began its journey tentatively until it found a side of the street its wheels went along without sliding.

Faith Graeff said, "You must be exhausted, Roger."

"Never mind me."

"I thank you. I wish Raymond hadn't asked you to do it."

"I would have, anyway."

"Why?"

"Faith, *why?*"

"Never mind."

"I wanted to. I was worried."

She said nothing to that. He rode beside the stretcher in silence for some time before he asked her, "Aren't you going to tell me anything about it?"

"I guess I'm very tired."

"You've never been too tired to talk in all the time I've known you."

"I daresay. I suppose you want to know what she's like."

"Who?"

"The little girl who went off on the Senator's arm. Am I right?"

"I'll tell you a secret; she's my employee. But I didn't know until this evening that she's also the Senator's fiancée. Did you hear what I just said? She's his fiancée!"

"Yes."

"Faith, what *is* she like?"

"Oh, she's—young. Unpolished. Vulnerable."

"I'll bet she threw his name around."

"She didn't mention the Senator."

"She didn't?"

"She didn't."

"There's a social *canyon* between them. Did you hear the way she talks?"

"Yes."

"You really are tired, aren't you, Faith?"

"Very. Of almost everything."

"I beg your pardon?"

"Roger, do you think it's true what Douglas wrote in his note?"

"His note?"

"His suicide note. . . . When he wrote that it wasn't anyone's fault."

"Oh, yes. That. We've never talked about that."

" 'It wasn't anyone's fault,' he wrote; 'I just can't make do.' That was one of my sayings. 'Make do.' I was always saying, 'We'll make do.' "

"Yes. . . . Well, Faith, I don't think suicide is anyone's *fault*. A person just gives up."

"I was thinking of something he used to say, when he was a small boy. He used to say, 'Is this me, I ask?' "

"Odd. What did he mean?"

"He was such a strange little boy, you know. One never knew exactly what he meant. But he would say that. And tonight I felt that way about myself. I think I know what he meant. . . . Such a strange, knowing little boy."

"Yes."

"He seemed always to know that life wasn't at all simple."

"Yes. What would you say when he said that?"

"I"—Mrs. Graeff took a deep breath, paused, let out the breath, and continued—"I would laugh and poke him in the stomach with my finger, and answer, 'Yes, of course it's you, *silly.*'"

They rode the rest of the distance to the hospital in silence, neither one able to think of anything more to say to the other.

# 47

When the Senator and Josie Swift left twenty-two-ninety-seven, Whistler turned to his wife and said, "Honey, you are truly sensational!"

He walked around his desk, across to the couch, where she was munching a chicken leg and putting things back in the wicker suitcase.

"Careful of the Soave," she said; "it's right near your foot, Will, what's left of the bottle. How do you like that football player taking all the credit for the rescue?"

He bent over and kissed her. "Who cares?"

"I care. He told that reporter on fifteen he helped evacuate Josie."

"He did go up the ladder after her."

"She said he nearly pushed her out of the way."

"Everything happened very fast."

"That big lug went up the ladder and left you and the Reverend to wrestle with Mrs. Graeff."

"He's not a reverend. Don't ask me what he is, but he's not a minister."

"He didn't get any credit, either. Did you see his hands? They were badly burned, and he just walked away from the doctor. Where'd he go?"

"Search me. Where'd he come from?"

"You two were the heroes. That big lug playing the hero!"

"Why shouldn't he? That's his business. Mine is to keep Whistle and the Whistlers above water. And I got off to a pretty elegant start tonight, thanks to you. Darling, that was a brilliant idea, bringing that picnic lunch down here! My God, did you see the Senator dig into your chicken?"

"Yes, and I didn't appreciate it. I brought it down here for you. All I could think of was how hungry you'd be, Will. When your name came over the radio, I made a dive for the picnic basket and the refrigerator door. I just loaded up, and it's a good thing. He ate like a pig."

"Did you hear him agree with me about the automobile industry's responsibility to do something about pollution?"

"Yes, yes."

"I made my point. Detroit's doing a lot more to foul the air than my little setup in Clifton. If they want to do something about air pollution, they should pick on the big fellows, not the little fellows. Let Detroit come out with electric cars. There are ninety million automobiles in use today; there's the heart of your air-pollution problem!"

"Yes, I heard. You nearly put *her* to sleep. She's awfully pretty, isn't she?"

"She wears too much perfume."

"She'll keep him on his toes."

Whistler laughed. "Or up on his elbows."

"Oh, everybody's going to be so anxious to make their dirty remarks about them. You know what? I don't think it'll bother them one bit And I genuinely liked them."

"Mariam, sweetheart, I'm glad you did."

"I know you are." She sighed, pretending exasperation.

"You're a wonderful, wonderful woman, baby, and I love you with all my heart."

"I heard. You want to have them to dinner."

"Would you make a pot roast? I figure him for potroast."

"You're always figuring, Will."

"Well, I'm a man who likes to use his head," said Whistler. "Do you know what you're supposed to say to that?"

"I say, let's go home, lover. I'm very tired of hearing all about air pollution and pot roast and all the rest of your business schemes. Just once, I wish you'd forget business. You never have as long as I've known you."

198

She got up and put her arms around him,, hugging him.

He said, "You're supposed to say to that, 'Well, don't that hurt your ears?'"

# 48

"Just a minute, Senator. *Senator?*"

Bob Anderson turned around on 45th Street and faced a New York columnist.

"Hello, Pete. I thought I was a pretty good escape artist; I didn't count on your being out this time of morning."

Josie Swift dropped a little behind Anderson.

"Senator, aren't you about to conduct an investigation?"

"You know what they say: the Senate opens with a prayer and closes with an investigation."

"But you are heading up a subcommittee that's about to look into air pollution?"

"So far, so good."

"Is William Whistler cooperating with you, Senator?"

"Pete, whatever gave you that idea?"

"Weren't you at the Gart Building this evening on his behalf?"

The Senator laughed. "Hardly."

"On whose?"

"Hers." He turned toward Josie. "The young lady's."

The columnist smiled as though he were going along with a joke. He said, "But you did just have a meeting with Mr. Whistler, didn't you?"

"We shared some fried chicken together, but we didn't talk turkey."

The Senator's cagey ways were often camouflaged with corn.

The columnist smiled wisely. "When will you talk turkey with him, Senator?"

"I haven't any plans along those lines."

"But you do plan to blow the whistle, so to speak, Senator, on the New Jersey manufacturers responsible for pollution in that state and this city?"

"We're going to look into it. Pete, I'm tired. Can we cut this short?"

"Do you mind if I mention the reason you were there at the Gart Building tonight, Senator?"

"Just make sure you have the right reason, Pete; don't make a damn fool of yourself."

"I won't make one of you either, Senator. I've always been for you; you know that."

The columnist gave a little salute as the Senator went on his way. The columnist was already busy writing in his head: "WHISTLE IN THE DARK . . . *The manufacturers of New Jersey, among them Whistle Foods, Inc., have a lot to lose when the Senate subcommittee investigating air pollution gets underway. It is a very dark picture, and perhaps it is only the light of coincidence that gives any illumination to the presence of Senator Robert Anderson at the scene of last night's—*"

"Maybe Fifth is clear by now, Jo; maybe we can get a cab there."

"That newspaperman's going to look silly, isn't he?"

"Or very sharp. Eventually."

"What do you mean?"

"He'll look silly tomorrow, because tomorrow I'm going to announce our engagement, if that's okay with you. Is it, Jo?"

"It was worth getting trapped in an elevator for that."

"I made up my mind in Whistler's office; there's no point in waiting."

"They're awfully nice, aren't they?"

"They're all right."

"But they don't like me for what I really am, do they?"

"Ask them tomorrow."

"Huh?"

"Tomorrow, when Whistler calls to ask us to dinner next week, so he can go to work on me over this air-pollution thing."

She laughed. "I get it."

"*Do* you?"

"Yes. But *we* like each other for what we really are, don't we?"

200

"If my hair wasn't already white, it would have turned white tonight." He put his arm around her as they turned into Fifth Avenue. "I don't ever want to lose you."

"You're not going to, either. . . . Bob?"

"There's a cab. What?"

"Why would that newspaperman look sharp eventually?"

"Mr. Ben Hyde was with my associate this morning. He had a lot to say. No one will ever know it was Mr. Hyde who said it, probably not even Will Whistler. Eventually what Mr. Hyde told us will come out in our hearings. I suppose there'll be those who'll remember the column Pete's probably going to write tonight. They'll think Whistler did cooperate with our committee, the way Pete's going to suggest."

"I almost told Mr. Whistler about Ben Hyde. Then I forgot."

"Learn to forget things like that, Jo; it's best."

"Why would people believe Mr. Whistler would tell on himself?"

"He'd be telling on a lot of others besides himself. People would believe he'd do it for immunity, or a period of grace; some would probably even believe we'd paid him. . . . *Taxi!*"

"Bob! How can we go to dinner at the Whistlers' next week knowing this?"

"We can't. We'll be on our honeymoon."

She said, and he said along with her, "Oh, wow."

# 49

Frank answered the phone himself.

"Frank? This is Dad."

"Oh, hi, Dad."

"Did I wake you up?"

"Ummm-hmmm."

"How are you?"

"Dad?"

"Yes, Dad! Who's it sound like, Batman?"

"Do you want to speak to Mother?"

"No, mister. I want to speak to you. How are you?"

"Okay."

"Just okay?"

"I was asleep."

"I'm in New York."

"Uh-huh."

"How'd you like to come up here?"

"Sometime."

"Not sometime. This weekend."

"I can't."

"What do you mean you *can't?* How'd you like to go to Hayden Planetarium? Get ready for the Sky Show! From Stonehenge to Palomar!"

"Huh?"

"Frank, how about getting an afternoon plane?"

"I can't. I'm going to the movies with some fellows."

"Mister, I'm inviting you to New York City."

"I promised them."

"You did, huh?"

"Yeah. . . . Do you want to speak to Mom?"

"I want to speak to you."

"Well . . . I'm here."

"How are you?"

"Okay."

"What've you been doing?"

"Nothing much."

"How's school?"

"Okay."

"You making all A's?"

"Some."

"What's your favorite subject?"

"Oh, I don't know. . . . Listen, here's Mom now. You can talk to Mom."

Gwen's voice then, husky from sleep, a cranky edge to it. "Oh, *Charlie.*"

He didn't say anything.

"Charlie, cut it out! Just let us go, Charlie."

He still said nothing.

"Do you know what time it is? I have to go to work in a few hours! Can't you let us go?"

202

"Go directly to jail," he said. "Do not pass go," he said. "Do not collect your two hundred."

Click.

He heard the dial tone and put the receiver back on its hook.

His hands were wrapped with bandages he had made by tearing his handkerchief in two. He could not see well without his glasses; their wreckage was in the pocket of his overcoat. He stepped out of the phone booth and walked the length of the lobby of the Gart Building slowly, out into the cold air.

The ambulances and fire trucks were gone; there were no television cameras left, no reporters; he had waited all that out in the phone booth, screwing up his courage to feed change into the slot. The snow had stopped; the wind had died down. The sky was breaking morning blue.

"Martin?"

He went on by her.

"Martin Luther Smoke? *Reverend* Smoke?"

Charlie stopped. She was a plump blond.

"Hi!" she said.

"Hi!"

"Know me?"

"Should I know you?"

"I waited at the hotel. Then I got on a subway and came up here. I thought maybe you didn't get my message."

He squinted at her with puzzlement.

She said, "Well, if you can be Martin Luther Smoke, Professor, I can be Salena, I guess. . . . I sent you a wire to tell you I was here. Did you get it? Then I just came up here, and all of this was going on with the elevator."

"Yes," he managed.

"So I waited over in Quinn's till they closed, and then I waited in the Cookery."

He could see that long ago she might have been that barefoot girl in the white peasant blouse with her breasts pressing forward, might ten years ago have had full hips and rounded belly and a waist pulled in by a wide red scarf, and she might have stood there in the field of bright-green and very seductive, very soft-looking grass.

She said, "I was curious to see you in the flesh."

"How are you, Lorine?"

"When I heard there was a Reverend Smoke in the elevator, I found it hard to believe."

"I can see why you would."

She fell in step with him as he walked down Sixth Avenue in the early morning.

She said, "I guess you didn't recognize me right off."

"Not right off."

"I'm older than I said. I stretched the truth a little."

"The truth, my pet," said Cary Grant, "is always in the eye of the beholder."